3/99

The Mysterious
Cape Cod
Manuscript

The Mysterious Cape Cod Manuscript

Marie Lee

AVALON BOOKS
THOMAS BOUREGY AND COMPANY, INC.
401 LAFAYETTE STREET
NEW YORK, NEW YORK 10003

10 9 8 7 6 5 4 3 2
PRINTED IN THE UNITED STATES OF AMERICA
ON ACID-FREE PAPER
BY HADDON CRAFTSMEN, SCRANTON, PENNSYLVANIA

For Jessica,
a delight of a daughter

Acknowledgments

Thank-you's are extended to Marcia Markland of Avalon Books for her unflagging confidence and support; and

To Bruce MacFarlane of MacSquid's for enlightening a novice as to the choice of a gun appropriate to the story.

Behold and see as you pass by
As you are now so once was I
As I am now so you must be
Think on Death and follow me.

—Epitaph on the tombstone of
Thomas Dyer
Old North Cemetery,
Truro, Massachusetts

Prologue

The three sisters sat in the cold and dark, gray garbed, surrounded by silence, the ghostly white silence that accompanies gently falling snow, its descent so slow as to appear tentative. This new location was not far from their original homesite, several moves in the past, but was more secure, distanced from the eroding ocean cliffs, immune to the thunderous surf, sheltered from the howling winds. Quiet, very quiet.

Except for this January night when the calm was shattered by a loud thump at the door, vulnerable since a band of marauding teenagers had kicked in the once-sturdy lock. Quiet again for a few minutes, then the sound of labored breathing and a faint scraping against the floor.

Footsteps retreated. The door was forcibly closed, its shattered wood protesting the incursion of the protruding, useless lock. The three sisters were left in their perpetual silence, harboring a dreadful secret.

Chapter One

"They're going to kill you," she warned.
"Who?"
"Not who. What. Those cigarettes."
"At least they won't nag me to death."
"Did I nag you, Joe?" queried Marguerite, her eyes betraying the vulnerability she vehemently denied.

It was twelve years since he had left her. On the first day of spring, he had packed his bags and jettisoned a wife and two children. His good-bye was uttered fleetingly as he hurried down the walk, coming upon her unexpectedly as she was turning over the dirt for a projected perennial border. Her fledgling garden, so eagerly anticipated, bore bitter fruit that summer.

"No, Meg, you never nagged."

He patted her hand in affirmation and noticed that she no longer wore a wedding ring.

"What happened to my mother's ring?"

Snap! Whoosh! Plop! "Ouch!"

Marguerite's hand flew to her eye, stinging from the sand blown into it by the fallen palm frond, symbolic of the tree's life cycle. Discard the dead fronds below; grow at the top; reach for the sun. Renew.

The Fort Lauderdale beach resembled a tropical atoll with palm trees along its length, their luxuriant fronds swaying in the ocean breezes, their flexible trunks bowing in obeisance to the ocean gales. Tourists fleeing the northern winter's cold and ice spent long hours on the beach soaking up the sun and a season's worth of memories before returning home to scrape ice from their car windows.

The offending palm frond startled Marguerite from her bittersweet reminiscence of that recent dinner with her ex-husband, Joe Smith, her first real contact with him since their divorce. A glance at the watch in her purse, carefully protected from encroaching sand, revealed that it was time to leave the beach.

She had a date! Not the usual date for bridge, or with a woman friend. A date with a man who appeared to be actively pursuing her. She was almost giddy with pleasure. And flattered.

They had met by chance at dinner as she and her friend Beatrice had completed the first day of their journey to Florida and stopped at a motel in Penns Grove, New Jersey. Exhausted after driving four hundred miles from Cape Cod, battling intermittent snow and poor visibility through a windshield splattered by every passing truck, they headed for the closest neon sign advertising food. Any place serving food would do. That was exactly what they got.

The restaurant made no pretense at grandeur. Formica-topped tables, anemic paper napkins, plates of food in a monochrome of tannish-gray, and surly waitresses made one eat and run. That was precisely what the management wanted. Tables were expected to turn over every forty-five minutes. Lingering for an hour was unacceptable and the waitress would be faulted with a sharp reprimand by the owner, who clocked every diner in his head as he simultaneously watched from the kitchen and passed out the platters of fried food.

Goldy's Place was appropriately named. It was a gold mine. Located strategically on the seasonal migration route—south in winter, north in summer, Disney World at all times—it was assured of a nightly stream of tired drivers looking for something to eat before they collapsed in their rooms to surf through unfamiliar television channels and retire early in preparation for the next day's grueling drive.

Lou Golding never worried about building a steady clientele. Tomorrow night there would be another stream of motorists, tired, hungry, anxious for the day to be over. No accountability. A gold mine!

Marguerite and Beatrice had to wait as a party of dawdlers,

having exceeded the forty-five-minute allocation, used a calculator to determine each one's individual bill. Amidst a heated discussion as to who had the extra coffee (no free refills here), the waitress was frantically clearing the table and pointedly suggesting that they settle their dispute at the register.

It was an uncomfortable wait for the two women as they alternately froze when the door behind them opened to admit another party of hungry travelers seeking comfort in a world of snowflakes and roasted when the door closed, causing them to sweat in their layers of clothing.

A lone male behind them commented without preamble, " 'Food is a weapon.'—Maxim Litvinov."

"Against whom?" queried Beatrice, her long earrings jangling as she whirled her head to face the stranger.

"Against whomever doesn't have it. In that case it was the Russians after World War I."

"And now?" she persisted, her hazel eyes flashing with the challenge of badinage initiated by this literate stranger.

"Us, dear lady, as we stand here faint and weary, at the mercy of hardened publicans."

"Who's next?" The voice of Mrs. Golding grated through the air. Convinced that her husband flirted with every waitress and female customer, although, in truth, he rarely left his post in the kitchen, Junie Golding doggedly fought the inevitability of fleeting youth. With too much hair, makeup, and heels, and too little dress—about two sizes too little—her forty-year-old self looked fifty.

"We are!" eagerly answered Marguerite.

"How many in your party?"

"Two."

"I have a table for four. Is there a party of four?" she hawked impatiently, ignoring Marguerite's protest.

"If I may intervene?" the stranger asked with a half smile. Addressing the formidable Mrs. Golding, he continued, "I am next after these ladies. If they can bear my company, I would be happy to join them and you can give us the vacant table."

"If they don't mind, why should I? Let's go."

And so the tragedy continued to unfold.

Chapter Two

"Your mother's ring is safe. It's in my box at the bank. If one of our children has a daughter I'll give it to her."
"We have a daughter. Why didn't you offer it to her?"
"I did."

At first, the stranger's attention was directed at Beatrice. The same height as Marguerite but slimmer, she appeared taller than her five feet four inches of elegance. Thick and wavy salt-and-pepper hair, strikingly grayer at the temples, was worn severely short, accentuated by her signature dangling earrings. A dermatologist's nightmare, she sported a perpetual suntan with a carefree air in an era of sunblock mania.

He openly studied her as she unwound the long hot-pink scarf from around her neck, removed the matching wool tam, the leather jacket, and the Irish sweater, revealing a yellow silk blouse with a soft frill running down the front topped by several strings of beads coordinated to the colors in her earrings. It was an unconventional but charming accompaniment to her well-worn western boots and jeans.

Marguerite, confident in the knowledge of her own quiet good looks, was unfazed at being outshone by the flamboyant Beatrice. She slipped off her down coat and knit hat, shook out her dark, curly hair to release it from the constraints imposed by the hat, tucked her classic gray flannel slacks neatly into her snow boots, debated whether to remove her green sweater, decided yes, and

5

peeled it off to uncover a white cotton shirt with a flower deli-
cately embroidered over the pocket. It was her namesake flower,
a marguerite, but it might as well have been a burdock, for no
one noticed.

He began the conversation with regrets that he could not offer
them a bottle of wine in appreciation of their hospitality but
doubted if this place even stocked cooking wine. They smiled.

He introduced himself as Nicholas Dante and said he would
like them to be his guests for this dinner but took no responsibility for its quality. They protested. He insisted. They yielded.

He amused them by quoting Ulysses S. Grant's description of
New England's climate as nine months of winter and three
months of cold weather. Beatrice laughed heartily. Marguerite
smiled.

He asked their destination. Beatrice replied, "Florida." Marguerite smiled faintly.

He told them he was also going to Florida and asked "Where
in Florida?" Beatrice replied, "Fort Lauderdale." Marguerite
glanced sidewise at her.

He was amazed at the coincidence. That was his destination,
too. "Where are you staying in Fort Lauderdale?"

Despite the insistent nudge against her thigh administered by
a cautious Marguerite, Beatrice replied, "The Sea Club."

Marguerite, no longer smiling and becoming uneasy, took the
initiative, hoping to catch him without an answer. "And where
are you staying?"

"Howard Johnson's," came the reply with no hint of guile.

The waitress was already clearing the limp, saturated salad that
lay barely touched on their plates and was slapping platters before
them. Although they had each selected a different entrée, the
dinners were indistinguishable fried meat or fish obscured by
french fries and soaked by the liquid from the canned corn running across the plate.

Ignoring the cold, doughy rolls accompanied by three minis-
cule pats of frozen butter, they turned their attention to eating,
gamely searching for substance under the potato mantle, politely
refraining from commenting as to quality or lack thereof. Conversation lagged.

He suggested coffee. Both women declined.

He asked for the check, left a tip too generous for the indifferent service and inferior food, walked to the cash register, and paid the bill.

They thanked him for the dinner and wished him a safe trip. He graciously complimented them on their company and made no attempt to escort them to their car but walked to his Lincoln, pulling away with a final wave as they slipped and slid along the parking lot.

Marguerite was relieved and began to think she was getting paranoiac. She must stop reading so many mystery novels.

Beatrice thought he was charming and hoped they would meet him again in Fort Lauderdale.

They did.

After an unremarkable trip—particularly unremarkable as to motels and food—they checked into the hotel, rummaged through their crammed suitcases without unpacking, and hurried into bathing suits.

The beach was directly across from their hotel, on the other side of Ocean Boulevard, a very busy road with two lanes of traffic in each direction and a center island to grant a reprieve to pedestrians scurrying across. Marguerite's vision was partially obscured by a large sun hat, beloved by her for its ability to be rolled up for packing. Beatrice had no such encumbrance, wearing only a bathing suit and long swinging earrings. She shepherded them onto the beach and settled in a spot midway between the water and the low, white art-deco fence enclosing the beach.

Within an hour, Beatrice spotted him walking along the water's edge, seemingly unaware of their proximity. "Nicholas!" she called out.

He appeared astonished at their presence but had hoped to meet them again, he admitted, unshaded black eyes reflecting sea and sky. Would they care to join him for post-beach cocktails in about two hours? Fine. No need to change. He would come by and they could go to one of the places along Ocean Boulevard. "Enjoy your afternoon, ladies."

It was obvious that Beatrice was the attraction. His attention was focused on her and she responded with voluminous information about herself while he discreetly prodded her with questions.

She was a widow with no children. Her husband, the late Cecil Owens, and she were from Michigan and both had worked for General Motors, she as an executive assistant to a vice president, he as a design engineer. After his sudden death from a heart attack, she had found it too painful to remain in the beautiful home they had shared. Recalling happy childhood memories of two summer vacations on Cape Cod with parents who doted on their only child, she took an extended vacation there during the summer after Cecil's death, found it amenable to her new life-style as a widow, and decided there was no longer a reason for her to remain in Michigan. She returned only to sell her home in Grosse Pointe and retire from her job. Eastham became home for her and a precious Siamese cat, Ling, killed six months ago by a heartless hit-and-run driver. Beatrice was alone now. Unspoken, but intimated, was her financial independence.

He had learned all this and more through cocktails and during dinner the next day to which he had invited them. Midway through dinner, the dynamics changed. His interest subtly shifted to Marguerite, who assumed he was merely being polite but found his charm seductive and responded despite her initial mis-givings.

A perceptive Beatrice sensed the shift in direction and gra-ciously accepted it. She assured Marguerite she had many friends in Florida and left early that afternoon to meet with a former business colleague in Boca Raton.

Marguerite Smith was surprised at herself. In her first winter trip south since retiring from teaching, she was acting like a giddy teenager. Nearing sixty but looking younger, she was still smart-ing from her abandonment by Joe so many years ago. She was even more surprised that it was Nicholas Dante who attracted her.

He was not a man she would have selected from a crowd. Not her type at all. His physique was unexceptional—medium height, average weight. His face was arresting. Dark, receding hair, which he made no effort to disguise with elaborate comb-overs, was worn unabashedly parted, straight and long, covering the upper ear. Dark eyes peered rather than gazed. A wide, narrow mouth was partially concealed by a full mustache. His expression was an inscrutable mix between frown and concentration, with the vertical frown lines between his pronounced eyebrows form-ing a perpendicular union with the horizontal concentration lines of his forehead. It was a formidable face, somewhat frightening in its serious mode. But his smile was dazzling and he knew to use it sparingly for greater effect.

Marguerite estimated that he was a few years younger than she, which presented a challenge. She had made a trip to the Galleria Mall that morning to buy a dress suitable for dinner at Le Dôme, the rooftop restaurant of The Four Seasons, celebrated for its imaginative cuisine and spectacular penthouse views of Fort Lauderdale and the Atlantic Ocean. Her social life was outpacing the casual wardrobe she had packed for the trip.

He was calling for her early tonight so that they would have time to stop at a Las Olas sidewalk café before dinner to sample one of their famous margaritas. It was with an uncharacteristic annoyance in her voice that she phoned the housekeeping department to complain that the maid had not returned with the extra set of clean towels she had requested. The towel that had been left in the morning was wet from the beach.

Chilled by the air conditioner, she removed her damp bathing suit and donned a bathrobe to await the maid. The room was vividly and sloppily decorated by items of Beatrice's eclectic wardrobe, discarded wantonly as she tried on and rejected one garment after another in various combinations to achieve that air of insouciance that was the signature of her appearance. Carefully clearing a chair of a chartreuse silk tank top and gray cotton knit gym shorts, Marguerite sat by the window staring at the beach in the fading light of winter, anticipating a delightful evening of dinner and dancing with Nick.

If only she could stop worrying about that recent meeting with Joe.

Chapter Three

A question fomented in his mind, furrowing his brow and opening his mouth. Before words could form, the answer erupted in his brain and his mouth closed, swallowing the unspoken question.

"I did," Marguerite had answered. She had offered their daughter, Alexandra, his mother's wedding ring and she had refused it. It was not a rejection of his mother but of him.

Alex had never forgiven him, although she had been twenty when he had left and long beyond any dependency on him beyond his paying her college bills, which he had continued to do.

Heavy silence ensued and Marguerite enjoyed it. It was his turn to hurt. A racking cough from Joe interrupted the stalemate. When the salvo ended, he was red-faced and drew from a pocket one of his monogrammed linen handkerchiefs to wipe the perspiration from his brow.

A waitress thundered over to their table, briskly asking what they wanted, pad in hand, seemingly in a rush, although on this snowy January night there were only two other tables occupied.

The college students who so ornamentally, sometimes ineptly, staffed the Cape Cod restaurants in summer were long gone. Restaurants that remained open were staffed by year-round professionals, more skilled but less playful.

Joe answered for both of them. "Two Beefeater martinis straight up, one with a twist, one with an olive. Two orders of

Wellfleet oysters on the half-shell, two small Caesar salads, two prime ribs, one rare, one medium, with baked potatoes.''

"That's a lot of food for one person, Joe." Turning to the waitress, Marguerite smoothly continued, "I'll have a salad with blue cheese dressing on the side and the duck, well done, no appetizer." The martini was spared.

"I ordered for you, Meg. I thought those were the things you liked."

"But you didn't ask, did you? I've learned to order for myself, Joe."

The unflappable waitress had seen it all before. "I'll cross out one oysters, one Caesar, and one prime rib. Whaddaya want, rare or medium?"

"Rare."

At the anticipated knock on the door, Marguerite rose from her chair and started across the room to meet the maid. Nick strode in without a word.

"Nick! You're early! I haven't even showered or dressed," she exclaimed, dismayed at her appearance—hair disheveled, no makeup, shapeless old robe.

"Don't bother. You're dressed fine for what I have in mind." He smiled, but it was only a flash of teeth. The eyes were not involved.

"And exactly what is that?" she inquired in her best put-offish schoolteacher voice, muted since their first date.

"Results, that's what."

"I don't understand. What results?" She pulled her skimpy robe more tightly around her.

Nick chuckled, an odd sound squeezing from between tightly drawn lips, raw, jarring, unexpected.

"Don't worry about your virtue. It's in no danger from me. All I want from you are some answers."

"About what?"

"I'll make it very simple," he said, enunciating each syllable slowly and emphatically. "Tell me everything, every word, of your conversation with Joe Smith when you had dinner with him."

Marguerite almost laughed. This was a disaster lightened by absurdity. She had been right, absolutely right, in her initial

assessment of Nicholas Dante. The absurdity was that she had
not trusted her instincts, usually so reliable.

"What concern is it of yours what I talk about to anyone?"
she asked huffily.

"My concern is whatever I make it. Right now it's Joe Smith."

"Is that why you were so nice to me?"

"Did you think it was your irresistible charm?"

"I was a little confused at first but I must admit I was beginning to hope so," she confessed with a hint of wistfulness.

"Marguerite, you disappoint me." He shook his head in a gesture of disapproval, dark eyebrows nearly touching. "I thought
you were smart enough to figure out I must be after something
besides you. You should be more careful of who you pick up in
restaurants."

"Pick up? You forced yourself on us!"

"And it was so easy, wasn't it?"

Embarrassed because he was correct, she lowered her eyelids
over sapphire-blue eyes, her most striking feature, closing off the
windows to the soul, blocking out the sight of the flesh-and-blood
manifestation of her gullibility.

"It was Beatrice who liked you. I was suspicious of you right
away. Why did you drop her?"

"Because she didn't have what I wanted and you do. Now
give."

Stalling for time until she figured out how to handle this situation, and energized by the anger which quickly replaced shame,
she commented lightly, "You're very good at whatever it is
you're doing. You certainly had us fooled. You must have prac-
ticed hard at being a gentleman."

" 'The prince of darkness is a gentleman'—*King Lear*," he
retorted. "Now just answer my question."

"Well, he asked me where his mother's wedding ring was and
I told him it was in the safe-deposit box. Then we did what
parents always do, even divorced ones, we talked about our children. Then . . ."

"Marguerite!" His voice was sharp. The dichotomy in his face
between dexter and sinister had faded. Sinister won. "No more
chatter! You've been babbling to me for days without telling me
anything. 'She speaks yet she says nothing'—*Romeo and Juliet*.
I have no more time to waste on you. I want to know everything
about the book Joe was looking for and I want to know which

one of your bridge friends has it. I already figured out it's not Beatrice. It's someone else and you're going to tell me who right now.''

"Beatrice! So that's why you were pursuing her and getting her life history. You were looking for something from her.''

"Correct. Was. But she's not the one. She's from the Midwest and so was her husband. They have no connection to New England. Too bad I had to drop her so fast. After her going to all that trouble to make sure I understood that she was available and well off. But it's another one of your friends who has the book Joe wanted and you're going to tell me which one. Is it Laura or is it George? You see, I *have* been paying attention.''

"I have no idea what you're talking about.'' A pounding heart and flushed face belied her air of nonchalance.

He smiled again. Not the drop-dead smile that had enchanted her. It was just deadly and accompanied by a move so quick and effortless that it was only when her arm hurt that she realized he had grabbed and twisted it behind her.

"Perhaps a broken arm would jog your memory,'' he hissed.

Emboldened by the knowledge that the maid would appear momentarily, she shrugged the one shoulder not immobilized and challenged him.

"You wouldn't dare! I'll scream. And you won't be able to get away by running out the door. I know your license plate number.''

"Of my rented car.''

She suspected he lied. His Lincoln had leather upholstery and other custom features, not the sterile interior of a rental.

"You're slipping, Nick. That's an obvious lie,'' she retorted boldly, though her shoulder screamed as he twisted harder.

"Don't play with me, Marguerite. 'Come not between the dragon and his wrath'—*King Lear*,'' he quoted, a chilly finality in the way he said it. He gave her arm a cruel jerk, forcing her to move to the right and against him to relieve the pressure. It was then that she became aware of the gun as she stumbled against its metallic hardness under his jacket.

There is no accounting for the vagaries of the human mind. Her first thought on feeling the gun was that she finally understood why his jackets were too loose, an imperfection in his otherwise impeccably fitted clothes.

"It's for the gun, of course. That's why your jacket doesn't fit right."

"Yes. Does it give you a little thrill to realize how close you've been to a monster?"

"Actually it makes me a little sad. I've been silly, but you're being stupid. You're the one who's going to jail. I hope the other inmates appreciate all those cute little quotes you've memorized."

"Jail, Marguerite? For what?"

"For assaulting me, carrying a gun, and threatening me."

"Wrong again. Teacher is slipping. You have no injuries except maybe a little bruise on your wrist—so far, that is. I'm licensed to carry a gun and as for threatening you, I doubt if you'll even want to mention that. You'd never be able to live it down. Especially in that hick town you live in."

"Why wouldn't I report you? You're threatening me."

"Because I'd become the injured party and you'd be a woman scorned. An older woman trying to ensnare a respectable younger man who was just trying to have a few days' peaceful vacation. She went crazy when he rejected her and he had to grab her arm to defend himself. I hope she doesn't get so violent that her arm gets broken. What a sad ending."

His look of feigned sorrow mocked her. The saucy confidence she had acquired deserted her. Once again he had outsmarted her. How much would she have to pay for a few days of pleasant company? Too much, evidently.

"I'm wasting precious time on you. Let's get this over with. Talk!" he demanded.

Before she could even think of a response, a knock at the door caused them both to stare at it nervously.

"It's the maid with towels," Marguerite reported. "I requested them. If I don't answer she'll use her key and come in anyway. You're finished with this little escapade."

"Not yet. Tell her to come in but don't move. I'll be standing right behind you."

"Come in," she called, her voice husky with fear.

"Unlock the door," responded a male voice.

"Ask who it is," whispered Nick, furious at having been tricked by Marguerite's insistence that it was the maid.

"Who's there?"

"It's the police. Open up. We have to talk to you."

Chapter Four

She regretted not getting the oysters. They looked delicious. Joe stubbornly resisted offering her one. Darn him! Marguerite had every intention of ordering oysters until he had presumed to order for her. She had to make the best of it now and tipped her cocktail glass to retrieve the two olives, an attempt to assuage her salivary glands.

"Do you still play bridge, Meg?"

"Yes, every Friday night."

"With the same partners you used to have during our summers there?"

The word "our" sent a shiver of memory through her. "I'm surprised you would even remember who they were."

"Let me see if I do," he mused. Slowly, with a thoughtful expression as if searching his memory, he enumerated, "Well, there was Laura Eldredge, Marge Kelly, and, uh, let me think, oh yes, George Atkinson." He looked triumphant at his feat of memory.

"Marge Kelly has gone. Moved to North Carolina. Beatrice Owens has taken her place. She's only here a couple of years. Very interesting woman. We've become good friends. In fact, I'm traveling to Florida with her. We're leaving the day after tomorrow. That's one of the reasons I didn't want to go out tonight, Joe. I have a million things to do."

"And the other reason, Meg?"

"I've buried the past, Joe. Don't disinter it."

15

*   *   *

"Thank heavens you're here!" she gasped, flinging open the door. "Who called you? Arrest him! He threatened me! And he has a gun!"

Turning to point accusingly at Nick, she was greeted by the sight of him, not cowering but confident, holding up for all to see a small leather folder hanging open to reveal a police badge from Brockton, Massachusetts.

"Officer, may I talk to you outside for a minute?" he asked in an appeasing tone of voice with a compassionate look tossed in Marguerite's direction.

"Glad to oblige," answered a uniformed police officer in a soft Southern accent, opening the door and gesturing to Nick as he did so.

"Don't let him go! He assaulted me!" she insisted, rubbing her shoulder, her voice in its normal range again though a touch hysterical.

"Why don't you sit down over there?" suggested one of the other two men, neither of whom were in uniform. His affiliation was unclear but the clipped speech and pronunciation of *there* as *thayah* left no doubt as to his New England origins.

As if to confirm her first impression, he introduced himself as Massachusetts State Police Sergeant Charles McEnerny, the Charles becoming Chahlz as in the rivah that flows between Bawstin and Cambridge and is the practice site of the Hahvid crew teams.

He looked out of place in the pastel ambience of south Florida. Wearing a dark-brown suit with a white shirt and green rep tie, a navy-blue parka draped over one arm, he had obviously wasted no time in coming here, not even checking into a hotel to unburden himself of his drab winter clothes.

The familiar accent comforted Marguerite and relieved her tension. McEnerny was of medium height and very slender with a luxuriance of pure white hair, prematurely turned and probably originally of the hue known familiarly as "Irish brown," with a propensity for endowing its bearers with white hair as early as in their twenties. Her own father had been similarly crowned. The pallid face, dusted with a faint residue of the freckles of youth, looked wan in this suntanned mecca.

Pale blue eyes were framed by wire-rimmed glasses. Pronounced ridges, one on each side, ran symmetrically from the bottom of the chin to mid-cheek. A faded scar over one eye, a souvenir of his early days as a longshoreman, and variously claimed to be from a fight over union representation, a falling pallet, or a barroom brawl, tinged his otherwise prim look with a hint of toughness.

"This is Massachusetts State Trooper Stephen Fleming," McEnerny was saying as she studied him and wondered why he was here.

The two men were physical contrasts. Fleming was tall, very tall, with lank light-brown hair falling listlessly into his deep-set hazel eyes; smooth skin; and lips in a perfect bow, imparting a look which was young, almost feminine. His size saved him, affirming his gender. And his feet. No dainty appendages were these. They planted him solidly to the ground. He walked as if his feet hurt. They usually did.

"Why are you here?" she asked, beginning to realize the implication of their being from Massachusetts.

Before McEnerny could answer, the door opened and the uniformed officer, sunglasses firmly in place, reentered—alone and carrying several clean towels. The maid had finally come.

"Where is he? Where's Nick?" Marguerite demanded.

"Why, he's gone home, ma'am. He won't be troublin' you anymore."

"Troubling me? Is that what you call it? He was twisting my arm. He carries a gun. Why isn't he under arrest?"

"He's licensed to carry a gun, with him bein' a policeman and all. As for threatenin' you, he denied that and explained why you were so upset and embarrassed when we came in. Maybe it would be best if you forgot the whole incident. But I'm forgettin' my manners. I'm Lyle Fairchild, Fort Lauderdale police. And here's your clean towels, ma'am," he added, proffering them to her, smiling as if presenting her with a gift.

"That's just wonderful! I'm assaulted, and when the police arrive they give me clean towels and let my assailant leave. Nick was right. He said no one would believe me. What did he tell you? That I was chasing him and he rejected my advances? That's what he threatened to say and he evidently got away with it. Did you really believe him? Or is this an example of that famous blue wall of silence? Cops taking care of other cops." In her anger and frustration, she had forgotten the officers from Massachusetts and her curiosity as to their mission.

A red flush beginning to show through his sun-bronzed face, Officer Fairchild sought to assuage her. "Ma'am, you'd be better off just forgettin' about him. Especially with you bein' a school-teacher and all." The longer Fairchild conversed with a Northerner, the more pronounced his drawl became. They seemed to expect it. Kept them off guard, too, on their assumption that no one who spoke like that could be intelligent.

"Oh, he told you that, too, did he? You must have had quite a chummy conversation. One man to another, huh?"

"He was quite a gentleman. Said he hoped we could keep this quiet and not cause you any distress."

"Oh, yes. He's *quite* a gentleman. I know a few quotes, too. 'Women and elephants never forget an injury.' Mr. Nicholas Dante will find out how true that is."

She was pacing now, back and forth, occasionally stooping to pick up one of Beatrice's garments that she brushed to the floor while squeezing past furniture and three men standing haplessly and crowding the room as she fumed and paced.

At this inopportune moment, the telephone rang. Much to McEnerny's chagrin, Marguerite picked it up. It was Beatrice.

"Marguerite, I was hoping to catch you before you left. Is Nick there?"

"Came and gone," was the cryptic answer.

"What do you mean, gone? Aren't you two going to dinner?"

"No, or anyplace else either."

"Sounds like you had a quarrel."

"More, much more than that."

"Okay, I guess you don't want to talk now. I'll tell you why I called. Is my address book anywhere in sight?"

"I'll look."

Marguerite moved some of the clothes covering all the surfaces and found a paisley-covered address book on the console.

"Yes, here it is."

"Great! Look under the Cs for Coughlin. Kenneth Coughlin. He moved to Boca but has an unlisted number. I'd like to call him."

"Here it is, Coughlin, K." She recited the number.

"Thanks. Don't let Nick upset you. Think of it as a learning experience."

"Yes, but what a hard lesson. 'Bye."

The phone call had calmed her. She would have to learn to be more like Beatrice.

McEnerny cleared his throat to gain her attention and ventured a neutral question.

"Are you Marguerite Smith?"

"Of course, I am," she flung impatiently at him. But the simple query and automatic response broke the spell. Her facial expression, in its anger mode with lines of fury appearing on her forehead and upper lip, transmogrified in stages, first shifting to the knotted forehead of puzzlement, finally to the wide-eyed, openmouthed look of fear and realization.

"Something is wrong. What is it? Is it one of my children? What happened?"

"No, it's not your children. It's Joseph Smith. He's dead."

She searched for the chair she had recently vacated and sat sideways on it, holding onto its back for support.

"Dead? He didn't seem that sick but I knew he had something, probably a touch of the flu. It must have turned into walking pneumonia and with the heart problems he had it killed him."

She was ruminating, talking only to herself. The three police officers remained awkwardly silent, waiting for her to initiate the next question. In police work, one could learn as much from what people did not ask as from what they did ask.

"Why did you come here to tell me this? Joe and I are divorced. For twelve years. He has another wife now. Didn't you know that?"

"We know it, Mrs. Smith," responded McEnerny, moving very close to her now, observing every line of her facial expression, every nuance of her words. The man whose familiar speech had provided comfort so recently was now adversarial. "But he didn't die of pneumonia. He was murdered. Understand? And you were the last person seen with him."

Chapter Five

A *s he savored the oysters, rather more ostentatiously than*
necessary, Marguerite observed him. Joseph Smith was a
very handsome man. Tall and still slender, with only his thinning
brown hair, invaded here and there by gray strands that replaced
the reddish-gold highlights and dulled their former sheen, to
mark the years. The amber eyes were the same. They seemed to
have come in a matched set with his hair. She had never seen
eyes that color on anyone else until their daughter Alexandra
was born.

The salads finally arrived. Starved though she was, Marguerite
resisted digging in heartily and settled for daintily picking at it.
She would not let him know how hungry the sight of those oysters
had made her.

"Does Laura still live in that mausoleum of hers?" he asked,
his face flushed, whether from the martini or his cold, Marguerite
could not decide.

"What you're calling a mausoleum is a historic house. It's
been in the family for over two hundred years," she replied in-
dignantly, defending a house she didn't like, with its small, dark
rooms, inadequate insulation, and musty smell despite the drafts
that permanently ventilated the inside air.

"Probably has the original roof, too. Laura always spent more
time taking care of those old family records than she did taking
care of that crumbling house. Does she still keep all those old
books and papers?"

20

"Yes, she does. Those old papers, as you call them, are important historical documents. Her ancestors were Puritans, here since the 1600s."

"There wouldn't have been enough Puritan descendants to survive if they all had her personality. Does she still beat you at bridge, Meg?"

"Only when she cheats."

"Murdered? Why would anyone want to murder Joe? Are you sure there isn't some mistake?" Her voice trembled.

"We're sure," replied McEnerny tersely.

Officer Fairchild opened his mouth preparatory to saying something soothing to Marguerite. McEnerny caught the motion and halted the incipient condolence with a furrowing of the brow and a flashing of those blue eyes, icy like only blue eyes can be, with a cold light bouncing off them as from an iceberg. The normally loquacious Fairchild remained silent. As did Trooper Fleming, who had yet to utter a word.

"How did he die?"

"Poisoning," answered McEnerny, as stingy with words as a telegram.

"Was it food poisoning? The oysters maybe. I didn't eat any. And with Joe's cold he might not have noticed if they were off. No, it couldn't have been. That was over a week ago. Unless, of course, he was sick a long time from the poisoning. But that's not murder, Officer. Unless you consider serving contaminated oysters murder."

"No, Mrs. Smith, it wasn't the oysters. It wasn't any kind of accidental poisoning. Understand? It was murder."

"How? How was he poisoned?"

"The lab hasn't completed the tests. But he was murdered all right."

"Why did you come all the way down here to see me? I can't help you. I've been away for over a week."

"I repeat, Mrs. Smith. You were the last person seen with him alive. We have three witnesses who swear that you were with him on the evening of January fifteenth, having dinner together in Orleans." His stare was relentless, unblinking.

"That's right, I was with him. But that doesn't mean I murdered him. Why would I want to kill Joe?"

"We're not accusing you of murdering him. We just need your

help and want to know everything that happened that night. Even if you're not aware of it, there might be some clue he dropped that would give us a lead to a motive or even to the murderer.''

Marguerite shifted position to gaze out the window, averting her eyes from the officers, not trusting herself to speak without crying. But she never cried and would not do so now. Lips compressed, eyes wide open to disperse the unwelcome moisture, she ignored the intrusive police presence.

Having lost her attention, McEnerny turned to Fleming and ordered, ''Call up room service. Get some sandwiches and coffee sent up here. Lots of coffee. It's dinnertime and this lady hasn't eaten yet.''

''Neither have we,'' ventured Fleming, his first words since entering the room.

Abandoning the shock treatment as having been ineffective, McEnerny ventured a display of solicitousness, trusting that it would encourage openness on her part. Some women crumbled when confronted with strength. Others responded to tenderness. Mrs. Smith was evidently the latter. No sweat. She would tell him what he wanted to know. They always did.

Turning back to Marguerite, who was still sitting sideways on the chair clutching its back, he entreated in a soft cajoling tone, ''Why don't you tell us everything you and Joe talked about. I'm sure you want to help us find out who murdered him.''

He underestimated Marguerite. Her mind had already raced through her last meeting with Joe and its implications. This policeman was smooth but lying. Two state policemen did not fly to Florida to ask a couple of questions that she could have answered on the phone. They did suspect her. And she had a motive. But did they know about it? She needed time to think.

Pulling her thin bathrobe around her, Marguerite addressed McEnerny but looked at Fairchild, whom she had guessed to be more chivalrous. ''Sgt. McEnerny, I haven't had time to change since leaving the beach. I was waiting for the towels. I'm cold,'' she added plaintively, and shivered to punctuate the remark. The shiver was only partially feigned. ''Do you mind if I dress first? Some warm clothes and hot coffee would make me feel better. Beatrice always has that air conditioner set too low.''

There was no stopping Fairchild this time. ''Of course we don't mind, ma'am. Why don't we just all step outside while you dress up?''

Marguerite intercepted the icicle look flying in the air toward Fairchild. She intervened. "That's not necessary. I can take my things into the bathroom," she volunteered, already opening drawers and gathering clothes—a turquoise knit shirt, long white pants, and a set of underwear tucked discreetly between the outer garments. Detouring to pick up the towels delivered by Fairchild, she rewarded him with a smile, a tacit thank-you for his courtesy.

Trooper Fleming was uneasy. Before leaving Massachusetts, they had been carefully instructed by Lt. Medeiros that Marguerite Smith was not a suspect. She was to be considered as a possible witness who might have some information leading to a suspect. They were to treat her accordingly.

Fleming had paid attention. McEnerny had not. To him everyone was a suspect. Every living creature that walked, crawled, swam, or flew had something to hide. He was intent on unearthing all those secrets while obscuring his own.

A suspect about to be questioned had to be read her rights; a witness did not. McEnerny was getting very close to the line. He would probably cross it. Though committed to guarding against such infringements, Stephen Fleming, recent law school graduate, hoped he didn't have to.

Though six inches taller and fifty pounds heavier, he was thoroughly intimidated by McEnerny. It was not the sergeant's rank or body that alarmed Fleming, it was his soul. McEnerny did not seem to have one. His intellect and emotions were clearly separated. One could look straight through those clear blue eyes and find—nothing. Only bottomless emptiness.

Marguerite was taking a long time to dress and McEnerny was impatient. He concluded she was stalling. He was right. She had dressed in two minutes and was seated on the edge of the tub, considering her options.

If they learned why Joe had visited her, it would be very easy to conclude that she had reason to kill him. Unless he had been murdered after she and Beatrice had left for Florida. She had to ask that question first. Once she knew the date of the murder, she could decide how much to reveal, telling the truth as far as possible. It was simpler that way.

If Joe had been murdered while she was still on the Cape, there were parts of their last conversation she did not want to reveal. That would be difficult. This McEnerny looked tough. She recognized him, not personally but as to type. In her youth in South

Boston, there were many young men like him, poor wannabes yearning for a better life. Some found it within the system, some without. Some never found it at all. McEnerny had taken the police route, a common one for young Irish-Americans.

Yes, he was tough but not infallible. He had made a mistake already when he so cavalierly ignored her allegations about Nick. If he had asked her why Nick was threatening her, she would have answered truthfully and told the whole story about her meeting with Joe. Before she knew he was murdered, she had nothing to hide. Now she was not so sure.

A knock at the bathroom door was followed by Fleming's voice. "Are you all right, Mrs. Smith? The coffee and sandwiches are here."

"I'm fine. I'll be right out."

With a run of the comb through her wind-tangled hair, a dabbing on of lipstick, and a pinch to her pallid cheeks, she was ready for them.

I've been an ex-wife for twelve years and any recent disagreement between Joe and me was strictly personal. I have nothing to hide, nothing to hide, nothing . . . she kept repeating silently as she strode erectly and shamly confident from the security of the bathroom, remembering to suck in her stomach as she walked.

Chapter Six

"And old George? Is he still complaining of his arthritis?" Joe inquired during the interval between the clearing of the salads and the serving of the entrées.

"Not much. Only when he's having a particularly bad spell."

The cough began again and Joe reached into the pocket of his beautifully tailored suit to retrieve the handkerchief thrust there so many times during this dinner.

He must still use the same tailor, she speculated. Joe's suits had always been made by a family of custom tailors who had served the Smiths for generations. Quietly elegant, his clothes imparted that look of belonging—to a social class, to an economic class, to the coterie that had flourished in Boston from its earliest days. Marguerite had been confounded by his ability to wear new clothes without their looking new, without that tacky, shiny, just-off-the-rack look. She tried for years to emulate him but never succeeded. She concluded that one had to be born to it.

"I wish I could get rid of this cough. It's bad for my heart."

"I didn't know you had a bad heart," Marguerite commented with a little catch in her throat.

"It's not serious. Just some angina. But this coughing is a strain. I'll have to get some cough medicine. Are any of the drugstores open at night?"

"I'm not sure, but one of them might be. If not, Stop & Shop is open."

"Good. Getting back to old George, does he still live in the same house? It was on Bridge Road, I think."

"Yes, he's still there."

"Big house for one man. He needs a wife."

"Some men cherish the memory of the wife they had."

Fairchild acted as host, which in a way he was. It was his town, his jurisdiction. He was not going to let these Northern boys run the whole show.

The remaining chairs had been cleared of clothes, which were now heaped on the bed like a tired rainbow, and the four of them sat at the small round table in front of the sliding glass door leading to the requisite terrace. Fairchild poured coffee, passed milk and sugar, and described the sandwich choices as he handed the tray around. He even attempted light conversation.

"And how has your visit to Fort Lauderdale been so far, ma'am?" he inquired, sounding like a member of the chamber of commerce and ignoring the reality that in the last few hours she had been assaulted (purportedly), advised of the murder of her ex-husband, and fingered as having been the last person with him.

"Just fine," she answered, joining the charade, but declining the sandwich while accepting the hot coffee. "You certainly have a beautiful beach."

"I think we should get back to the reason we're here," interjected MeEnerny, also taking only coffee. He and Marguerite were like two toreadors preparing for the corrida, stomachs empty, reflexes caffeinated. "Now, Mrs. Smith, if you would just answer some questions. We really need your help," he concluded with uncustomary humility, still role-playing.

"Of course," she answered with a faint smile, not a smile of joy, just a smile of politeness, with the corners of her mouth barely creasing and her lips remaining closed. "But would you mind telling me when Joe was mur . . . uh, died? I was so shocked that I don't even remember what you said."

"I didn't say."

"Then please tell me now," she persisted.

"I didn't say because we don't know." Even in his friendly mode, McEnerny resisted giving information.

"I'm afraid I don't understand. When was he found?"

"His body was discovered on January twenty-first."

Marguerite tried hard to disguise it, but the sigh of relief escaped audibly from her lungs.

Counting backward on her fingers, she concluded, "I told you I couldn't help you. That's the day I arrived in Fort Lauderdale. We checked into this hotel. You can verify it if you want. Although I guess you already have."

They had. As well as the fact that Marguerite had personally filled out and signed her registration card.

"You're not paying attention, Mrs. Smith. I said the body was found on January twenty-first. Understand? I didn't say when he was murdered." Irritability had surfaced. Catching its sarcastic overtone, McEnerny squashed it in a renewed show of concern. "I know how upsetting this must be for you, having just been notified of the murder of a member of your family, your children's father, but we really need your help."

Marguerite started. She had forgotten about the children. She had to notify them.

McEnerny continued on, "The only reason I didn't give you the date of death is that we don't know it. I'm being completely honest with you"—Fleming turned his head away before he winced—"and telling you everything we know. The body had been in an unheated place for some time. It was frozen. That makes it difficult to nail down the date of death. Understand? That's why we need you to help us."

Her cheeks could have used another pinching. Joe, the love of her life, had been murdered and then discarded somewhere until his body froze, unattended and unmourned. But her mind was not as bereft of blood as was her skin. The synapses were screaming, "You're a suspect! Don't let them know you had a motive!"

"What can I do to help you?" she asked calmly.

McEnerny's neurons were not idle either. He noted with satisfaction that she never asked where the body was found, one of those omissions he considered significant.

"Did you often see your ex-husband?" he began softly.

"No, not often."

"When did you see him last, before January fifteenth?"

"Oh, let me think," she pondered, one hand to the side of her forehead. "I think it was some years ago."

"How many years?"

"It was at our daughter's college graduation." She neglected to mention that Joe had been there despite Alexandra's refusal to send him an invitation.

"And when was that?"

"That was, oh, eleven years ago."

"And from eleven years ago to January fifteenth, you never saw him."

"That's correct. Officer Fairchild, would you mind passing me the plate of sandwiches? I'd like a half of the chicken. I couldn't eat any before but that coffee has warmed me and I'm feeling a little hungry. Of course, I'm sure this isn't anything like real Southern chicken. No one can fix chicken like a Southern cook can."

"That's kind of you to say, Mrs. Smith," Fairchild replied with a half bow from his sitting position.

"Could we forget the chicken? I have important business here. Understand?" McEnerny was having difficulty keeping up his end of the polite pas de deux.

"After all those years, why did Joe decide to take you to dinner that particular night?"

He caught Fleming's head rising from the pad on which he was taking notes—McEnerny hated taking notes—and softened the question. "I only ask this because his state of mind and his actions may be a clue to the reason for his murder." Fleming resumed writing but not before he edged the back of his shoes off his feet.

She finished chewing a bite of the sandwich before she replied, using the time to seek a truthful answer. "I wondered that myself." It was the absolute truth.

"Didn't you ask?"

"Joe was a financial advisor with many clients, some on Cape Cod. Mostly retirees who used to live in Boston or Brookline." True again.

"Did he just knock on the door on a snowy night in January?"

"No, he called the day before."

"And despite the fact that you hadn't seen him in eleven years you agreed to go to dinner with him."

"Yes, I did."

"Why?"

"Why not?" Their eyes locked, her rich blues against his pale ones. Fire against ice. The whine of the air conditioner was the only sound in the room. Chewing stopped. Breathing was suppressed. It ended in a draw, both ocular combatants looking away in the same instant.

Fleming and Fairchild almost cheered. McEnerny was one of them. Mrs. Smith might be a murderer, but for one brief interval she had put the insufferable sergeant in his place.

It was a Pyrrhic victory. McEnerny had ascertained she was hiding something. No dame ever stood up to him like that. This one was hard as nails under that ladylike pose. It would make his ultimate victory sweeter. And victory was assured, because Charles McEnerny was harder than nails.

Chapter Seven

"You seem to be making a survey of my friends. Is there a point to all these questions, Joe?" she inquired as she paused in her dissection of the duck, browned to her taste, not half raw as some of the new chefs insisted on serving it.

Joe's appetite was off. He had barely touched the prime rib, rare and bloody as he preferred. The bottom of his plate had turned red from the oozing juices. It matched the red that distorted the whites of his eyes, angry from the allergens invading his body.

"Yes, Meg, there is. There's something I'd like you to do."

"What?"

"I'd like you to borrow a book for me."

"From where?"

"From one of your friends."

"Why don't you borrow it yourself? You know all of them. Except Beatrice, of course. But how would you know Beatrice had anything you would want? I don't understand."

"It's a little complicated. I can't do it myself because I don't want the person to know that this book has been borrowed. You can do it because you go to the house to play bridge."

Her eyes widened. "You don't want me to borrow a book. You want me to steal one!"

In the nearly empty restaurant her voice carried and two women at one of the other occupied tables turned to look.

Joe laughed as if she had said something funny and smiled at

30

the gaping women while shrugging his shoulders as if in amusement at Marguerite's funny statement. They smiled back and turned away to resume their conversation, two local businesswomen enjoying the luxury of a leisurely dinner in the off-season.

"Don't get so excited, Meg. I just want to borrow something that is sitting unused, probably being eaten by bookworms."

"Is it a valuable book? Do you plan to sell it?"

"The book has no intrinsic value. It's nothing in itself. But it has some information in it I need."

"Then why can't I just ask to borrow it?"

"Because it's important that no one know what's in there. Someone could beat me out on it. I'm talking about millions, Meg," he whispered, the frantic tone a stranger to his lexicon of cultured speech patterns.

"Who has this book you're so hot to get?"

"I can't tell you that until you've agreed to help me."

"Then you might as well finish your dinner, Joe. This conversation is ended. The answer is no."

"I don't think so, Meg. I think you're going to want to help me."

Refilling his coffee cup, McEnerny began anew.

"Did he pick you up or did you meet him at the restaurant?"

"He picked me up. At seven twenty-five. I know the exact time because I was watching the clock. He was supposed to be there at seven."

"Did he say why he was late?"

"Yes. He said he had an unexpected meeting at the last minute. He didn't say who with."

"Tell us everything you can remember about your conversation."

"Well, he asked me about his mother's ring and wanted to know where it was. I told him it was in the bank and I was planning to give it to a granddaughter if we ever have one. Then he asked why I didn't give it to our daughter when she got married since I don't wear it anymore. I told him I did offer it to her but—"

"Wait!" McEnerny interrupted, hands upraised. "Is this ring valuable?"

"It's probably worth a few thousand dollars, maybe more. Joe was more concerned with its sentimental value. It has been in his family a long time.''

"Did he want it back?''

"He never asked for it. If he had I would have given it to him.''

A dead end.

"Let's skip the ring. What else did you talk about?''

"Bridge. He wanted to know if I still played bridge.''

"Do you?''

"Oh, yes. Every Friday.''

"What else?''

"He asked if I still play in the same foursome. I told him Marge Kelly had moved to North Carolina and Beatrice Owens had taken her place. Then he asked if Laura and George still played and I told him yes. Then—''

"Do you play for money?''

"Laura play for money? Are you serious?''

"Let's skip the bridge. What else?''

Marguerite crowed inwardly and paused to take another bite of sandwich until she could control the elation in her voice. Charles McEnerny was so bored with her he was dismissing the first significant part of her conversation with Joe—the members of her bridge group.

"He had a terrible cough and asked me if there was a drugstore open. I told him there might be and Stop & Shop definitely would be. It's open twenty-four hours a day. His cough—''

"Let's skip the cough. What else?'' He was drowning in chatter. Useless, meaningless chatter.

As she paused to recall the next topic of conversation, Fleming gratefully used the time to remove his jacket and brush the damp hair from his forehead. He wished he could remove his tie but knew he would be risking a scathing tongue-lashing as soon as the sergeant had him alone. McEnerny never reacted to weather, hot or cold, and still had on his woolen jacket with tie firmly in place.

Fairchild, a native Southerner, found the winter weather refreshing and looked crisp and cool in his starched, short-sleeved uniform shirt. His dark hair was unparted and combed straight back in an unrelieved smoothness. The sunglasses had finally been removed and tucked in his shirt pocket, revealing wide-spaced brown eyes retreating from a nose slightly larger than average, balanced by full lips and a thrusting chin. Fairchild was good-looking without the responsibility of being handsome.

Although he refrained from participating in the questioning, he was paying more careful attention than his laid-back attitude would indicate. A lifelong hunter, he measured people in terms of the web of life, the dynamics of predator and prey. In this contest Marguerite was a sparrow, McEnerny, with hooded eyes, a hawk. Against all odds, sometimes the sparrow escaped. If this one did, he intended to keep her in his sights.

Perhaps he would even talk again with Nicholas Dante. Though he had not detained him, there was something about the man that made him uneasy, brother officer though he was. Fairchild sensed in Nick the sullen guardedness and hopeful seductiveness of the predatory male. Florida was a haven for men like this, with more than its share of lonely and well-off women.

Either Nick or Marguerite was lying. If she was lying about Nick, she might be lying now. If she had told the truth about Nick, she might be in need of protection. In the meantime, he took another sandwich. He might be missing a home-cooked dinner but the overtime he was racking up was worth it.

She resumed her narrative. "I told him I was going to Florida in two days with Beatrice."

"Did he ask you to do anything for him in Florida? Or to carry home anything for him from Florida?"

Marguerite reacted with shock. "Sergeant, are you talking about drugs? Joe would never deal in drugs and he would certainly know enough not to ask me to participate if he did."

"Okay, let's skip the drugs. Did he appear to be in fear for his life?"

"Only from the cough. He said it was straining his heart because he had angina."

"Did he mention any enemies, anyone who might be a danger to him?"

"No."

"What time did you leave the restaurant?"

"About nine-thirty or a quarter to ten."

"Did you go straight home?"

"Yes."

"What happened to the cough medicine?"

"I guess he forgot about it."

He stared at her, long and hard, silent, unmoving, except for his hands, which flexed and relaxed repeatedly. He was anxious for the kill and moved in.

"Tell me what you fought about in the restaurant. The fight that made you both forget the cough medicine." Simply said, no emphasis. Fleming tensed.

"Fought? What do you mean, fought?" The sparrow was in the hawk's sights.

"We have a witness, three in fact, who say you had a fight, made threatening remarks, and left without waiting for the coffee you ordered. Decaffeinated," he could not resist adding, showing off.

"Are you accusing me of something? Are you charging me with murder because I had some words with my ex-husband? Because if you are, I'm going to stop even talking to you."

"No, no, not at all," McEnerny countered, palms uplifted and opened in a gesture meant to calm and to attest to his truthfulness. "But if he was upset because of some problems he was having, that would help us. Understand?"

"Husbands and wives, even ex-ones, argue over a lot of things. Mostly trivial. Are you married, Sergeant?"

Fairchild harrumphed. Fleming relaxed. McEnerny dodged.

"What time did you get home?"

"Before ten. I let Rusty out—that's my dog—but she didn't stay out long. The ground was snowy and she hates to get her feet wet. Then I watched the ten-o'clock news."

"Did Joe Smith come into the house with you?"

"No."

"Did you see him again or hear from him before you left for Florida?"

"No."

"Did you leave your house again that night?"

"No."

"Can anyone confirm that?"

"Of course not!"

"No phone calls?"

"No, oh, wait a minute. I did make one. Shortly after I returned home. There was a message on my answering machine to call Beatrice. She needed the address where we were staying in Florida. I called to give it to her."

"Any incoming calls?"

"No."

"Is there anything you can tell us about a reason for someone to murder him?"

No one but me, she thought, but said, "I know nothing about his murder."

"That's all for now, Mrs. Smith. We'll drop by tomorrow with a statement for you to sign."

She was not that easily dismissed.

"Sergeant, where was Joe murdered?" she asked softly.

"We don't know yet." He looked as sour as the acid gurgling in his empty stomach. One of the significant omissions had just evaporated.

"Well, where was he found?" she persisted.

"In Eastham. In the lighthouse."

"Which lighthouse?"

"One of the Three Sisters."

"But they're always locked," she blurted unthinkingly.

His interest was piqued. "You seem very familiar with those lighthouses. How do you know they're locked?"

Trying to speak casually to cover her blunder, she answered, "That's no secret. Every so often, usually during National Maritime Week, all the lighthouses are open to the public. Last year I went to the Three Sisters for an early tour and the guide had to find a park ranger to unlock the doors."

McEnerny did not intend to linger and subject himself to more of her questions. Not believing in prolonged farewells, he walked to the door and left without looking to see whether the other two men were following him. He knew they would.

As fear and tension ebbed from Marguerite's consciousness, sorrow trickled in, filling the vacuum. She should have hated Joe by now, but an emotion gestated at the age of nineteen was not easily aborted. He was the standard by which she measured every other man, and all had been found wanting. He was the albatross that doomed every attempt she had made at dating after their divorce.

This orgy of regret culminated in tears that began to run down her cheeks, unnoticed until she tasted their salt in her mouth. She made a desultory attempt to wipe them away, then abandoned herself to their luxury. It was finally time to cry.

She was deprived of that time. A loud rapping at the door and the abrasive voice of McEnerny intervened.

"It's the police, Mrs. Smith. Open up."

They had not gone far, only to a telephone in the lobby from where the sergeant had called his headquarters in Massachusetts to issue a verbal report. He received more than he gave and hurried upstairs again to confront Marguerite.

She opened the door, red-eyed, wet-faced, using the sleeve of her shirt to swipe her cheeks and eyes.

He swaggered in; there was no other word for it.

"Let's start over, Mrs. Smith. I think you forgot to tell us something. Tell us what Joe and you discussed about your house. Understand?"

Chapter Eight

"*You have no hold over me, Joe. The answer is no, positively and absolutely no. If you want to steal something, then do it. Leave me out of it. But if one of my friends' houses is broken into I'll know who's behind it and tell the police.*" *Her lips trembled as this threat escaped past them. Could she really turn him in?*

"*What do you know about real estate law, Meg?*"

"*Very little. Why?*"

"*I suppose you don't know the difference between joint tenants and tenants in common.*"

"*No, I don't. What does it matter to me?*"

"*Oh, it matters, particularly to you. You see, if a house is owned as joint tenants, the property can only be conveyed or sold by the agreement of both people or by a court of law acting upon a request for the partitioning of the property.*"

Joe was warming to the lecture. His coughing subsided; his eyes were animated. He had abandoned his customary erect posture to lean forward so that he would not be heard in the quiet restaurant.

"*On the other hand if property is owned by two people as tenants in common, each owns half and owns it independently of the other half. Either one of the partners can sell his share to someone else, to anyone he chooses,*" *he concluded in triumph.*

"*Joe, I think you're delirious. This mumbo jumbo about tenants this and tenants that has nothing to do with me. I received*

*the house in our divorce settlement. It's the only thing I got. I
never asked you for anything else."*

*"That was foolish of you, Meg. You could have gotten more.
And now you'll end up with even less. You should always pay
attention to the mumbo jumbo. That's where all the good stuff is
hidden."*

Her first impulse was to deny everything, the instinct for self-
preservation battling her innate honesty. This impulse dissolved
almost as quickly as it had wafted through her mind. They knew!

Fleming stepped into a position slightly behind Marguerite and
out of her sight but directly in the line of McEnerny's vision. He
gestured to his pocket as he partially withdrew from it a small
card.

The sergeant silently cursed Fleming and bemoaned the decision to pair them for this investigation. With a free hand he could
probably settle the whole matter right now. This woman was at
the breaking point. Reluctantly, grudgingly, he nodded.

Fleming moved around in front of Marguerite and after his
characteristic gesture of pushing the hair out of his eyes began
to read, "You have the right to remain silent. . . ."

It was almost a relief. It was out in the open. She was a suspect.
The rules had been established by that dog-eared card. The adren-
aline of fear cleared her mind of suffocating emotions like sorrow
and self-pity.

"Sgt. McEnerny," began Marguerite, in the voice formerly
reserved to address wayward pupils, "I have nothing further to
say to you until I consult with an attorney. Since my attorney is
in Massachusetts, and since this incident occurred in Massachusetts, I shall return there as soon as I am able to make arrangements. I have a friend staying with me and she will be forced to
alter her plans as well. If you leave a telephone number with me,
I shall call you tomorrow. Unless you plan to arrest me right
now."

His face was a mask, betraying neither disappointment nor anger. "We'll call you, early," he commented in a flat voice, more
threatening because of its coldness. His glasses had shifted a frac-
tion lower on his nose, causing the wire frame to underline and
highlight the scar over his eye. Still carrying his winter parka, he
turned and left.

Fleming followed, turning back to Marguerite with an undecided smile, part disappointment, part sympathy.

Fairchild exited with a "Good evenin', ma'am."

As soon as they left, she regretted their leaving. Fear enveloped her, overshadowing any relief at being free of questioning and suspicions.

Joe had been murdered! Not because of some silly dispute over her house. *She* didn't murder him. But he had been trying to frighten her in order to get some book he wanted. From whom? What was in it? Was it valuable enough for Joe to have been murdered over it?

Nick must know. She would call him and ask. He said he was staying at Howard Johnson's. Unless that was a lie, too.

The number was easily obtained. The directions for making calls from the hotel took a little longer to decipher as she slogged through the possibilities on the little card.

"Howard Johnson Ocean's Edge Resort."

"Would you please connect . . . Fool!" she exclaimed aloud.

"Pardon me?"

"Oh, I didn't mean you. I meant me. I mean, er, I have the wrong number. Sorry to bother you." She replaced the receiver gently, apologetically.

What was I thinking, calling Nick? He threatened to break my arm. He has a gun. Since the police don't seem to know the exact date of Joe's murder, Nick might even be the murderer. Then he followed me because he didn't get the information he wanted from Joe. He seems to think I know who has that book. He's probably going to come back after he's sure the police are gone for the night. My call would have been the all-clear signal. Think, Marguerite, think!

Footsteps, soft on the rug but perceptible, came down the hall, slowing as they approached her door. She ran to it, turned the deadbolt, and attached the chain. The door to the next room opened and closed; the television came on.

She wished Beatrice were there. In the meantime, she had to get out of this room. Even with three locks on the door, she felt insecure. It would be safer to be around people. Grabbing her purse, she abandoned the room and ran into the hallway, usually resounding with the chatter of happy vacationers, now ominously empty even though it was only nine o'clock. As she rang for the elevator she prayed someone would be on it. If not, she would pass it by and wait for another. She debated using the stairway but decided that was even more dangerous.

At last a down elevator settled on her floor, opening to reveal a young couple wearing socks but no shoes, in-line skates slung over their shoulders, and protective pads on knees, elbows, and wrists. No helmets, however. Nothing to hide or restrain their shiny blond hair, streaked even more so by the sun, hers flying loosely, long all around, his cut short on the sides and long in the back. As distressed as she was, Marguerite took it all in and thought their safety priorities interesting.

Now what? Peering into the nightclub, she noted it was about half full, but would probably crowd up as the late diners sauntered in. She wasn't in the mood for a festive atmosphere, for being the specter at the feast, and turned away, choosing to sit in the lobby to await Beatrice.

Ensconced among tropical trees and caged birds, with people passing to and fro, she felt less vulnerable but more isolated. Everyone was with someone. She needed a someone to help her but was far from home and unsure if there was help even there. The police would be waiting for her. Oh, where was Beatrice?

Resigned to the wait, she settled back amidst the enveloping foliage with half-closed eyes, starting at every break in the rhythmn of the noises. At ten o'clock she roused from this lethargy long enough to telephone her children—Cornelius in Seattle, Alexandra in Washington, D.C.—and advise them of their father's death, while dodging any reference to her present predicament despite the yearning to cry "Help!"

With her energy fading, she returned gratefully to her post in the jungle, waiting for Beatrice. The next time she looked at her watch it was eleven o'clock. She might have missed Beatrice, hidden as she was among the luxuriant plants, eyes closing involuntarily.

Inquiring at the desk for messages, she was handed one from Beatrice, who had called an hour ago. She was with an old friend and had decided to say overnight in Boca Raton. An old friend named Ken, conjectured Marguerite.

Weariness dulling her fear, Marguerite decided to go to bed. She would secure all the door locks and put the bar across the glass sliders. It was silly to think that Nick could force his way in through all that hardware. She would be perfectly safe.

Exiting the elevator on her floor, she had second thoughts. It had been two hours since she had left her room. Only the single door lock had been engaged. Those locks were notoriously easy to open. Especially for a policeman. Nick could even have gained entry to the room by showing his badge to a gullible chambermaid. Some of them had trouble with English but Nick's charm and dazzling smile spoke a universal language. It certainly fooled her!

The nearer she got to her room, the more trepidation she felt. As she stood ouside the door, hesitating, a sound emanated either from her room or one next to it. She turned and fled, this time not stopping in the lobby but heading right out the door and into a passing taxi.

"Where to?" the driver inquired as he flipped the meter arm.

"Just drive away. I'll tell you later."

Chapter Nine

The waitress cleared their places, his dinner lying uneaten, her plate cleaned. He declined to have his prime rib wrapped up to take with him. She said she would take it for her dog.

"You see, Meg, we own our house as tenants in common and I intend to sell my half. What do you think the house is worth now, two hundred thousand, maybe two-twenty-five?"

"You can't sell anything. I own the house. You signed it over to me. I have the papers."

"I'm afraid that what you have is a forgery. I never signed anything. I've just been letting you live there all these years. And, of course, you're a half owner. You'll acquire a roommate."

"Joe, my lawyer received those papers from your lawyer. How could they be a forgery? Your lawyer knows they're not. He saw you sign them."

"Unfortunately for you, that's not the way it happened. I was traveling a lot at that time, if you remember, and a lot of the papers were being mailed back and forth between me and my lawyer. That one must have gone astray and I never saw it. Someone must have signed it for me. I'm still a half owner."

"That won't work, Joe. I know the lawyer you used and he would never be a party to a fraud like this. Roger Wilcox will remember you signed it and won't lie for you."

"I guess you don't read the obituaries, Meg. At least not the

42

Boston ones. Roger Wilcox is dead. Now let's talk a little more about that book I want you to borrow for me."

Marguerite emptied the contents of her pocketbook onto the front desk. No glasses. She remembered using them to look up the telephone number of Howard Johnson's in her ill-considered notion to contact Nick. She must have left them on the nightstand when she fled the room.

The clerk, whose name tag identified him as William Morrison III, was making impatient noises and fidgeting. It certainly was not due to the press of work. At this late hour Marguerite was the only one commanding his attention.

A vein-swollen face with its look of flushed alcoholic excess provided a road map to his slow decline and this temporary way stop as night manager of the Hotel Tropicana—an economy hotel, blocks from the beach, no pool, no extras. It was temporary because this no-star hotel had a minimum of overhead guaranteeing a maximum of profit providing the occupancy rate was high. It was a harbor for spontaneous travelers, last-minute arrivals, free spirits without reservations. Night clerk was an important cog, too important to entrust to an alcoholic. His propensity for this addiction would no doubt be discovered and he would fall one notch further in his slide to the bottom.

"You can fill it out for me," she suggested, pushing the registration card and pen toward him.

"Name?" he asked in a bored voice.

"Mar . . . Margaret Johnson," she offered, catching her paranoiac self in mid-word.

"Address?"

She improvised a fictitious street in a fictitious town in New Hampshire.

"License plate?"

"None. I came by cab."

"Credit card number?"

"I'll pay cash."

He studied her. A lone woman, arriving late at night with no luggage and paying cash. If she had been younger, he would have been obliged by management rules to question her further, see some identification. But this woman was too old to be in that profession. Let her go. It was nice to have a cash customer.

William Morrison III handed her a key, gestured vaguely in

the direction of the room, and hurried into his haven behind the desk where he pressed the button to activate the neon NO VACANCY sign. Now he could have some peace.

The door to the room was yawning open. She began to retreat but caught herself, feeling foolish. No one could possibly have known she was coming here to this particular room. The maid must have left it open. Nevertheless, she left the door ajar as she snapped on every light and checked the bathroom and under the two queen-sized beds. Empty except for dust balls.

Relieved at the lack of a terrace, she engaged the three locks and dropped into bed in her underwear. She assumed she would never sleep—but she did, though fitfully and with images of Joe in various guises slipping across her dreamscape.

Lyle Fairchild was not enjoying the basketball game. Instead of watching Shaq leap for a dunk he was seeing Marguerite Smith opening the door for them, obviously relieved at their presence.

Had they, or rather he, made a mistake in letting Dante go? So intent were they on a murder investigation that they might have overlooked another crime. Or maybe even a connection to the same crime.

Joe Smith had been murdered in Massachusetts. Nicholas Dante was from Massachusetts. Was it only a coincidence that he had met Marguerite Smith in Florida? And why was a policeman from another state carrying a gun on vacation? And on a date with a lady? He had decided almost immediately upon meeting her that she merited being called a lady. Maybe he ought to check on her. See if she was okay.

During the next commercial, at about eleven-twenty, he dialed the Sea Club and rang her room. No answer. Not unusual for someone on vacation, but she looked too distressed to be out socializing.

Still uneasy, he called the desk, identified himself, and asked if anyone had seen her.

"Why, yes," answered the desk clerk. "We're so busy I don't usually notice people coming or going but I did notice her because she was sitting in the lobby for so long. Looked as if she was waiting for someone. Then she came to the desk and asked if there were any messages. I gave her one that was left in her box. About ten minutes later I saw her hurrying out and waving a taxi."

"You wouldn't happen to know what was in the message, would you?"

"No, I didn't take it."

"Was anyone with her when she left the hotel?"

"No, she was alone. Is anything wrong?"

"I guess not. Everything seems fine."

He hung up, shaking his head at her resilience. He hoped it wasn't Nick she was hurrying to meet. Well, she certainly was old enough to know better. He hoped so, he really hoped so, as play resumed.

Chapter Ten

"You can't get away with this, Joe."

"I already have. I've been to see the lawyer who took over Wilcox's practice—Raymond Carlyle. He's checked the file. The only other supposed witness to this fake signing was a secretary. Poor thing. She has Alzheimer's. Can't remember anything."

"I have a lawyer, too, and he's not dead or senile. He'll put a stop to this nonsense. I can't believe you're doing this to me. Why? What's so important in that book?"

"I told you, it's worth millions."

"Even if it is, why are you so desperate to get it? You make a lot of money. You've always had money."

"Had is the operative word, Meg. My life has been expensive lately. That mansion we bought sucks in money like a vacuum. It's been rehabbed from top to bottom and then, of course, we had to have the most expensive decorator in Boston do twelve rooms, some of which I never step foot in. And then there are the two Mercedes, membership in The Country Club in Brookline, the house in Maine, and assorted other necessities of life."

Marguerite felt better than she had in twelve years. It was only her innate good manners that kept the smug look off her face.

"You can cut down on those expenses, Joe. You don't have to become a thief."

"It's not so simple. There are other problems. I tried to make

46

money too fast and made some speculative investments. High return, high risk.''

"And they turned bad.'' She still knew how to finish his sentences. A moment's reflection added another phrase. "And some of it was other people's money.''

"Yes. It wasn't illegal. I had carte blanche to invest the money. But if word of this gets out I'll be ruined. Most of the people who entrust their money to us are conservative. They'll pull out. Maybe even sue us. And I've lost most of my own money. I'm broke, Meg. Too old to start all over, and anyway my heart is giving me warning signals. That's why I need your help. Get me that book and I'll forget about selling my share of the house.''

"What about your inheritance? Did you lose that, too?''

"No danger of that. My old man was such a tightwad that after he paid for our educations he figured he did enough for us. He put the money in a trust so that we only receive the interest. When I die my share goes to my children. You must remember that. I told you about it.''

She nodded in agreement. "Yes, I do remember. But I thought you might have found a way to break it.''

"No way! It's ironclad. I can be penalized even for trying to break it. Evidently, he didn't trust my brother and me to provide for our families.''

"He was right, wasn't he?''

The airplane ride provided a kaleidoscope of climate zones along the East Coast: the lush green landscape of Florida with skies of blue dotted by puffy white clouds; the brown winter grass of the Carolinas where the skies were still blue, but a brittle winter blue; the white snow-covered landscape of Massachusetts, the skies a gloomy dun color.

It was seven o'clock when the taxi deposited Marguerite and her mass of luggage in the driveway after an expensive ride from the Plymouth & Brockton bus station in Hyannis. With no move on the part of the driver to assist her, she made two trips from the cab into the house since she could not roll the bags over the snow-dotted gravel driveway and had to carry them.

The snow was mostly melted; it never lasted long on Cape Cod, but it left a wet, slushy mess and her feet were soaked when she finally locked and bolted the door behind her. Her fear had traveled with her as excess baggage.

She was exhausted. She wanted to go to bed. She wanted to pick up Rusty. Most of all, she wanted to go back in time to January fourteenth and say no when Joe invited her to dinner.

First, though, she had to turn up the heat. The flannel slacks and wool sweater, so onerous when she boarded in Florida, were not enough to warm her now. George Atkinson's house would be warm. She could go there to pick up Rusty and kill time till her house warmed, but she dare not. She felt obliged to warn him and Laura about Nick, but had to talk first to Portia.

Tomorrow would be soon enough. Nick would not know she had flown home so quickly and Beatrice had checked out of the hotel at the same time as Marguerite. She had gone to stay a few days with her friend in Boca Raton and from there would make other plans.

Of course, that Florida policeman was another matter. He was probably giving Nick a road map of her itinerary. On second thought, Fairchild might not know anything because he was not with the state troopers when they came to her room this morning with a statement for her to sign. McEnerny must have had that nice young Fleming up all night typing it.

She had gone to the airport as a standby, uncertain as to whether she would get a flight today. Luckily, more people arrived in Florida on this Friday than left, so she waited only two hours.

But first things first. What about dinner? The kitchen had been cleared of perishables before she left, but she had a well-stocked freezer and cupboard. Perusing the freezer, she spotted the last container of tomatoes, surplus from her summer garden, chopped and ready to use. Pasta would be just the thing. Carbohydrates were feel-good foods and she could use a little of that.

There was no fresh garlic but she had received a bottle of garlic-flavored olive oil in a Christmas package and that would do. In a matter of minutes, the water was boiling and the sauce was bubbling—her tomatoes flavored by red pepper flakes, black olives, anchovies, and capers. After all, she told herself, she had to keep up her strength.

Dinner dispatched and cleared, it was time to call her niece, Portia Newcomb, a lawyer. Portia was the only child of Marguerite's one sibling, Denis, who had wanted to be a poet and a lawyer. He married young and became neither but named his daughter Portia, a name symbolizing the confluence of his dreams. Motherless at ten, orphaned at eighteen, her closest relative and steadfast mentor had been Marguerite. Now married to Jebediah Newcomb, a scion of an old Boston family, and with two children, aged six and eight, she had a family of her own but remained devoted to her aunt.

Marguerite had spoken with her briefly from the Fort Lauderdale airport but had merely outlined the problem. She was afraid to miss hearing her name called for a flight. She now detailed the whole story, beginning with her dinner with Joe. Perhaps not the whole story. Embarrassment precluded her from supplying all the details of that stupid infatuation with Nick.

"The first thing we have to do is get you a lawyer, Aunt Meg."

"I have a lawyer. You."

"I mean a criminal lawyer."

The mean word shocked Marguerite. "But I'm not a criminal," she protested.

"Of course you're not. But if you have to defend yourself against a criminal offense you'll need someone who specializes in it. I'm sure it will never come to that, but having the right lawyer is the best way to avoid a problem. I asked around the office today and have a couple of names I'd like you to consider."

"Portia, there is no one I would trust more than you."

"Then your trust is misguided. I work in estates. Before that I worked on corporate mergers. I've never even been in a criminal court except as an observer when I was in law school. You deserve better than that."

"I might need one of your fancy criminal lawyers if I had really done something, but I'm innocent. The case will be a snap. You can do it."

"No, I can't, Aunt Meg. There's another problem," she confessed after a long pause. "Raymond Carlyle, Uncle Joe's lawyer, is with our firm. There's a conflict."

"B-but he can't be. He bought the practice of Joe's former lawyer, Roger Wilcox, and Roger wasn't with any firm other than himself."

"That's right. But Ray built up his estate practice so much that our firm wooed him and brought him in as a partner."

"But Joe's dead. That case is over."

"Not necessarily. His widow might decide to pursue this. In any event, Ray will be questioned. Aunt Meg, if I represent you, it might only end up hurting you. Even if I quit my job right now, and I would be willing to do that for you, I still wouldn't be qualified to handle a criminal case, especially a murder case.''

The words were finally spoken. Marguerite might be the defendant in a murder case. Portia was still talking.

''Let me tell you who I think would best represent you. I suggest—''

''Never mind, Portia. There's no time for that. I have to be at police headquarters at ten o'clock tomorrow morning for questioning. I've already delayed it long enough to get home from Florida. I'll call Andrew Mullen, the lawyer who handles my business here.''

She knew that he was out of the country. On January sixteenth, the day after her dinner with Joe, she had spoken with him about Joe's claim that he still owned half of her house and was about to sell it. Andrew had chuckled and told her that was a new low in his experiences of divorce cases, but she had nothing to worry about. The papers were good and he would vouch for them. Besides, at the time the divorce decree was issued, the court made a final disposition of the property. The house was hers.

''Could he sue me now and claim that there was a misrepresentation of the facts or a forgery?'' she had asked.

''Anyone can sue you for anything, Marguerite. The question is whether they have any grounds for winning a suit or even to avoid getting it thrown out of court. In your case there are no grounds. I would be surprised if it ever went to trial. Go to Florida and forget about it. Call me when you get home if you have any more threats from him. I'll be out of the country myself for three weeks starting tomorrow.''

She wished she were as confident as he. The problem had nagged at her all during her trip.

''Is he experienced in criminal work?'' asked Portia with concern in her voice.

''I'm sure he is. Small-town lawyers do a little bit of everything, whatever comes their way.''

''If you're sure you're all right, Aunt Meg. You know I'd be there in a minute if I thought I could help.''

''I'll be just fine, Portia,'' Marguerite fabricated. ''Call you tomorrow.''

''Aunt Meg, I'd like to offer one piece of advice if I may. Don't repeat to anyone what you said to me about your problem with the house being over because Uncle Joe is dead. It does give you a motive for murder.''

Marguerite replaced the phone with a great melancholy enveloping her.

Et tu, Brute!

Chapter Eleven

*T*he waitress placed the dessert menus on the table. They ordered only coffee, decaffeinated for both.

"What's your decision, Meg? Someone loses a musty book that isn't doing anybody any good right now, or you lose half your house?" He sounded anxious, not as sure of her as he had been earlier in the evening.

"Let's be sensible, Joe. I'd like to help you but I won't steal from my friends for you, or from anyone for that matter. Why don't we both go to whomever has this book you want, explain its value, and both of you agree to split the proceeds."

"No way! I did all the work on this. No one would even know about it except for me and that book would probably be thrown away when the owner dies. If I tell the person about this, I can be cut out. Besides, there's someone else already trying to get in on this. People get very greedy around money."

"Yes. Some people even steal and blackmail for it," she remarked pointedly. "Is that your final decision? You won't reconsider?"

"No deals. It'll be done my way."

"Then it won't be done at all. At least not with my help. I don't think I want that coffee, after all. I'd like to go home." She slid out of the booth, taking her coat with her.

"Tomorrow my half of the house goes up for sale," he warned.

"You do what you have to do, Joe, and I'll take care of myself.

*Just leave me alone!'' Her voice was rising. The two business-
women turned around to look.*

"Ssh, Meg. You're making a scene.''

*"I'm planning to make more than that. I will not be black-
mailed. You're going to be sorry you ever called me. I'm going
to get you out of my life for good!'' The waitress was hovering
nervously.*

*Marguerite, her coat and wool hat in place by now, hurried
out of the restaurant. Joe quickly paid the bill and ran after her.
She was walking in the direction of home, four miles away. The
temperature had dropped below freezing, and the snow was ice
underfoot, solidified into crests and troughs. He pulled the car
alongside her and opened the door. She climbed in without a
word, secretly relieved at having been rescued from the ice field.
The ride was silent.*

*As he pulled into her driveway, he made one last attempt.
"Sleep on it, Meg. I'll call you tomorrow.''*

*She slipped from the car as wordlessly as she had entered and
gingerly walked and skidded to her house without looking back.*

Seven o'clock was not too early to telephone George Atkinson.
He arose every day at six o'clock to the clarion call of his arthritic
joints. After dressing slowly and painfully, he walked for half an
hour, sometimes with a cane, sometimes without, depending on
the whims of bone, cartilage, and lubricating fluids. Today was
a cane day as he thrust before him a lovingly carved tree branch
cum cane, a relic of Hurricane Bob, to gain secure footing on the
ice before each hesitant step. With his other hand he held Marguerite's dog loosely on a leash.

The leash was more for George's peace of mind than out of
necessity of restraining Rusty. She had no desire to run away.
Ever since she had appeared on the Smiths' Boston doorway, an
abandoned puppy with soulful eyes, she had been a homebody,
reluctant to stray lest she find herself once again without a refuge.
The Atkinson house was temporarily home and she would stay
close to her guardian until instructed otherwise.

When the phone rang at seven, with Marguerite's voice greeting him, George assumed she was calling from Florida to check
on her dog's well-being.

"Marguerite, there is no need to get up at dawn to see if I'm
mistreating Rusty. She's right here; do you want to talk to her?''

he teased, his cheeks forming smooth little mounds on each side, the kind ladies loved to pinch when he was a little boy.

"That's not why I called, George. I'm home. Put the coffee on. I'll bring the doughnuts and be there in about fifteen minutes."

"Home? I thought you were going for a month. What happened?"

"It's a long story. Make lots of coffee."

Already showered and dressed after the longest sleepless night she could remember, Marguerite had decided her course of action sans legal advice. She was innocent; in fact, she was a victim of the machinations of Joe and Nick (however did *he* fit into this scheme?).

Her first priority was to prevent harm to anyone else. Beatrice was out of the loop at some unknown location in Florida and safe for now, but George and Laura were sitting ducks. She had to warn them immediately because Nick would probably know by now that she had left Florida to return home. Long accustomed to the security of their town, she doubted if their doors and windows were locked. As for herself, she would sleep better with Rusty back in the house to bark at strange noises.

As suspected, George's door was unlocked and she walked in to be greeted by the smell of coffee, freshly ground coffee if she knew George. His frail physique attested to a small appetite but it was a selective one.

Rusty was the first to greet Marguerite, barking with a happy sound and jumping on her to claim ownership.

"Come on in and sit down, Marguerite," urged George, beckoning to a table located in a glass outcropping of the spacious kitchen and surrounded by potted citrus trees.

He had the good manners not to ply her with questions as he poured coffee and put the doughnuts onto a Limoges plate after breaking off a treat for Rusty. It was the dog's destiny to be spoiled.

"George, I walked right in here. The door wasn't locked."

He smoothed his thin hair which sparely covered his crown, did the same for his luxuriant, gray beard, tugged the lobe of a capacious ear, and pushed his glasses higher on his nose so that they rested in the familiar grooves.

"When haven't you been able to walk in here during the day without the door being unlocked?"

"I know, George, but perhaps you ought to be more careful."

"What's on your mind, Marguerite? What's happened to bring you home from vacation worrying about locked doors? Has your house been broken into?"

"I wish that's all it was. But it's worse, much worse. My ex-husband has been murdered, I was the last person seen with him, and he wanted some book which someone else threatened to break my arm to get while I was in Florida."

"Whoa, Marguerite, let's start all over. I knew Joe was dead. It was in the papers. Found right here in Eastham at the Three Sisters. Suspicious circumstances, they said. As if any fool wouldn't know it's suspicious for a body to be found in a lighthouse. But the papers didn't mention you. And what's this about a gun and a book? Start at the beginning."

She did. It was such a relief to tell someone the whole story.

"That's why I'm worried about you, George. I don't know who has this book and Nick doesn't know either, but he knows it's one of the people I play bridge with. He's decided it isn't Beatrice, so that leaves only you and Laura. He has a gun. You could be in danger. I have to be at the police station at ten o'clock this morning and I'll tell them everything, but the last time I tried to tell the police about Nick they didn't believe me."

"Does this Nick character know where I live?"

"Probably not, but you're in the phone book. He'll find you."

"It would be a waste of his time if he did. I have nothing in my library of any value. Not any real value, that is. I have some leather-bound books, and some signed first editions. And, of course, I have my father's books. He was a journalist but wrote a couple of books. The whole kit and caboodle is probably worth about five thousand dollars, tops. Laura has a whole houseful of books but she's not a collector, not of rare books anyway. She's more like a repository of family history. Her collection would be of value to someone who wanted to write a history of Eastham and its inhabitants, her family in particular, but that would take a scholar and the results wouldn't be particularly profitable. My own feeling is that either Joe was mistaken about something we had or he was just using this as an excuse to get money out of you by threatening to sell your house from under you."

"He didn't ask me for any money. And I certainly don't have the kind he needed."

"Maybe, maybe not. You could pick up quite a bit by mortgaging your house. Maybe that was his game."

"But someone did murder him, George. It must have been connected with this scheme of his."

"Not necessarily. He told you he lost a lot of money, some of it other people's money. You don't know whose money that was or what he might have done to cover it up. People get pretty upset when they think they've been swindled. He might even have been into the loan sharks."

"Then why didn't he ask me to mortgage my home?"

"He knew you'd say no if he just asked you. First he had to frighten you somehow to soften you up. Didn't he say he would call you the next day? That was probably when he was going to ask you."

"But he never called."

"Must have gotten himself murdered first."

"And Nick?"

"Probably someone Joe owed money to and was trying to stall with this story of some valuable book. After having to show his identity to those policemen, I doubt if you'll hear from Nick again."

"You make a lot of sense, George. But I'm still uneasy. I have to warn Laura. Some of her windows are so old they don't even close tightly, let alone lock." A slight raising of the eyebrows tainted her expression of concern. Marguerite chafed at the knowledge that Laura was her equal at bridge, a game Marguerite had long been accustomed to winning. She considered Laura's talking the hand or "coffee-housing" as cheating. Laura bridled at Marguerite's criticism. George mediated.

"Why don't you let me talk to Laura? I'll go over there now and break it to her gently without scaring the dickens out of her. You have enough problems, having to go to the police and all. What time did you say you had to be there?"

"Ten. Oh my goodness, it's after nine already and I have to get Rusty home and freshen up a little." Marguerite was gathering up plates and cups, looking a little flustered as she did so.

"Just leave everything there," exclaimed a disconcerted George as he saw the china so lovingly collected by his late wife being hurriedly stacked and transported to the kitchen counter. "I'll take care of it. You'd better get started. Doesn't pay to make the police wait. Do you have a lawyer?"

"Everything's taken care of," she assured him, not wishing to burden George any further with the problems she had unwittingly thrust upon him.

Her answering machine regurgitated two messages: one from her daughter, Alexandra, urging Marguerite to call her; one from Portia with the same request.

Later, she decided, as she changed out of her corduroy slacks and into a butternut and black tweed skirt with a butternut silk shirt and black cropped jacket. *I'll call them later. Alex just wants to criticize me for getting into this mess and Portia wants to tell me how bad she feels about not being here. It's too late for apologies.*

She should have been here.

Chapter Twelve

"*Bonjour,* Marguerite."

"*Bonjour,* Frank," she responded to Francis Nadeau, Police Chief of Eastham.

They had begun speaking together in French about two years ago when, quite by accident, as he unsuccessfully attempted to locate library books written in French, she had been standing in line behind him and volunteered to lend him some of hers. She had been fluent in French since childhood, thanks to her French-Canadian mother, and had refined her knowledge during intensive college courses leading to a minor in that language. Frank was a beginner, seeking to recapture the language of his Acadian ancestors forced out of Nova Scotia over two hundred years ago to settle in New England.

"*Comment allez-vous?*" (How are you?) he continued formally.

"*Est-ce que vous êtes sérieux?*" (Are you serious?) she responded with disbelief in her voice.

"You're right, Marguerite. Forgive me." Clearly embarrassed at having overlooked the gravity of her being here at all, he turned away and gestured toward the other occupant of the room. "You know Lt. Medeiros of the State Police homicide division, don't you?"

"Yes, we'll have to stop meeting like this." She smiled faintly at Albert Medeiros, who was dressed in a rumpled herringbone jacket, open, she suspected, because he had added a little more to his increasing girth. He was a comfortable-looking man with crinkly dark hair threaded with gray, lustrous dark eyes, and a face weathered by sun and wind, indicative of off-hours spent on the water working with his fishermen brothers. He was of medium height, his formerly muscular build becoming a little flabby as it increased in size.

Medeiros was in marked contrast to Frank, who wore his brown hair cut short, almost military short, and fought every half-inch of waistline expansion. When on duty, he wore a uniform, pressed and creased as if for inspection. His leisure clothes were something else, worn and torn to a point his wife considered disreputable, but he balanced these two sides of his persona without apparent conflict. Perhaps it was his army experience during the Vietnam War that developed this dichotomy—all spit and polish during basic training, then almost two years mucking about in the swamps and jungles.

Marguerite looked around the room as if searching for someone, then commented, ''I expected Sgt. McEnerny to be here.''

''Are you disappointed?'' asked Medeiros playfully, mindful of the sergeant's grating personality.

''Not in the least. Understand?''

They did and showed it by involuntary grins, quickly erased as they recovered their professional demeanors.

''He's tied up with a wedding today. We had to get on with this,'' Medeiros elaborated, hands waving vaguely in the air, his words not clarifying the unspeakable ''this.''

''Wedding?'' inquired Marguerite. ''Is the sergeant getting married?'' A hint of disbelief underlined her question.

''No, he's giving the bride away. His niece. Her father's dead. He put in for this day months ago.''

The buzzer on the chief's desk sounded insistently. With an annoyed look at it, he switched on the intercom and growled, ''I thought I told you not to interrupt me and to hold my calls.''

''It's important,'' crackled the apologetic voice of the dispatcher. ''Mrs. Smith's lawyer is here.''

''Send him in. Why can't these lawyers be on time?'' he groused.

Mouth agape, Marguerite turned to face the door, certain there was some mistake.

''Portia!'' she gasped as her niece entered the room. ''What are you doing here?''

"Representing you, Aunt Meg. I called you early this morning but you didn't return my call. Sorry I'm late."

"But, the problem we talked about. You can't represent me."

"Probably not as well as you deserve, but better than nobody. I called Andrew Mullen's office. He's out of the country. Let's get down to the business at hand," she commented brusquely as she removed her long winter coat, revealing a green suit trimmed with navy blue, and a navy blue sheath peeking out from the neckline. "What have you said so far, Aunt Meg?"

"Nothing, actually. We haven't started."

"Good." Turning to the police officers, she requested with authority in her voice, "Could you leave us? I would like some time alone with my client."

Marguerite was astonished at this assertive side of Portia. About an inch taller than Marguerite, she appeared smaller due to the delicacy of her bone structure. Her facial features were finely drawn like her mother's had been, but drawn on a template of her father's physiognomy. The brown hair and green eyes were Denis' too, and strangely comforted Marguerite.

"That's not necessary, Portia. I've had plenty of time to think. Joe has been murdered, but not by me. The only way I can end this nightmare is to tell the police everything I know and help them find the guilty person. I'm glad you're here, though."

"Is my aunt a suspect?" Portia demanded of Medeiros.

"Everyone's a suspect until a case is solved," he answered ambiguously. "All we know right now is that she was the last person seen with him and she apparently had a motive. We need to hear her side of the story."

"Is she being charged with anything?"

"Not at this time."

"Since she's innocent, she will, of course, cooperate fully." Portia pulled over a chair and sat next to Marguerite.

Frank cleared his throat, obviously unhappy about his next duty. "I believe you were read your rights in Florida but I'll repeat them for you." He proceeded to do so, deeply regretting the necessity of offending this woman he had come to consider his friend. Would they ever converse happily again, him struggling along in French, she patiently correcting him?

Medeiros, aware of the struggle in Frank's mind, took over the questioning. "Why don't you just start at the beginning, from the time Joe contacted you. Your statement will be recorded on tape.''

Marguerite began, hesitantly at first, gradually picking up speed. She recounted their unhappy dinner, the fateful meeting with Nick, his initial interest in Beatrice and later shift to her, concluding with the episode in her hotel room and the timely arrival of the police.

"Did you tell the officers about his threatening you?" asked Medeiros.

"Lieutenant, if I'm correct, you have in front of you a copy of my signed statement. In which case, you can see that I added that information in my own handwriting because they omitted it. In fact, they shrugged it off. That Florida policeman seemed to think he was protecting my reputation. The nerve of him!" Her feistiness had not deserted her.

"You may be right about that," agreed Medeiros casually. "But I don't see anything in here about Joe asking you to steal a certain book for him or else he would take part of your house away."

She was prepared for this question and answered it immediately. "You're perfectly right. That's because when I came to that topic and started to tell them that Joe asked about my bridge partners, McEnerny became impatient and cut me off. He said to skip that subject and go on. Of course, I did what he asked," she concluded meekly, blue eyes focused shamelessly on Medeiros. "I was in a state of shock."

Marguerite was indeed in a state of shock—right now. Shock at the degree of subterfuge in which she had indulged in order to hide the truth from McEnerny and in which she was now indulging to reveal the truth to Medeiros.

"I understand that officer was rude, Lieutenant," offered Portia. "My aunt had just learned her former husband had been murdered, and without even letting her recover from that shock, he started to importune her about a recent meeting with the victim, the father of her children. Insensitive at best, harassment at worst."

Portia had willfully hit the right button, used the dreaded buzz-word—harassment. Police and prosecutors alike knew that the strongest case could turn to Jell-O when a defendant cried harassment, especially a defendant like Marguerite Smith—intelligent, articulate, mature, a former schoolteacher, no smears on her escutcheon, not even a traffic violation. Portia Newcomb might not be a criminal lawyer, but she knew the drill.

"Counselor, I know you're concerned about Mrs. Smith," soothed Medeiros, "and so are we. She said herself that she thinks she's in danger from this Dante character. She's also worried about her two friends. It might seem kinder if we could observe a period of mourning, but in the long run we wouldn't be doing our duty. A man has been murdered. The killer is still loose. The best thing we can do for everybody is to find him and put him away. Mrs. Smith wants that herself."

The door to the office opened slowly, tentatively, and the head of a young policeman squeezed itself into the smallest space possible.

"I didn't hear any knock, Morgan," barked Frank Nadeau.

"Excuse me. I knocked but I guess you didn't hear me," apologized David Morgan, two years a policeman, terrified of the chief, his face turning an embarrassed crimson at every real or perceived criticism. David did not know and Frank would never admit that he was very fond of this artist-turned-policeman and considered him intelligent and perceptive. Frank's harshness was an attempt to toughen up this sensitive young man before he got eaten up alive in a rugged profession.

"Knock louder! Assert yourself!"

"Right, Chief," David promised, slipping a little further through the door, his slender frame not requiring much of an opening. "I have very important information if I could see you for a minute. I know you'll want to hear this."

"I'd better," warned Frank as he arose and left the office, relieved to be out of Marguerite's anguished presence.

He was gone for about fifteen minutes, an interminable time to Marguerite. Medeiros had switched off the tape recorder and Portia took her aunt's hand, sending encouraging smiles in her direction, noting the unfamiliar creases on Marguerite's brow and mouth.

Frank burst into his office with an expression of annoyance and asked hostilely, "Counselor, is that your BMW in the parking lot, license plate SHIPS-2?"

"Why, yes it is," confirmed Portia. "Am I parked in a reserved spot?"

"Not at all. But I'm sure my colleague and I would be interested to know why you were at the Sunset Motel on the evening of January fifteenth, asking for the room of one Joseph Smith, the same Joseph Smith whose murder we're investigating."

Chapter Thirteen

Marguerite walked around the post, bypassing the chain across the entrance road to the present location of the historic Three Sisters lighthouses. The chain bore the sign FIRE ROAD and was meant to discourage vehicles, not pedestrians. Rusty forged ahead, eager to scout this new territory.

A yellow police tape surrounded the first lighthouse, the tape torn and flapping between two of the stakes set in the frozen ground to demarcate a zone of forbidden entrance. The door was secured by an intrusive police padlock that replaced the more discreet former lock, kicked in by perpetrators unknown. The crude entry was probably not the work of the murderer of Joseph Smith, since an array of empty beer cans, discovered at the same time as the body, attested to the building having been the site of a recent drinking party.

The Three Sisters had been commissioned in 1837 to assist the coastal and fishing vessels that sailed too close to the curving shore to see the beacons of Highland Light in Truro or Chatham Light. Ralph Waldo Emerson wrote of visiting the keeper some years before the Civil War and hearing from him that there was resistance to the building of a lighthouse on this coast, as it would ruin the wrecking business.

Typical of the back side of Cape Cod, the sand bank eroded beneath them and they were replaced by three movable wooden towers that acquired the nickname Three Sisters because they were gray with black light towers and from the sea looked like three nuns. In time, two of the lights had been extinguished, the towers sold and moved, and a flashing light installed in the remaining tower. This met the same fate as its sisters when it was replaced by a taller lighthouse, the present Nauset Light, which was itself in danger from continuing erosion and from the Coast Guard's decision to decommission it.

The National Park Service acquired and reunited the Three Sisters. They rest in retirement in a parklike setting not far from their original site but sheltered from wind and water, their feet on solid ground, safe for now from the encroaching Atlantic Ocean, which moved landward about three feet a year, devouring the coastal dune.

Now there was another footnote to the history of the Three Sisters—the discovery of a murdered man in the sister nearest the road.

Why, Marguerite wondered, *why here?* Who would bother to transport a body to this spot and drag it from the road into this building? Unless he was poisoned here. Nonsense! Why would Joe come here voluntarily and permit himself to be poisoned? He had to be dead already. Perhaps he wasn't dragged far, though. A vehicle could drive around the post and approach very close to the building. And if Joe had been murdered the night she met him, it had been snowing, a guarantee that tire tracks and footprints would be covered.

Normally effusive and upbeat, Marguerite was dejected. This old lighthouse, so lovingly preserved, had been a tomb for her handsome, elegant Joe, his body a frozen carcass tossed carelessly among discarded beer cans. She still used the word "my," never having gotten out of the habit of loving him, their recent disagreement of no more impact than one snowflake in a blizzard.

Her emotions had been sorely tried: angered at Joe's demands, devastated by his death; thrilled by the attention from Nick, embarrassed by her own naïveté, frightened by his threats. And now Portia.

Had she been betrayed by Portia, or had Portia tried to protect her, thereby jeopardizing a legal career? Always protective of Portia, Marguerite inclined toward the latter, adding guilt to her portfolio of problems.

As Rusty sniffed and explored the ground surrounding the two other sisters, Marguerite contemplated the morning's events and experienced a cold that had less to do with the weather than with what was inside herself. Confronted by Frank Nadeau's revelation about her car's presence at Joe Smith's motel the evening of his dinner with Marguerite, Portia blanched, her normally pale freckles standing out in relief against an ashen skin. For a full three minutes there was silence, the asynchronous inspiration and expiration of eight lungs the only sounds in the strained atmosphere.

"Yes, I was there," she finally admitted.

"What were you doing there?" asked Medeiros quietly.

"Waiting for my Uncle Joe."

"Why? Why were you waiting for him?"

"That is privileged information. I decline to answer," she replied flatly, avoiding her aunt's eyes.

"Was Joseph Smith your client?"

"Not mine individually, but he was a client of the firm Hopkins, Potter and McNamara, in which I am an associate."

Neither Frank nor Medeiros recognized the law firm. That would have pleased the partners. The firm was high class and low key, handling the business and personal affairs of the very rich or the very old families, some of whose prestige had outlasted their money. Tabloid-shy, Hopkins et al. handled no criminal matters and found other representation for clients who had the bad taste to find themselves on the wrong side of the law, while continuing to handle the miscreants' business affairs and retaining the anonymity they craved. Publicity was anathema. The rich knew who they were.

"Is Raymond Carlyle a member of that firm?" queried Medeiros.

"Yes, he is," replied Portia.

"It is our understanding that Mr. Carlyle was Joseph Smith's lawyer and that he was representing him in a matter directly related to Marguerite Smith, your aunt. Is this correct?"

"I have already cited lawyer-client confidentiality," she answered stubbornly.

"No way, counselor," retorted Medeiros more harshly. "Number one, your so-called client is dead. Number two, if he was your client, what are you doing here representing Mrs. Smith, whose interests might be in direct conflict with Joseph Smith's? Number three, he was really the client of Raymond Carlyle, who called us when he heard Joseph Smith was murdered because he thought he might have some information as to a motive. Which motive, by the way, involves Marguerite Smith. We didn't know he was with the law firm you just mentioned. He just gave us his own name and telephone number.''

''So that's why McEnerny came back to my room after he had left it,'' Marguerite interrupted, clarifying events for herself. ''He called you and learned what that lawyer was claiming.'' She still had enough control of her mental processes to remember to use the word ''claiming.'' Nothing had been confirmed yet.

Despite herself, Portia chuckled. ''They'll be furious.''

''Who?''

''The partners. They hate publicity. If their name gets in the paper, Carlyle is finished.''

''And how about you?'' asked Medeiros sharply. ''Are you finished, too? Your seem to have involved yourself in a murder case.''

''A murder I had nothing to do with. And neither did my aunt.''

''In that case you'd be better off telling us what you know. All of it,'' he warned.

''Am I a suspect?''

''No more than anyone else at this time. However, if you would feel better, I'll read you your rights.''

Portia waved off the suggestion. ''I know them.'' Speaking directly into the tape recorder, she added, ''I will, of course, cooperate fully so that you can find the person who committed this horrible crime.''

Medeiros, determined to retain control of this interrogation, also spoke formally into the microphone. ''Please note, Portia Newcomb, an attorney, is familiar with her rights and has waived them.'' He nodded to Portia. She had permission to continue.

Avoiding Marguerite's anguished look, Portia hesitantly told her story. She had seen her Uncle Joe enter Raymond Carlyle's office several times in early January. She knew that the Smiths, an old Boston family, had used the law firm Pennbrook and Knowles for several generations.

Except for Joe's divorce. Joe had gone to Roger Wilcox for that. Roger died about three years ago and Raymond Carlyle bought the practice from his widow. Subsequently, Carlyle had joined Hopkins et al. and, upon spotting her uncle, Portia assumed Joe's divorce had come along in the files.

Joe probably didn't know she was with this firm, since she had no contact with him. Curious though she was as to the reason for his visits, she was conscious of the confidentiality between lawyer and client and refrained from acting on her curiosity. Until January fourteenth.

She had telephoned Marguerite that afternoon, ostensibly to wish her a good trip south, covertly to learn if Marguerite would mention any problems with Joe. She had been right when she wanted to be wrong. Joe had called Marguerite to invite her to dinner the following evening, when he would be on the Cape to visit clients. He had been on the Cape many times in the years since their divorce but had never contacted Marguerite. Portia's nerves tingled. Something was wrong.

After an anguished debate with herself, Portia concluded that no harm would be done if she just glanced at the file. If it portended no harm to Marguerite she would forget about it.

After everyone left that evening she entered Carlyle's office. The file was on his desk and easy to spot. Roger Wilcox had been an old-fashioned lawyer who continued to use file folders tied with ribbon. Carlyle had not bothered to replace this folder, probably considering it a dead case.

She had difficulty deciphering the notes, handwritten on yellow legal paper, very sketchy, but indicating three meetings. It was necessary to delve further into the file to make sense of the cryptic notes.

Joe was claiming he had never agreed to give Marguerite the house and had not signed any papers indicating such. Furthermore, he asserted, at the divorce hearing the judge had mumbled throughout and Joe, very nervous and assuming his lawyer was protecting him, did not listen closely enough. His lawyer grossly misrepresented the agreement. Joe's understanding of the settlement was that Marguerite could live in the house but he maintained half ownership. Could he sell his half?

Portia was certain Carlyle would have advised against any such action or claim, but he had made no notes in the file as to his opinion or advice and she dare not ask him. After a troubled night, Portia decided her obligation to her aunt was paramount and she would face Joe Smith, person-to-person, confront him, tell him his claim was baseless and she knew he was only bluffing, frightening Marguerite for some purpose Portia could not fathom.

"Portia, why didn't you tell—" Marguerite's question was short-circuited by an intent look from Portia.

"How did you know where he was staying?" prodded Medeiros.

"I called his office in the morning intending to see him before he left for the Cape. They told me he had gone directly from home. I said I had important business and asked where I could contact him."

"What time did you get to the Sunset Motel?"

"Chief?" she inquired playfully, turning to Frank Nadeau, her eyebrows raised quizzically. "When did I get there?"

"No games, counselor," intervened Medeiros, suspecting that she was fishing to find out how much they knew.

"I arrived about five o'clock."

"And what did you do?" Medeiros prompted, as if coaching a child.

"I went into the office and asked for Joe Smith's room. They evidently have some policy about not revealing room numbers, so the desk clerk dialed his room instead of telling me. There was no answer. I knew there was no use asking again for the room number but there was no need. He was very careless and dialed the room number so that I could see it. I left the office and drove my car over to park in front of Uncle Joe's room. The light was on so I knocked, thinking that he might have been in the shower when the phone rang. There was no answer so I sat in the car and waited."

"Was his car in front of his room?"

"I don't know what kind of a car he has."

"Was there any car parked in front of his room?"

"Only mine. But there was a car parked two doors away. I had thought that one might be his but I guess it wasn't."

"Were there a lot of cars at the motel?"

"In January? No, of course not."

"Then why did you think he might have parked two doors away?" persisted Medeiros.

"I really didn't think much about it at all. Perhaps there was a delivery truck in front of his room. Maybe one of the staff parked there. I don't know."

"How long did you wait?"

"Until about seven-thirty."

"It was snowing and freezing out. Weren't you cold?"

"I certainly was. Every once in a while I turned on the engine and the heater to warm myself."

Medeiros hesitated, unsure of how to continue. He had not had a conference with Frank and did not know the details. That was a mistake. They should have talked first. Too late now. He did not want to interrupt the interrogation. Frank rescued him.

"Did you enter your uncle's room at any time?"

"How could I? I had no key."

Neither policeman was impressed with that defense. On a snowy Tuesday night in mid-January, the night clerk was likely to be in the small back office cozily watching television instead of the keys. She had already proven adept in obtaining the room number.

Frank paused to assess what he had learned from Officer Morgan. Chuck, the night maintenance man at the motel, had spotted her car that night. There had been only two rooms occupied on this frigid night and her car was in front of one of them. A car buff, he immediately noticed the Beemer and its custom license plate, SHIPS-2.

He had been out sick for a couple of days and just learned that the police were inquiring about that night. He remembered it clearly because it was the first snow of the winter and he couldn't find his window scraper.

No, Chuck could not tell them the exact time he noticed her car, but it was probably about five-thirty, right after he came on duty. A woman was sitting in the car but he did not see her clearly enough to identify. The BMW was still there when he had to answer a call from the other occupied room about a running toilet. He was not wearing a watch—the battery had run out—but he recognized the television show that was playing in that room, so the time was between seven and eight. He noticed that the woman was no longer in the car and the light in the room was on. There was a car parked beyond hers but he couldn't see it clearly because her car was blocking his view and he was running with his head ducked down because of the snow.

"Did you leave your car at any time during this period you were waiting?" Frank resumed.

"I left the car about seven-thirty and went into the lobby."

"Why?"

"To use the ladies' room."

"Did you use anything else while you were there?"

"Yes, the telephone."

"Who did you call?"

Portia hesitated. She made several false starts to speak but each time her mouth clamped shut. Finally, with an apologetic look at Marguerite, she answered.

''My aunt.''

Chapter Fourteen

I n two hours they had received more significant information than they had obtained in the six days since Joe's body had been discovered. But they were unhappy.

Neither Frank nor Medeiros wanted the murderer to be Marguerite or Portia. Police liked to arrest bad guys. These seemed like the good guys. But you never knew.

The average citizen was more likely to be murdered by a family member or acquaintance than by a stranger. The spouse was the first suspect. Ex-spouses rated highly, too.

"Well, what do you think, Al?" asked Frank, leaning far back in his chair, sipping a cup of coffee poured from the station's communal pot, trying to relax after a particularly painful interrogation.

Medeiros removed his jacket as the heat hissed on. He hated warm rooms and closed windows, preferring the fresh salty air he had imbibed since birth in his native Provincetown. He also hated stale coffee but was making an attempt at drinking it to quiet his hunger pangs. It was past noontime and his stomach tolerated no changes in its regular feeding schedule. Medeiros swallowed, grimaced, and answered thoughtfully.

"Both ladies had motive and opportunity. We don't know if they had the means because we don't know the type of poison it was. I wish that lab would hurry up," he groused. "And poison is popular with the gals."

"You're right, Al, but I wish it wasn't in this case. She's a friend of mine!'' he exclaimed. ''Why would she murder some-one over half a house when she'd probably win the case anyway? That claim of her ex's sounds like a crock.''

''People have been murdered over a parking spot, Frank. Or a pair of sneakers. We're talking about a hundred thou here. A nice piece of change. Besides, maybe there's another motive. If she's telling the truth about that book he was looking for, maybe she wanted a cut of whatever he was expecting and he wouldn't ante up, so she offed him. Planned to get the book herself. We only have her word that she doesn't know who has it or what's in it.''

''Then why would she tell us about any of this?'' Frank que-ried.

''She had to tell us about meeting him for dinner because there were witnesses. Ditto for the fight they had. She probably didn't intend to say anything about the book but she hadn't counted on this Nick fellow. By the way, we have to locate him. Sounds like he knows a lot. She must be more scared of him than of us, so she decided to tell us enough to protect her. You notice she didn't say anything about the house or the book when she was ques-tioned in Florida. Murderers do make mistakes. That's why we catch them.''

''But she claims she called her lawyer the day before she left for Florida and asked him about Joe's claim to the house. He told her she had nothing to worry about. Why would she even tell him about the house if Joe was dead already?''

''We have to check out that story. She could have called him to show she wasn't hiding anything. After all, she knew it would come out in the open because Joe consulted his lawyer,'' Al concluded.

''How does the niece fit into this?'' wondered Frank. ''If only that guy at the motel could be more exact. He knows the light was on in Joe's room when Portia wasn't in her car but doesn't know if it was on when he first saw her sitting out there. He knows there was a car parked near hers but couldn't see it too well. Joe drove a Mercedes. If this guy had gotten a look at it he would have known what it was. He digs cars. The room was near the main office. The car could have been the night clerk's. He claims her BMW was there without her in it sometime between seven and eight. She says she left her car to call her aunt at seven-thirty and there was no answer. She figured Joe had picked Mar-guerite up by then so there was no point in leaving a message and she left. If she's not telling the truth and stayed there after seven-thirty, possibly in Joe's room, she was most likely waiting for him to return. Maybe waiting to poison him.''

"She could have done it, too. She admitted she didn't get home till midnight. Maybe later. There's no witnesses. Not even her husband, which wouldn't be too useful anyway. The trip supposedly took hours because of the snowstorm—an accident delay on Route 3; she had to find a gas station; she had to find a place to get something to eat; she had to telephone her husband to tell him not to wait up for her. You name it, she had to do it. The only thing we can check is the accident, but there were probably a lot of them on a bad night like that. She paid cash for the gas, doesn't remember the station and doesn't remember the convenience store she stopped for a sandwich. Doesn't even know which exit she got off Route 3, only that it was in Plymouth. That's a big place and there's more than one exit for it." Al sighed, his stomach growled, and Frank nodded his head, reluctantly in agreement.

"That means Portia had the opportunity to poison him before or after his dinner with Marguerite," he deduced.

"Depending on the type of poison that was used," reminded Al, "and how quickly it works. We still have to wait for the lab. There's one thing you've forgotten, Frank. Marguerite had the same opportunities. Even more. She had dinner with him. He probably went to the gents' at least once. She could have slipped something into his food or drink."

"I haven't forgotten that, Al. But there's some problems with that theory. One is that Marguerite did return home after dinner as she claims and made a phone call to Beatrice. McEnerny checked that out with Beatrice when they were in Florida. Wouldn't she have stayed with him if she poisoned him and wanted to hide the body? Another is Joe's car. It's still missing although our guys have the description and tag numbers and have checked all the parking lots. His stuff was taken out of the room, too, and the key dropped in the early checkout slot. Just like he left on his own. How could Marguerite do all that? You know how hard it is to move a dead man and put him in a car. The medical examiner says he weighed one-seventy. And where's the car?''

"Those aren't such hard problems, Frank. Maybe she did return home at ten as she claims and made a phone call. How do we know she stayed there? She could have driven her own car to the motel and gone into Joe's room on the excuse that she was reconsidering his proposal but actually to be there when the poison took effect and get him out of the room and hidden until she left for Florida.''

''Al, her car isn't exactly inconspicuous. It's a red convertible.''

''She could've parked someplace nearby. Another possibility is that she didn't poison him at dinner and did stay home that night. Joe checked out on his own early the next morning and drove to Marguerite's for a final answer. She fixed breakfast for him—his last breakfast. That's more likely since she wouldn't have known the night she went to dinner that she had a reason to kill him.''

''Maybe. But she still would've had to carry a dead body into a car, drive to the Three Sisters, and drag him out of the car and into the lighthouse in daylight.''

''She could have let him walk to the car if he was feeling sick from the poison and told him she would take him to a doctor. Then she drove around till he died, stashed the car in the driveway of a house closed for the winter, and came back after dark to move him to the lighthouse to delay the body turning up till she was gone south and had an alibi. She might have been walking around there with that dog of hers and saw the broken lock. If she drove around the chain right up to the steps she wouldn't have to drag him far. By the way, you'd better have the patrols start looking in driveways for the car. Especially houses within walking distance of hers.''

They sat silently for a while, each contemplating the unthinkable, hating this aspect of police work. Al put down his cup, having finished off the cold coffee in one gulp as if it were medicine, and offered one more thought to his depressed friend.

''Frank, there's one more option. The niece owes her aunt big time since Marguerite got her husband out of a jam with that murdered archaeologist.* What goes around comes around. Maybe it was Portia's turn to help her aunt. The two of them could move a body and empty a room. They could even ditch a

*The Curious Cape Cod Skull

car far away from the motel because one could follow in another car. In fact, this makes the most sense of all.''

   ''Except for one thing,'' objected Frank.

   ''What?''

   ''I know Marguerite didn't do it.''

Chapter Fifteen

Plump, round drops of rain fell softly, washing away the slushy remains of the snow. The initial rain was hazardous, creating a slippery footing as surface water concealed underlying ice. Unbalanced by several bags of groceries, Marguerite walked rapidly from the car toward her house to avoid a soaking. Rusty, hating the rain, stood at the front door barking, encouraging Marguerite to walk faster.

She slipped and fell, scattering cans and produce over the walk and the adjacent garden. Rusty abandoned her refuge under the eaves, ran to Marguerite, and licked her face, joining in the fun of this new game. Embarrassed at her clumsiness, Marguerite scrambled to her feet hoping no one saw her. But someone did.

Within two minutes after she fell, she heard a male voice behind her inquiring, "Are you okay, Mrs. Smith?"

Momentarily confused, she swiveled around to face the voice's body, which eluded recognition. Her driveway and walk were invisible from any other house except the cottage across the narrow dirt side road that was unoccupied during the winters. Except for this winter, she remembered.

As her legs steadied, her mind cleared and she realized that this was the man who had taken the cottage for a winter rental. Ed Rogers. He had introduced himself when he moved in, explained that he was an artist who needed to get away from the distractions of city living so that he could work in peace for a few months to complete some paintings for a spring showing at a Boston gallery, and asked her where he could find a Laundro-mat. Further contacts had been confined to a passing wave, and then she had left for Florida.

Thwarted in her attempt to hide her fall, she laughed with him at the groceries decorating the ground. They both stooped to re-trieve them from amidst the slushy gravel of the walk and the blackened, frozen perennial stumps of the summer garden, then carried them dripping into the house. Rusty signaled her approval of their new playmate by licking his ungloved hand each time he reached to pick up an item, impeding the progress of the cleanup. The dripping people, dog, and groceries finally assembled in the kitchen, Marguerite stashed as he cleaned and dried the wounded purchases, both of them joking over the state of each item. It was her first release from tension in days, comic relief though it was.

She estimated him to be in his late thirties or early forties. Blond hair, softly curled, hung in fine tendrils to just below the ears. With green eyes, a fine nose, and perfect teeth, so perfect that had he been an actor she would have suspected artifice, he had an aspect at once pleasing and restful. No little flaws or moles on which the eye would focus and distract from the whole. About five-feet-eleven and slender with well-toned muscles hovering discreetly beneath fair skin and revealed by the close-fitting, short-sleeved polo shirt he was wearing on this winter's day, he looked more like a model than a painter.

Her reprieve was brief. A police car pulled into the driveway and Frank Nadeau knocked at the door. She knew he was not here for a French lesson, and her stomach recoiled. What now?

After introducing himself to Ed and surveying him as police-men do to strangers in their midst, he asked to speak privately with Marguerite. Ed excused himself and went back across the road to his cottage.

"To what do I owe this pleasure, Frank?" she asked warily.

Frank hemmed and hawed, his eyes roaming the room, finally settling on a colorful painting of a tropical setting. "Sure is a bright picture. Looks kinda Caribbean."

"It is."

"Have you been there often?"

"No. Just once. Why do you ask?"

"Well, I, er, just wondered if you brought back any other sou-venirs. Like necklaces or rosary beads. Anything like that. Maybe something made out of seeds."

"I'd never buy anything made of seeds. Some of them have insect larvae hidden inside and some are even poi . . . sonous," she completed after a long mid-word pause. Sitting down, hand supporting forehead, she murmured, "Joe was poisoned, wasn't he? With some kind of a seed."

"Yeah. Medeiros got the report after you left. He was poisoned with something called abrin that's found in a tropical plant. The rosary pea. Funny name for something so deadly. But they make it into rosary beads and other stuff like necklaces. People have died by chewing on the seeds. Usually children. That's how they pinned it down so soon. One of the new assistants to the medical examiner had seen a case in the hospital where he interned. A three-year-old. Died from chewing on his mother's rosary beads. This doc was in on the autopsy. Recognized the same signs in Smith, so they were able to alert the tox lab what to look for."

"And you came right to me to learn if I'd been to the Caribbean. Do you know how many people travel there every year? Especially from New England in winter?"

"Thousands. But their ex-husbands don't turn up dead. Believe me, Marguerite, I'm on your side. I came here hoping you'd never been there so it would be harder to connect you with this. Not only have you been there but you know about the poisonous seeds. Now we're back to square one."

"How was it given to him? I can't imagine him eating a strange seed. He's not a child."

"We don't know. But the seeds are very hard and if they're swallowed whole they usually pass right through the digestive system without harm. They have to be broken up. I would think he would've tasted something funny."

"Not necessarily. He had a bad cold—in fact, I thought it was the flu—and his taste was off. He didn't eat most of his dinner. Except for those oysters, of course." She still chafed at that deprivation despite the fact that she lived in the next town and could have their famous oysters at any time.

"Frank, what else can you tell me about the investigation?"

"Nothing, Marguerite. I probably shouldn't have told you this much but I expect that the results will be in the papers anyway. Medeiros is in charge of the investigation, not me. I'm here as your friend. Take this seriously. Get yourself a lawyer."

She ignored his remark, eager for more information. "I have one more question, Frank. It shouldn't be a secret because I can look it up in a toxicology book. But you could save me the time. How long does this poison take to react?''

''That's part of the puzzle. It could be hours or it could be a couple of days. Depends on the number of seeds and how much they were broken up. Depends on the person, too. Size, age, general health.''

''Just one more question. I swear just one,'' she promised, holding up her hand as for an oath when he made a face. ''What are the symptoms?''

''There's a whole batch of them.'' He retrieved from his pocket a wrinkled slip of paper and read, ''Nausea, vomiting, diarrhea, abdominal pain, dilation of the pupils, ulcerating and bleeding of the mouth. In severe cases, convulsions, coma, and death. And no more questions,'' he warned.

''There you have it!'' she exclaimed triumphantly. ''Joe had already been poisoned when I met him. He hardly touched his dinner—probably nauseated. And he went to the men's room several times. Must have been diarrhea or stomach cramps. Both, most likely. And if his mouth was ulcerated, that would explain why he could eat the oysters but nothing else. They're soft and smooth. He always ate them straight, too. No cocktail sauce. That means I didn't do it!''

''Even if you had corroboration on all those facts, and I doubt if you do, you still have a problem. There's no evidence right now as to what time he got to your house before you went out to dinner. He could have been poisoned then. We're trying to track down his appointments but it's been slow going. A couple of the people left for vacation afterward. Just like you did. Of course, if you're right it puts another suspect right in the limelight. The person who was looking for him and waiting at his hotel. Portia.''

Wordlessly, Marguerite watched Frank leave the house, carefully turned the latch to lock it, and chastised herself for her careless tongue, which had implicated Portia. She had to get herself together and help both of them out of this mess.

The knock at the door was soft, as if not really sure it wanted to be heard. ''Is everything okay, Mrs. Smith?'' inquired Ed when she opened the door. ''I saw the police car drive away and thought you might have bad news.''

''Oh, nothing too serious,'' she uttered impulsively, feeling almost amused at the absurdity of herself or Portia being considered murderers. Or was it murderesses? No, she liked murderers better. ''It seems my ex-husband was poisoned, his body dumped in the lighthouse, and discovered after I was in Florida. And I seem to be a suspect, along with my niece. Other than that everything is hunky-dory.''

Green eyes wide, mouth agape, he merely stared at her. In her heightened state of sensitivity, she finally located a flaw in that perfect face. One eyebrow lifted higher than the other. His imperfection made her feel expansive.

''Ed, why don't you stay and have dinner with me tonight? No, it's not a bother,'' she assured him as she saw his mouth change shape to verbalize a protest. ''It would actually be a help to me. I need to be distracted from this problem, and cooking clears my head. I'll keep it simple. How about that chicken you rescued from the ice? With brown rice, a few peas, and a red pepper for color. The only condition is that we don't discuss murder or poison. Deal?''

''I'll take a chance and eat with you,'' he quipped, grinning mischievously.

Chapter Sixteen

The tide was out, enabling Marguerite to walk on the path around Salt Pond, her low rubber puddle-jumpers making a sucking sound each time she lifted a foot, extricating it from the muddy residue of melted snow and high tides. It was not really a pond at all, but an inlet from the ocean filtered through Nauset Marsh and subject to the lunar ebb and flow of the ocean.

It was an auspicious Sunday morning. The sun shone, the temperature rose, and the sky was blue, albeit a washed-out wintry blue. What a difference the sun made! She understood the primal urge to worship it and felt renewed, resilient, ready to tackle her mounting problems.

Marguerite walked jauntily despite the clumsy footwear and the clutching earth. No one could seriously think she murdered Joe. Or that Portia did, either. But someone had and she would not be free of suspicion until that someone was discovered. Whether the police objected or not, she had to help solve this.

As she reached the highest point of the walk, the expanse of Nauset Marsh became visible in its beauty and in its savagery as a feeding ground for birds who shopped its bounty for mollusks or fish, each according to preference and availability, competitive in the urge to survive and ensure their own genes a place in the future pool for their species. She sat on one of the benches strategically placed for viewing the marsh and watched nature's performance while calculating her own.

She already had a couple of answers. For one thing, she

thought she knew how Joe was poisoned. The seeds were broken up and steeped in a tisane, a type of tea made by soaking herbs, flowers, and spices in hot water.

He had been introduced to tisanes by her own mother, Genevieve LeGrand, who used them as curative agents in a time of limited medical care, varying the ingredients to suit the symptoms. Joe had been delighted by the intriguing flavors of a tisane, each one different from the last, and drank them regularly.

Though she had told Frank that the symptoms Joe displayed at dinner with her were consistent with those of the poison, it was also possible, even likely upon reflection, that at least some of those symptoms were, as she had originally assumed, from a cold or flu. In that case, Joe might very well have made himself a tisane that had been tampered with, or accepted one from someone else who visited him. Packets of the herbal ingredients could be bought commercially and, with an infusion heater, only required a cup and water to prepare. His taste buds were desensitized and the mixture of strong flavors like lemon, mint, thyme, and rosemary would disguise any strange taste from the seeds.

Should she tell the police? The negatives weighed in very heavily. Her mother had introduced Joe to them. She herself was thoroughly familiar with tisanes and grew many of the requisite herbs, a fact Frank was sure to remember, especially since she liberally flavored her iced teas with them, causing him to compliment her every time he sampled one. Better wait a while until she could figure out who doctored Joe's drink.

Frank had inadvertently supplied her with the answer to another question that had puzzled her. Why didn't they know when Joe had been murdered? She had understood part of the problem from the beginning. His body had been frozen and the normal measurable processes of decay halted.

But what about stomach contents? Freezing would have preserved those. His dinner on the night of January fifteenth was well documented. Frank had dashed her hope of exoneration by stomach contents other than oysters and martini when he read the symptoms of poisoning by abrin, prominent among which was nausea. Joe's stomach was probably empty due to vomiting. No help at all.

There was no way around it. She had to track down that book Joe and Nick were so hot to get. Trying to contact Nick was out of the question. She was terrified of him. He might be the murderer.

Searching through George and Laura's books would be no help either, since she had no idea of what to look for. Furthermore, Joe had been certain that the person who owned the book was unaware of its value.

The only solution was to start at the other end—Joe's end. Track down what he had been investigating. There were two people most likely to know, his brother Wilson, and his wife Veronica. Wilson would be no problem. He and Marguerite had become friends as well as in-laws.

But Veronica? How would she greet an ex-wife, the last person known to be with her murdered husband? And, if Joe was telling the truth, he died broke. Even the income from the trust fund would disappear, as the money would pass to Joe's children, Neil and Alex.

She had been sitting long enough for her feet to become cold and her seat damp. Time to leave. She had to visit Laura. George had promised to do that but Marguerite sensed that he did not take her warning seriously. Besides, she might obtain a little information at the same time.

The walk back was quicker than the stroll out. She suddenly had a sense of urgency and the woods no longer seemed friendly. At every rustle of a squirrel or bird, she jumped. *Just because you're paranoiac,* she cautioned herself, *it doesn't mean they're not out to get you.*

A red blinking light on the message machine awaited her.

"Mother, it's Alex. I can never find you at home and you have not answered my calls. I had to phone Portia to see if she knew where you were. You seem to have gotten in over your head this time. Preston and I are on our way. We're flying to Logan and renting a car from there. Try to keep out of any more trouble until we arrive."

The State Department is coming to the rescue. I must be in worse shape than I thought, pondered Marguerite. *But at least there'll be someone besides myself to question Veronica. Wait till Alex hears that.*

Chapter Seventeen

The house sat in sleepy decay, closer to the road than was fashionable today, but perfectly placed two hundred years ago for easy access to the wagon track. It was an "add-on" house, typical of its era. A young couple would build a half Cape house, characterized by two front windows and a door, accommodating a front room and a kitchen—both served by fireplaces from a central chimney—and an unheated bedroom tucked between them. As the family grew, so did the house, becoming a three-quarter Cape, then a full Cape with two windows on each side of a central door. With each addition, the chimney grew, completing its circle with fireplaces serving each room adjacent to it. The Eldredge house eventually acquired wings, one on each side, unmatching and asymmetrical.

The house had never been remodeled or gutted, so the original section had low ceilings and tiny closetless rooms, the next section marginally larger rooms, and the two wings, added at different times, came equipped with a bathroom each and small clothes closets. It was an impractical, uncomfortable house.

Marguerite spotted Laura's old Dodge in the driveway and was relieved that she was home from church, probably not as relieved as the minister, though. Laura's ancestors were among the earliest residents of Eastham and had been prominent in the founding of the church at which she worshipped. Almost three and a half centuries and several buildings later, Laura guarded the church as if the sweat and blood of her forebears were in every beam and board. She regarded each passing minister as an interloper, while *she* represented continuity.

It was even worse for the ministers' wives, who felt compelled to consult Laura before every change of paint or paper in the parsonage although that building had no connection to the history of the original church, having been willed to the parish in the 1940s.

Laura opened the door before Marguerite reached it. No one pulled unnoticed into her driveway.

"I thought you'd be coming around. Looks like you and that Owens woman cut quite a swath through Florida." Laura referred to Beatrice as "that Owens woman" even though they had been playing bridge together for two years. "Getting mixed up in a murder and with the Mafia."

"May I come in, Laura?" Marguerite inquired with civility. She had prepared herself to be insulted.

Laura stepped aside and waved toward the small back parlor. That room and the kitchen were the only nearly comfortable rooms during winter in that ill-heated, drafty house.

Laura was as ungainly as her house. Tall, gaunt, with steel-gray hair tightly braided and coiled in the back and pale gray eyes, she had a face that was all edges—sharp nose, sharp chin, facial bones on which the skin fit too tightly.

Still dressed for church, she wore a wrinkled woolen skirt, tan with a muted red design hinting at a plaid. Her warm sweater top was a hue between mustard and jaundice, imparting a yellowish tint to her bony face, colored today with lipstick that was bleeding into the crevices above her mouth. Perversely, she wore lipstick only to church. Opaque black stockings and sturdy flat-heeled shoes completed her Sunday best.

Marguerite seated herself on the edge of an old horsehair sofa and explained, "First of all, Laura, Joe's murder occurred in Eastham, not in Florida, and I had nothing to do with it. Secondly, I don't know anything about a Mafia connection and neither do you. You're just making that up."

Sniff. "Where there's smoke there's fire, I always say."

"Yes, you do always say that," agreed Marguerite. "But I came here to make sure you understand that there really is some danger and you should take care. Nick Dante has a gun and is dangerous. Are you locking your doors and windows?"

"Don't be foolish, Marguerite. You know that some of these

windows don't even have locks. But I can take care of myself. I have a gun, too, you know. Several of them. Father taught all of us to shoot when we were young. Even took us hunting on the days he wasn't out on his fishing boat. Was a lot easier then. Not so many do-gooders telling everybody what they could do.''

"Be careful, Laura. Sometimes a gun gets used on the one who owns it."

"Not on me! Too many amateurs using guns today."

"I guess you're right," agreed Marguerite, determined to be conciliatory. "Did George tell you about a book that some people think is very valuable?"

Sniff. " 'Course he did. Insisted on looking through all mine to search for it. Spent several hours doing it before he got all stiff and quit."

"Did he find anything?"

" 'Course not. He didn't even know what he was looking for."

Marguerite was disappointed. Laura paused, then added dryly, "But I solved the problem anyway."

"You did?"

"Sure. It just took some good common sense, which you and George lack. Since neither George nor I have a book that is worth much in itself, I figured it must be information someone wants, not the book itself. He said you claim the book is worth millions. What's worth millions on Cape Cod? There's no oil under these sands and if there's gold no one's found it yet. Must be the ocean."

"I don't understand, Laura. No one owns the ocean," protested a puzzled Marguerite.

Sniff. " 'Course you don't understand. No common sense. What's valuable about the ocean? The view. Oceanfront property is worth millions. Mostly to people who don't know any better than to build a house where it's sure to get washed away. There's very little of it left and now with the National Park here there's less than ever. Suppose someone found a way to claim a huge amount of oceanfront land. He'd be a millionaire many times over."

"But what has this got to do with you or George?"

"Nothing to do with George. Plenty to do with me. I have lots of records. Going back to the mid-1600s when Eastham was first settled by Pilgrims. Some of my stuff may be the only records in existence because papers get lost, burned, discarded, and even rot away.

"After the delegation from Plymouth bought the land here from the Indians on behalf of the congregation in Plymouth, the court granted all this land to the church or those that came to dwell here. The settlers then divvied it up among themselves. Suppose someone has an idea that it wasn't done right or someone, maybe one of his ancestors, was cheated. There always was some question about Billingsgate. This was north of the territory purchased but the Indians didn't claim ownership of it, so the Pilgrims did. Or it may concern a later property dispute. If the person could find the right records, he might have claim to hundreds of acres. That's worth a lot of money in itself and if any of it is waterfront, it would be an incredible amount. I must have the papers to back up the claim."

"Could anyone claim land after all that time?"

"They could *claim* it. *Proving* it would be a little more difficult and would take a lot of time. Meanwhile there would be a lot of frightened property owners who would be blaming the government for their problems. If they had enough clout they could even force the state or the federal government or a combination of both to offer a settlement. That's what's so valuable. My land records," she concluded triumphantly, justifying her years of stewardship.

"Then you have to put them somewhere in safekeeping and let it be known that you don't have them anymore. That would protect you. Let's call the police."

Sniff. "The police! That's the last thing I'll do. Let them paw through all my precious books with their clumsy hands. Never! I've been taking care of them all my life and will continue to do so. Besides, I have hundreds of books and almost as many boxes of papers. I don't even know what period of time we're concerned with here. I intend to sort them out, though, and separate the land records from the personal journals. That will be a start."

"Laura, that could take weeks, maybe months. In the meantime, you'd be in danger from whoever wants those records."

"I doubt it. One look at all this stuff and he'd know it'd be useless to try to find anything without me. He'd need a truck to take everything away and years to read through it all. So you see, I'm safe. I'm the only one who can make sense of those records." She was actually smiling, her strong, slightly overlapping teeth revealed between narrow lips that seldom parted more than the minimum required for laconic speech.

"Don't be so sure of that. If someone knew exactly what he was looking for it wouldn't be as difficult as you think."

"I was taking care of myself and everyone else in my family as far back as I can remember. I can still fend for myself," Laura proclaimed adamantly.

Marguerite nodded, aware of Laura's past though fearful of her future. Laura's mother had died young from pneumonia, leaving Laura with the responsibility of caring for the house, her father, and two younger brothers as well as the records for her father's fishing boat. Her brothers, Joshua and Isaac, hated fishing. Seeking a way off the water, they secured financing to operate a fish processing plant and Laura had an additional job—the plant's books.

When the fishing industry declined, they managed to sell to an optimist and opened a seafood restaurant in Yarmouth that featured only seafood from Cape Cod waters, including underutilized species—no shrimp, no mahimahi. Laura learned the intricacies of restaurant bookkeeping.

By this time her father had died and her brothers married and left home. After they opened a second restaurant in Falmouth, they retired Laura and put the increasingly complex business matters into the hands of a professional accountant. It never occurred to them that Laura had little else in her life except her work for them. In fact, they had never thought much about Laura at all.

"Okay, Laura, but do you mind if I at least let the police know what you told me? It might help me. They seem to think I had something to do with this mess."

"That's because you're always showing off with them. If you acted sensible and kept out of their way they wouldn't give you a second thought. As for carrying on with your ex-husband, you should know better," Laura scolded.

The information she had received made Marguerite feel magnanimous despite the chastisement and the calumny. "You're wrong about any carrying on with an ex-husband, but maybe you're right about getting myself involved with the police." She was thinking of Nick. "You've been a great help. Thanks, Laura," added Marguerite as she rose to leave.

"See if you can find anyone to make a bridge fourth," Laura called after the departing figure. "That Owens woman will probably flit around for the rest of the winter."

Chapter Eighteen

Marguerite made reservations instead of dinner for her daughter and son-in-law who arrived Sunday afternoon with four pieces of Vuitton luggage and two laptop computers complete with modem. The lobster huts and clam shacks, Preston's favorite haunts on Cape Cod, were closed and shuttered for the winter.

The Captain Linnell House, historic and elegant, was originally the home of a clipper captain and now home to fine dining. Dinner was on her, and Marguerite deflected Alex's questions until they had ordered coffee and dessert wine, Preston's favorite—d'Yquem. She declined to join them.

They had one small sip of the expensive wine before she disrupted their after-dinner aura of contentment. "As I see it, the only reason the police are bothering me is because they know that I was with Joe that night and they don't know anything he did after that. Or even before that. Like why was he late picking me up? Who detained him? Who had a motive to kill him? Those are the things we have to find out."

As she paused to take a sip of her coffee, Preston, wide-eyed at the suggestion that "we" had to find things out, ventured his own suggestion. "I think the first thing we have to do is get you a proper lawyer."

He stressed the word "proper," evidently considering both Marguerite's vacationing lawyer and her compromised niece as having failed the test. For Preston, being proper had a multitude of extensions, all of them important in his life.

Of old North Carolina lineage and a graduate of Duke University, he had met and married Alexandra in Washington, D.C., where they now made their home in the Georgetown section. Her career as a college professor of English literature and his at the State Department melded to suit them both. His frequent travels abroad provided her with the solitude she required to write, a necessity for her profession, a balm to her angst.

Six feet tall, Preston had very light blond hair and hazelnut-colored eyes of almost the same shade as his tortoise-framed glasses. His smooth, guileless face was fuller than one expected with his slim physique, the hues and curves of youth having lingered on into manhood. When he smiled, the corners of his mouth turned up to meet the creases in his cheeks, creating an altogether happy look like a child's smiley drawing. This and his easygoing conversational manner belied his steel-trap mind, making him a natural diplomat.

"I don't think so, Preston," Marguerite replied to his suggestion about a lawyer. "A lawyer would either advise me to tell the police what I knew, which I've already done, or to tell them nothing else, in which case they'll be convinced I'm guilty. The only way out of this for me is to find out the truth or, at the very least, to drum up some other suspects for them to worry about. I've already gotten some information today from Laura. I'll tell Frank her idea about the book tomorrow. I'd better tell you now."

The story took a little time, necessitating more coffee but, thankfully for Marguerite, no more d'Yquem. "So you see," she concluded, "I already learned something they don't know."

"Has it occurred to you, Mother, that if you are correct about Dad's murder being connected with some phantom book of great value that the closer you come to that book, the more danger you're in?"

Marguerite looked at Alex with a heaviness in her heart. So like Joe in appearance—the same amber eyes and hair, the same tall, slim physique with its effortless grace of movement—Alex lacked his easy charm, his air of bonhomie.

"Yes, it has occurred to me. It's also occurred to me that maybe this phantom book has nothing to do with his murder. There might have been lots of other people with a reason for

murder. How about a wife, a girlfriend, a business competitor or
business associate, and, maybe most of all, an investor whose
money Joe lost? A person's whole life can be ruined if he loses
all his money. Tomorrow we start tracking these people down.
I'll go see Wilson. He would know the most about the business
end of this mystery. I'd like you to see Veronica. Get some in-
sights on the personal part of Joe's life.''

Alex groaned as Marguerite feared she would. The wine wasn't
working. ''Oh, no! How can I visit her? I've never even spoken
to her except when Dad introduced her to me at my graduation.
I wasn't even polite to her.''

''You've grown up a lot since then. You'll know how to talk
to her.'' Marguerite dismissed Alex's protests and turned to Preston. ''You can be a great help by driving us. I figure you can
drop me off at Joe's office in Boston, then drive Alex to Chestnut
Hill and come back for me when Alex is finished. I can spend
as much time as I have to with Wilson. We always have a lot to
talk about.'' Focusing back on Alex, she directed, ''You'll need
to call Veronica though, first thing in the morning, or you might
not catch her at home.''

''But I don't even know what to ask her,'' moaned Alex dis-
mally.

''Don't worry about a thing,'' her mother responded encouragingly. ''I'll make up a list of things we need to know. You can
memorize them on the way there. Just pretend you're cramming
for a test.''

Satisfied with her night's work, Marguerite paid the check
which had been sitting on the table for some time and ushered
them out of the restaurant.

The ride home was unnaturally quiet, each thinking of the mor-
row's mission. Marguerite was glad to hear the phone ringing as
she opened the door, since it gave her an excuse to rush in and
leave the disgruntled couple to commiserate.

It was Ed Rogers, her winter neighbor. ''Sorry to bother you,
but I was wondering if you had yesterday's *New York Times*. I
heard there was a great bridge hand in it by Omar Sharif.''

''No, I had too many things happening to me yesterday to even
buy a newspaper. Are you a bridge player?''

''I play a little but I'm trying to improve myself. That's why
I read those hands.''

''I have a bridge group that usually plays on Fridays if we're all here. There's one person missing now. If the others would like to play this Friday, would you like to join us?''

''I don't think so. I'm not up to your caliber.''

''Don't worry about it. You can be my partner. They can't complain about that. It'll give Laura a chance to win honestly for a change.''

''If you think it's okay,'' he answered with hesitance in his voice.

''It's okay. I'll take a chance and play brige with you,'' she replied, mimicking his words of yesterday.

Chapter Nineteen

He came for her early Monday morning, before they had finished breakfast. Preston and Alex had their heads buried in newspapers; Marguerite was engrossed in a list she was making—questions she wanted Alex to ask Veronica.

David Morgan rapped at the door with more authority than he felt. He was fond of Marguerite, who could be relied on for a cold glass of iced tea on a summer's day. An artist who became a policeman to satisfy his habit of liking to eat regularly, he had adapted well but every once in a while he had a conflict between his emotions and his duty. Today was one of those times.

"Good morning, David," Marguerite greeted him brightly. "You're just in time for some breakfast," she continued, although suspicious that David had not come for coffee.

"Uh, no thank you, Mrs. Smith," he murmured, nervously twirling his cap in his hands. "I'm sorry to bother you so early, but they'd like you to come down to the station."

They, not we. David was distancing himself from the request. She noticed. "Who exactly are they?"

"Well, the chief, of course. But mostly Sgt. McEnerny."

Her spirits sank. Wouldn't this ever end?

"Well, you might just as well have that coffee anyway. It will take me a few minutes to get ready," she told him, clearing her place and setting out a cup and saucer for the uncomfortable policeman.

"Preston!" intoned Alex in a commanding voice. "Do something!"

"Yes, of course," he said coolly, his voice reflecting State Department understatement colored with Southern inflections. "Marguerite, you don't have to answer any of their questions without a lawyer. Why not postpone this and we'll discuss further the advisability of hiring an attorney."

"It's no use, Preston," she sighed resignedly. "That will only bring McEnerny here and I'd rather not entertain him. Besides, I've already told them everything I know except for Laura's theory about her books. I'll tell them that. There's nothing else they can possibly want from me."

She discovered that there was a lot they wanted from her as soon as she entered the chief's office, accompanied by Preston, who had delayed the anxious Officer Morgan long enough to dress as if for a diplomatic mission. His three-piece striped gray suit, starched white shirt, small-patterned dark red tie, and shiny black-laced shoes raised eyebrows in this assemblage of police officers accustomed to the less formal attire of Cape Cod lawyers, for a lawyer was what they assumed he was.

Nicholas Dante had been murdered, his body discovered awash on the bank of a man-made canal in Fort Lauderdale. The owners of one of those multimillion-dollar canal houses had docked their multimillion-dollar yacht after a week-long sailing trip and discovered the body near their landing while disembarking at noon on Saturday.

He was identified easily since his laminated ID and police badge were in his pocket. Although not assigned to homicide, Lyle Fairchild had heard the name from a police buddy with whom he had gone fishing Sunday morning. The connection to Marguerite was made. He informed the homicide division of that as well as the fact that she had not been in her room when he called shortly after eleven and had been spotted leaving the hotel and getting into a cab. Still shaking his head in surprise at this turn of events, he wondered if he had read Marguerite wrong. Or if she had really murdered Dante. Or killed him in self defense. Her complaint should have been taken more seriously.

Aghast at the violence surrounding her, Marguerite experienced a horrified blankness and turned helplessly to Preston, who spoke for her.

"As I understand it, that is the man who threatened Mrs. Smith and whom you let go. Very likely he's also the person who killed her ex-husband. We're all relieved we can put this problem behind us now.''

''It's not behind you yet,'' warned Sgt. McEnerny with a granite expression. ''We have a lot of questions to ask Mrs. Smith. This is the second man she's threatened who turned up dead. Something about elephants not forgetting, wasn't it?''

''She left Florida on Friday morning. What could she possibly tell you about this horrid incident?''

McEnerny warmed to the duel. He was dressed in an old gray suit, shiny at all the points of wear, with a new-looking azure tie that added color to his pale blue eyes. Even in her shocked state, Marguerite noted the tie and decided it must have been a gift. Probably from that niece he gave away.

His annoying mannerisms were intact, however. He sat astride a chair, facing its back with fingers tapping an insistent tattoo on the top while he talked.

''She can tell us where she was Thursday night for starters. That's when the doc says he was killed. Late Thursday night or early Friday morning. Sometime before six o'clock. That's the closest he can come so far. Rigor mortis was over, so he must have been dead at least thirty hours. The body was partly in water and partly out so it was in two different temperatures and had two different sets of creatures feeding on it. They've got the bug doctors figuring that out.''

Marguerite shuddered at the implications of a human, even one as duplicitous as Nick, becoming carrion for crabs and flies and other scavengers. She was about to speak when Preston smoothly preempted her.

''Sergeant, I am still not sure why you brought Mrs. Smith down here. Especially since you're questioning her about a crime that occurred in Florida. Isn't that a little out of your jurisdiction?''

''Normally, yes. But this here crime seems linked to one that did occur in my jurisdiction, as you call it. Also, I've been in contact with Lauderdale homicide. They asked me to do them a favor and see if I could find out anything about Dante's whereabouts. Now if you'll just let me do my job.''

''Not yet, Sergeant. I have one more question. Is she a suspect in either murder?''

McEnerny was wary of the word ''suspect.'' It brought too

many privileges. "She's a material witness," he responded cagily.

"To what?" inquired Preston evenly, rattling McEnerny, who preferred outright confrontation.

"That's what we're trying to find out, if you'd shut up for a minute. Understand?"

Marguerite's aversion to McEnerny had stimulated her shocked system into recovery. "It's okay, Preston, I have nothing to hide. The sooner they solve this case, the sooner the murders will stop. They haven't had much success so far"—this with a sly glance at the sergeant—"so evidently they need my help."

"Would you like some coffee, Marguerite?" asked Frank Nadeau, speaking for the first time.

"No thank you, Frank. I already had coffee at home. *Café délicieux,*" she added with a meaningful glance at the muddy concoction in his cup. "How was he killed?" she inquired, hoping it was not poisoning.

"He was shot. Now, where did you go on Thursday night after we left you at about eight-forty?" resumed McEnerny.

"Down to the lobby. I was waiting for Beatrice to return."

"Why didn't you wait in your room?"

"I was afraid, afraid Nick would return. He threatened to break my arm, remember?"

"How long did you wait there?"

"Until about eleven. Then I picked up a message at the desk from Beatrice that she wasn't coming home. So I went upstairs."

"And you stayed upstairs?" He was grinning like the Cheshire cat.

She knew he knew the answer. "No, I was afraid to enter the room. I left and went to another hotel for the night."

"Did you leave the hotel to meet Nicholas Dante?"

"Don't be absurd! He was the person I was afraid of."

"So afraid that you called his hotel from your room at exactly eight-forty-seven, shortly after we left you. Were you arranging to meet him?"

"I didn't call him. I dialed the number of his hotel thinking he could tell me what was going on. Then I realized he could have murdered Joe and hung up. I never spoke to him." Her chin thrust out aggressively, daring him to contradict her.

"That's one possibility. There's another way of looking at it. You called him and asked him to meet you in the lobby. You went down there but he never showed. Then you got a message from him to meet you somewhere else so you left and got a cab to meet him.''

''Sergeant!'' admonished Preston. ''Mrs. Smith came here voluntarily as a good citizen to assist the police. You seem to be implying that Mrs. Smith had something to do with his murder.''

''You misunderstand me,'' McEnerny replied in an aggrieved voice. ''I only think she met him and spent some time with him but is too embarrased to admit it. I only want to know because if she could tell us when she left him it would help establish the time of death a little closer. She might even know where he was going when he left her. Understand?''

''I undertand perfectly,'' interjected Marguerite. ''You are still convinced that Nick was not a threat to me and that I made up that story.''

He was embarrassed by her acuity and quickly asked another question to hide it. ''What's the name of the hotel you claim you stayed at?''

''I stayed at the Tropicana.''

''Did you fill out a card to register?''

''No. I forgot my glasses so the clerk filled it out.''

''Did you pay with a credit card?''

''No. I paid cash.''

''Do you always pay hotel rooms in cash?''

''Not always.''

''Then why this particular time?''

Marguerite fidgeted, realizing how bad her answer was going to sound. ''Because I didn't use my real name. I was afraid Nick would find me if I did. I used the name Margaret Johnson.''

''And you were alone?'' he asked archly.

''Yes, I was alone,'' she answered angrily.

''That'll be easy enough to check out. And when we do we'll get back to you. Understand?''

Chapter Twenty

Alex was remorseful even before the police car pulled away. Why couldn't she ever get it right? This professor of English literature, creator of flowing prose, could never garner the words to repair a tragic flaw in her relationship with her mother.

In her childhood it had been Mother who made the rules and Daddy who could be relied upon to bend them for Alex, his princess. Mother was the heavy. When Joe left, Alex was long past childhood but not past her devotion to him, and harbored the secret belief that Marguerite had driven him away. Time had shown her the error of her reasoning but had not diminished the petulance with which Alex responded to her mother's every suggestion.

Regretting the griping she had done about Marguerite's plans for today, she decided to act rather than react. Her mother needed help.

Her first priority was determined by Rusty, who kept running to the door then back to Alex, nudging her leg each time. It had been Alex who befriended the abandoned puppy seeking shelter on their doorstep so many years ago and who had then cavalierly bequeathed the care of the dog to her mother. Dogs, just like mothers, were forgiving.

The day was clear, the ground had dried, and Rusty was exuberant at taking a different route today. Alex noticed none of this as she walked down the road planning her approach to Veronica in the phone call that was next on her list of things to do.

The ensuing conversation with Veronica was mutually unenthusiastic, though Alex, as the petitioner, tried to hide her distaste. Veronica would see her about noon; she hoped she would be home from the hairdresser by then; if not, Alex would just have to wait somewhere.

One more phone call assured Alex that her Uncle Wilson would be in his office today and would expect Marguerite. Now, if only the police would stop grilling her mother.

Preston and Marguerite arrived before Alex's thought was even stored in memory. An introspective Marguerite was startled when her formerly reluctant daughter hurried her into the house announcing that they had to leave immediately, the appointments were all arranged.

The commuter rush hour over, traffic was moderate, and Marguerite was deposited at the familiar State Street building before she had thoroughly considered the ramifications of another murder linked to her. Quickly repeating to Preston the directions to Chestnut Hill, she breezily wished Alex luck and strode toward the door with a confidence in her walk that she lacked in her psyche.

It was as if she had been there only yesterday. The same office furniture, the same pictures on the wall—mostly sailing scenes, some anonymous, some with Joe and Wilson, one with her in it. He must have forgotten to take that down, she thought. Most familiar of all was the same secretary, Mildred Jones, who had been hired by their father right out of secretarial school and stayed on with the brothers. Her interest in the firm was so proprietary, they had jokingly taken to referring to it as Smith & Jones.

After a greeting that for Mildred was effusive, Marguerite went into Wilson's office. He was two years younger than Joe, two inches shorter, but approximately the same weight, the extra pounds on a smaller frame settled around the neck and the waistline. Like many men of his physique, he wore his belt below his corporation, causing the pants to bag at the ankles and the seat, an altogether comfortable and comforting look to Marguerite who was glad he did not resemble Joe. With coarse dark hair, nearly all gray, and blue eyes, the dissimilarity was complete.

After a mutual exchange of condolences she hesitated, not knowing what to say next. He knew exactly what to say, skirting the problem before them and complimenting her on how well she looked, saying she could still be voted the best-looking girl in her Radcliffe class.

This leap from the intolerable present to the fairy-tale past when Marguerite Fallon, a working-class student from South Boston attending Radcliffe on an academic scholarship, met Joseph Daniel Smith, a Boston Brahmin and Harvard student, unleashed a flood of remembrances.

"Do you ever go back to your old neighborhood, Meg?"

"Not since my parents died. Except for recently when I went to St. Brigid's for a funeral."

"I remember your wedding. The church was packed. You had a lot of friends."

"Not that many. Most people came out of curiosity. Everyone wanted to see the grand family into which I was marrying. What a disappointment you all were." She laughed.

"Disappointment?"

"Sure. Everyone came out in that bitter cold day to see the swells. What a surprise when all of the women in your family were wearing serviceable woolen winter coats and plain pumps. Why, my side of the aisle was resplendent with all those rented fur stoles and new satin or taffeta dresses." Her eyes were aglow at the memory.

"I guess we've always disappointed you, Meg."

"No, Wilson. Those were the best years of my life."

She permitted herself only a moment's reflection before getting to the point of her visit.

"Wilson, the police think I murdered Joe. They're also hinting that I murdered someone called Nicholas Dante who followed me to Florida and tried to find out what Joe wanted from me. I didn't do either of these things. You know I would never murder anyone, especially Joe."

"I know, Meg. They were here questioning me about his visit to Cape Cod and about his relationship with you. But I didn't know anything about another murder."

"Neither did I until a couple of hours ago." Briefly she updated Wilson on Nick and her encounters with him. "There's someone with a motive for murder, two murders. Or maybe there were two murderers. Both Joe and Nick were asking me about a valuable book one of my friends supposedly has. But they didn't tell me who had it or what was in it. I need to know more about that. Joe also told me he had business problems, that he was broke and needed the money he could get from finding that book. Was Joe really in financial trouble?''

Wilson hesitated, weighing his answer. ''Meg, you know it's not our policy to discuss private affairs, but I'd like to help you out so I'll bend the rules. Yes, Joe was in trouble. His expenses were exceeding his income so he started making unwise investments. Unfortunately, he also made them for his clients, looking for bigger commissions. He guessed wrong.''

''I noticed you said *his* clients. Weren't they yours, too? Aren't you a partner?''

Clearly embarrassed, he almost stuttered his answer. ''Why yes, of course I am. But I haven't suffered the losses he did. None of my personal money was invested. I control that myself. I also have my law practice which is separate.''

Marguerite tried to mollify him. ''I realize you weren't involved in Joe's mistakes, Wilson. I'm just trying to find out if one of these disgruntled investors could have had a reason to kill him, just out of sheer anger.''

''No, Meg. I've thought about that a lot. The police asked me the same question. Most of his clients were elderly. They could never have pulled it off. Besides, no one knew about the money problem yet. Joe was still able to cover it up by issuing incomplete statements and blaming it on the computer. I didn't know how he was doing that until I went through his papers after he died.''

Visibly disappointed, Marguerite tried another avenue. ''How about that book everyone seems to want? Do you know anything about that?''

Wilson was clearly in a quandary. He pushed his glasses up and rubbed his eyes as if clearing his head. Resetting the glasses, he moved the papers around on his desk, putting them in a neat pile. Marguerite smelled blood.

''Meg, I'm in a bind. Our clients''—she noticed it was now *our* clients—''expect confidentiality. But I'd like to help you. Joe did have some book he was excited about. He got it from a client who was emptying out her house and selling it because she was too old to keep it up and was moving to a managed-care facility. He handled her money for years.''

''What was in the book?''

''I don't know. I'm not sure if Joe knew either because it was written in German. I know he was making some efforts to translate it. In fact, he was becoming rather obsessed with it.''

''Where is that book?''

''I don't know. It wasn't in his desk or in the safe. Maybe he had to give it back to the client.''

''Who was the she?''

There was no answer. Wilson fidgeted with some pencils.

''Wilson, do you understand that I'm a murder suspect? Two murders, in fact. I'm innocent, but I'm convinced I have to take matters into my own hands to prove it. Please help me,'' she implored, her penetrating gaze piercing the armor of his reluctance.

''Okay, Meg. I guess it's not revealing a confidence anyway since this was not part of the business we were conducting for her. Her name is Grace McGuire and she lives in Winthrop. I can get her address for you from Joe's Rolodex. I don't know how much longer she'll be there, because her house is for sale.''

''Did you tell the police about this?''

''No. They didn't ask. They were just interested in his business dealings, his appointments on the Cape, and his relationship with you.''

''What did you tell them about his relationship with me?''

''I said that as far as I knew, there wasn't any.''

''Thanks for your help, Wilson.'' She started to rise then sat down again. There was still something on her mind but she hated to ask, fully aware of how protective the Smiths were about personal matters. She asked anyway.

''There's one more thing. In most murders the first suspect is the spouse. How about in this case? Was everything all right with him and Veronica?''

Wilson laughingly answered, ''I thought you were slipping, Meg, and weren't going to ask.''

''And I know you're not slipping and don't want to answer. Do I have to give you my desperate plea again?''

''No, I guess not. Joe's dead, There's nothing I can do for him now. Maybe I can help you. To answer your question, everything was not okay. It really never was, but it was getting worse. She spent him into this mess he got into. He wanted to divorce her but couldn't until he got his finances straight. She didn't know the situation he was in but would have found out in a divorce action because she would have been demanding money and he would have had to reveal his assets, or lack of them. Then the worms would be out of the can and everyone would have known, including his clients. He couldn't risk divorcing her until he made good his losses.''

''I think there's more, Wilson. Something you haven't told me yet. If Joe was so anxious to have a divorce there must have been another woman. Who was she?''

''Leah,'' he answered simply. ''I don't know her last name. But she works at the Boston Public Library, the main one. I think in the reference department. He met her there while he was trying to unravel that blasted book. Then he stopped talking about her but I would hear him call her. That's when he became secretive.''

''Would I be right in assuming you didn't mention this to the police?''

''Of course I didn't mention it,'' he answered indignantly. ''They didn't ask, and it's none of their business. This is a family matter.''

Chapter Twenty-one

Officer Morgan had never seen a coyote. He knew they lived in Eastham, prowled at night, left behind balls of fur in place of the family cat, but he had never sighted one. That is why he was so excited when he saw an animal running across the road toward a food stand closed and shuttered for the winter. It was like a dog yet not a dog. Close enough for kinship. Bigger than a fox. Must be the elusive coyote.

He wheeled into the empty parking lot with a squeal of tires. The animal heard his noisy approach and ran for cover behind the stand. Driving slowly, David followed the edge of the parking lot to where the paved area narrowed to a single lane leading behind the stand. A cautionary sign on each side of the drive warned, *No Entrance. Delivery Trucks Only.* Hot on the trail of his first coyote, David continued around the stand.

And there it was. Parked in the U made by the encircling building, and hugging the wall so closely that the tires on the right side were resting on two crushed juniper bushes, was the missing Mercedes—Joe Smith's car.

David jumped from his cruiser and walked around the car on the three accessible sides, peering in but remembering not to touch anything. There was nothing remarkable to see. The car appeared empty. If the murdered man's bags were in the car, they must be in the trunk and he dared not look or the chief would have his head. Trying his best to sound cool, he radioed the discovery to headquarters, remembering to use all the correct police jargon.

While David sat contentedly in his car waiting for the tow truck and the accolades due him, the forgotten coyote peeked out from behind a Dumpster and observed this creature trapped in a big metal box. With a burst of speed, he scooted from his hiding place and headed for a nearby copse of pine trees, the young officer glimpsing only a fleeing tail and left in the uncertainty of whether or not he had seen a coyote.

It was of no importance. He had seen a Mercedes.

Chapter Twenty-two

This was not the Veronica Alex remembered. In their only previous meeting, at Alex's college graduation to which Joe had stubbornly insisted on bringing his new trophy wife, Veronica had been smashing. Twenty years younger than Joe, petite, dimpled, with tawny blond hair worn long and draped over one eye, she flashed a provocative smile that hinted at a saucy vulgarity.

Eleven years had wrought a change disproportionate to the time span. She had gained weight, not much, but on her small frame it had settled in the middle, resulting in a barrel shape with a round torso and thin appendages. Her formerly sleek hair, which Alex had guiltily envied and secretly tried to emulate, was cut in short spikes and tortured into two shades of blond, much lighter than her natural color, looking like ash and ashier, contrasting jarringly with dark brushes of false eyelashes and purple eye shadow.

She was dressed in pale shades, white leggings that accentuated the slender legs, with a white-and-tan long knit top that attempted to disguise the expanded waistline. Spike-heeled tan boots added several inches to her diminutive stature and completed the hard look which she had so expensively and unwittingly attained.

"You might as well come in as long as you're here," was the ungracious reception extended to Alex.

"Thank you for seeing me, Veronica," replied Alex, following her stepmother, only eight years her senior, into a large central reception hall with a magnificent staircase ending in a grand swirl of a landing dominated by an antique mahogany newel post. Accustomed to the narrow spaces of her Georgetown house, Alex could only gape at this expanse.

Veronica led her down the wide hall past a living room so large it had two crystal chandeliers. Spotting a gold harp backlighted from a sheerly curtained window, Alex stopped to look at the exquisite room. Her hostess smiled, exhibiting those fetching dimples.

Painted in an unusual shade of periwinkle blue, the walls had white molding and woodwork. The polished oak floor was covered in several places by area rugs highlighting the seating groups, each with its own round, white marble table, surrounded by chairs, some upholstered in a cotton of the same hue as the walls, others gessoed white with silk upholstery in yellow or lavender. An immaculate white fireplace had not a smudge of smoke to sully it. If anyone had ever sat in this room he left no imprint.

"Those chandeliers cost five thousand each," bragged Veronica. "And that harp, I don't even like to mention the price."

But you will, thought Alex.

"Fifteen thousand just to sit there. We don't even play it," she volunteered boastfully, proud of their conspicuous extravagance. "Let's go into the garden room."

With the same sheer white curtains and large windows as the living room, but with a red brick floor covered by a seagrass rug, this room was a decorator's idea of casual. Walls of apple green, furniture in white and pale beige with apple-green pillows, and another white marble table created a look as pristine as the living room. In neither room was there a book, a newspaper, a magazine, a radio, stereo, or television, anything that gave evidence of human habitation. Nor was there a plant in the garden room.

Without preamble, Veronica blurted, "I guess you came about the money."

"What money?"

"Dan's trust fund. You know it goes to you and Neil."

Alex was momentarily confused by the name Dan but quickly remembered that upon his marriage her father had started signing himself as J. Daniel Smith. He had always hated being plain Joseph Smith. New wife, new name.

"Yes, I know. But that's not why I came." Alex swallowed

hard, trying to summon the resolve she had felt that morning. "I wasn't advised of any funeral for my father. Will there be one?"

"He's been buried if that's what you mean. It was done quietly. I didn't feel up to holding a wake after all that scandal."

"What scandal?"

"Him being murdered and all. And after spending the night with his ex-wife."

That barb was the impetus Alex needed. "Veronica, I know you're very upset but my mother hadn't seen Dad in eleven years. She only went to dinner with him. He left her before ten o'clock, alive, and drove off. She never saw him again. Someone did murder him but it wasn't my mother. That means someone else did and that someone is still loose and looking for a book Dad knew about that appears to be valuable. It's why he called my mother. He thought she had some knowledge of it, but she didn't. The murderer might even think you know something and come after you. You're in danger, Veronica."

This two-pronged approach was Marguerite's idea—the lure of money, the fear of harm. Veronica did not answer immediately. She had long considered mother and daughter her enemies. Why trust them now? She threw out a feeler.

"What book?"

"Didn't the police tell you anything about it?"

Alex's remark was calculated to frighten Veronica a little more. She guessed that the police had not seen Veronica since Marguerite's revelation about the book and she wanted Veronica to think that the police were not concerned about her safety.

"I don't know, but Dad evidently thought it was worth a lot of money," Alex continued. "Maybe he was right and was murdered because of it. If he had something here in the house or if you know anything that could lead to it, you might be able to claim all or part of the money."

"Lord knows I could use it." She snorted. "Do you know that he lost all his money? Every bit of it. I found out after he died. I think that brother of his was happy to break the news. He never did like me."

"Everything? How about this house? And insurance?"

"The house is mortgaged for more than I could probably get if I have to sell in a hurry. The insurance is only fifty thousand. He was so used to having money, I guess he never thought I'd need anything. And to think he was going to leave me in the lurch.''

Alex quickly picked up on this. "Leave you? Was he divorcing you?"

"No, of course not," Veronica insisted nervously. "I was just referring to in case he died like he did."

Alex was not convinced and stored the information. "How about the book I mentioned?"

"He was interested in some old book. It looked like it was falling apart. And it was in German. He spent a lot of time having it translated. He suddenly loved the library." Her voice underlined the word "loved." More data for Alex's mental file.

"Is the book here?"

"No," she said too quickly.

Alex wished Preston had come in instead of waiting in the car. This was just the sort of thing he was good at.

"Veronica, neither my mother nor I want any money that might be discovered as a result of what Dad was looking for. We don't need it. But you apparently do. Why don't you help us? If we all work together maybe we can find the real killer and whatever he was looking for. You might be entitled to something he found."

Alex very much doubted this, but she had no other bait.

"What would I have to do?"

"First, look for the book Dad had. It could solve the whole problem."

"I'll try. But I'll have to get into his safe. Would you believe he never gave me the combination?"

Alex believed it. There was a lot she was learning about her father.

"A lock company could help you with that. You mentioned that he was spending a lot of time at the library. Is it possible someone there was helping him translate? Maybe that person has the book."

The answer took a long time coming. "There might have been someone. I think I heard him mention the name Leah. She was just the librarian."

The admission was obviously painful. Alex decided not to dwell on it. "Do you know if Dad received any threats or harassing phone calls or letters?"

"Humph." She grunted. "I'd be the last to know. He kept

himself closed up in that den of his. Wouldn't even let the decorator do it over.''

Alex had finally discovered where her father lived. It had plainly not been in any of the rooms she had seen.

''Veronica, I know you have a lot to think about now, but give this a little more thought after I've gone. Try to find that book and recall anything, no matter how insignificant, that might give us a clue to someone who wanted him dead. Either someone who would benefit or someone who hated him. I'll call you in a day or two or you can call me at my mother's. Just ask for me,'' she added, knowing that Veronica would not want to talk to Marguerite.

As Alex rose, preparatory to taking her leave, Veronica addressed her softly, ''You know, you look just like him. He was so handsome.'' Moisture dimmed her eyes. ''You even dress like him,'' she remarked, gesturing toward Alex's brown tweed suit, yellow oxford shirt, and rust-colored V-necked sweater.

With tears running freely, Veronica continued, ''I never could please him with the way I dressed or did anything even though I really tried. It's funny, a man falls for you because of how you look then marries you and tries to change you.''

Embarrassed at the tears and the confession, Alex tried to comfort her. ''I spent hours and hours trying to copy your hairdo when I first met you, Veronica. I guess we're never satisfied with what we have.''

They walked to the door together, each with a little more understanding toward the other. They had both loved Joseph Smith and he had tired of them along with Marguerite and perhaps other women. As Alex struggled into her winter coat, Veronica had one bitter suggestion.

''If you're looking for someone who benefitted from Dan's death, you'd better look at that brother of his. They had insurance on each other. Wilson stands to get one million bucks. How's them apples? I get a lousy fifty thou and have to pay all the bills. I think the police should take a good look at Mr. Wilson Snob Smith.''

Chapter Twenty-three

It was that quiet time in the day of a restaurant, the yawn between lunch and dinner, so they obtained immediate seating at the Union Oyster House. Boston's oldest restaurant, it opened in 1826 in a building that had previously housed a dress goods business, the oldest newspaper in the United States, the paymaster for the Continental Army, and an exiled future king of France who taught French to Boston's fashionable young ladies.

Preston glanced longingly at the raw bar as they entered but permitted himself to be shepherded upstairs to a comfortable booth. It was lobsters for all, boiled for Marguerite and Preston, a casserole of lazy man's lobster for Alex. While they waited they nibbled on the hot Oyster House sampler—a selection of clams, oysters, and shrimp in various guises. And, of course, they talked; that is, one of them talked and two listened.

Marguerite was bursting with her three pieces of news: Joe had been excited about an old book written in German that he obtained from an elderly client, Grace McGuire; he had had a girl-friend named Leah who worked in the Boston Public Library and helped him translate the book; and he had planned to divorce Veronica as soon as he straightened out his finances.

"We finally have something tangible," pronounced Marguerite as she transferred to her plate one clam Casino and one grilled oyster. "Although it's also getting more complicated. We now have two books to locate, one Joe already had that was written in German, and one he was looking for and hoping to get my help to obtain. The first book must have led him to the second. But at least we know where to start looking. Tomorrow I'll visit Grace McGuire and you two can try to find Leah the librarian. I think it's better for me to stay clear of wives and girlfriends, don't you?''

Just in time, Alex suppressed a complaint. The resolve to help her mother had almost collapsed after only six hours.

Marguerite paused very briefly to try the clam before continuing her rapid narration. ''According to Wilson, Veronica didn't know about the financial mess Joe was in or the impending divorce. It's unfortunate she didn't know about the divorce. She would have made a wonderful suspect and gotten the police off my case for a while. A younger wife killing her wealthy husband before he divorced her so she could get all the money instead of fighting for a settlement. She has no children to get support for, either. But if she didn't know about his plans to divorce her, that won't work. Unless, of course, it was the other way around and she has a boyfriend and wanted a divorce and the money, too. We'd have to find out about the boyfriend, though. I suppose one of us could watch her house and follow her for a few days. She's bound to—''

''No, no, no!'' cried Preston, pausing with a chunk of lobster speared to the fork emerging from the melted butter, and suspecting correctly that Marguerite had him in mind for this shadowing assignment. ''I'm not going to sit outside that house and spy on her. I'd probably be arrested for stalking.''

''You're absolutely right, Preston. You wouldn't be the person for that job,'' agreed Marguerite, picking up her oyster.

Unsure of whether her husband had been insulted or complimented, Alex entered the conversation. She had sat quietly during her mother's summation, but internally she was an engine revving expectantly, waiting for a chance to burst forth. ''I found out a few things myself, Mother. First of all, I'm positive Veronica did know about the divorce. She slipped and tried to cover it but later admitted that Dad knew someone named Leah who was helping him translate a book, the same one you mentioned written in German. 'Only the librarian,' she called her, but I have a hunch she suspected more than that.''

Marguerite was mildly impressed. Alex tried harder.

''I think you're right about her not knowing Dad had lost his money. She was very disturbed about it. Evidently Uncle Wilson broke the news to her. She claims Dad was only insured for fifty thousand dollars and they have a lot of debts.''

Good information, better than Marguerite had anticipated from Alex. It gave Veronica the motive Marguerite was hoping to attribute to her. But Alex's hunch was not evidence. Not much use at all.

Alex knew something about building a story to its climax. In a deliberately understated manner, she concluded her account. ''Veronica told me one more thing that might interest you. Dad and his brother had partnership insurance. Uncle Wilson stands to get one million dollars.''

She had finally caught her mother's attention.

Chapter Twenty-four

It was early when they assembled in Chief Nadeau's office, early enough for the coffee to be reasonably fresh, much to Al Medeiros's relief. He had brought muffins—cranberry-banana, baked by his daughter Gloria the night before. Sgt. McEnerny settled for his usual black coffee, causing a shudder to run through Medeiros. Even when fresh, police station coffee required a brave man to drink it black.

This Tuesday morning, January twenty-ninth, was eight days after the discovery of the body of Joseph Smith, two days after they had learned of Nick Dante's murder in Florida, and one day after the discovery of Joe's car. They had notebooks full of information, uncoordinated and disparate. It was time to organize.

As officer-in-charge, Medeiros started the information session. But not until he downed his first muffin and washed it down with coffee.

The murder of Joe Smith, their chief problem, had several strange aspects, one of the strangest of which was that no one had reported him missing for three days. He left for Cape Cod on Tuesday, January fifteenth for a one-night stay and never returned. The body wasn't discovered until January twenty-first when a man walking his dog noticed the splintered door and broken lock on the lighthouse and reported it to the park service.

Upon questioning, neither Joe's wife nor his brother offered a cogent explanation as to why they had waited three days to report him missing. Both admitted to having called the motel and being

115

told that he checked out early Wednesday morning. When asked why they weren't concerned about his whereabouts, they muttered similar explanations about thinking he had business elsewhere but no specifics were forthcoming. Something was amiss.

Although the poison could have been administered any time from a few hours to a couple of days before Joe showed symptoms, the murderer or an accomplice had been with Joe sometime on the night of January fifteenth or the early morning of January sixteenth to take charge of the sick man and hide his body. This was the time period on which the police were focusing.

Neither Veronica nor Wilson had an alibi. Veronica claimed to have been at home alone without incoming or outgoing phone calls. Ditto for Wilson, whose wife, Emily, was out of town helping (possibly hindering, he suggested) their daughter cope with her first baby. She had called him at the office at five o'clock on January fifteenth and he claimed to have gone home after that, neither seeing nor speaking with anyone all night. Strange behavior for a man who didn't cook and loved to eat.

Frank had been listening closely, hoping for some break in this case that would lead away from Marguerite. He responded eagerly to the information about Veronica and Wilson.

"As I see it, Al, there are two possible reasons for their actions. One, they were both in on his murder for the usual reasons, lust or money. Maybe both. Or, two, they knew about his money problems and thought he took a powder so they weren't saying anything. They were giving him a chance to get away first."

Medeiros thought it through before replying. "If they're both in on the murder, money probably wasn't the motive for Wilson. But it might have been for Veronica if she didn't know about Joe's money problems. Maybe she wanted the money and Wilson wanted her. He was at that age, you know, when a younger woman makes you feel good."

"How about you, Al, are you at that age?" Frank teased.

"I'd like to be but my wife would kill me."

Medeiros turned serious again. "There's one more thing. We checked on Joe's insurance for his wife. It's only fifty grand. Barely enough to pay off their cars. No motive there."

As to Portia's story of a four- to five-hour trip home, it could neither be proved nor disproved. There were several accidents that snowy night on Route 3, one of which tied up traffic for a considerable time. Its occurrence at eight-thirty would have coincided with Portia being on the road if she left Eastham as she claimed at seven-thirty. Paradoxically, she could have arrived home at approximately the same time if she had left much later, say after ten o'clock, if she had been waiting for Joe to return from his dinner with Marguerite and poisoned him soon after. The accidents had been cleared up, the roads sanded, and the snow had abated somewhat, making a fast trip possible if one discounted her supposed stops for gas and food.

Marguerite's situation was also unresolved. Her lawyer and his wife were traveling by car through the south of France. He would probably call his office sometime during the week but his secretary could not be sure when it might be. Mr. Mullen took his vacations seriously. The secretary could not, more likely would not, confirm or deny whether Mr. Mullen had even spoken with Marguerite Smith on January sixteenth when she claimed to have been reassured by him that she had no problem about Joe's claim with regard to the house.

McEnerny recounted his and Fleming's interviews with George Atkinson and Laura Eldredge about Marguerite's story of a valuable book. George assured them he had no book of value; Laura assured them that every book and paper she possessed was valuable and launched into her theory of long-forgotten land records. Though dubious of their relevance, McEnerny had permitted her to show them her treasures, but recoiled at the sheer volume— room after room of old books crammed onto lopsided shelves and box after box of papers in crumbling cartons. Convinced that she was seeking a sense of importance, he told her if she found anything connected to the case to let them know. She was delighted to have an assignment. Joe's Mercedes, discovered only yesterday, was receiving a full-scale investigation—fibers, prints, dirt, everything. So far they had been told that his overnight bag was in the trunk along with his cellular phone. A preliminary look at the fibers suggested that a white towel had been placed over the driver's seat. It was of a type commonly used by motels, and Fleming was to obtain a towel from the Sunset Motel today for the lab to make a comparison. If the towel had been placed on the seat by the murderer before moving the car, they were dealing with a very sophisticated murderer who was unlikely to have left any traces in the car.

"That doesn't sound like it could be Marguerite," ventured

Frank, still defending his friend. "It sounds more like a pro. What would she know about fibers on a car seat?"

"You'd be surprised," commented Medeiros, brushing crumbs from his Christmas tie. "Have you read any mystery stories lately? My wife reads all of them. They have so much technical stuff in them I think I could send her out to work a case."

"Maybe you're right," Frank agreed reluctantly. "How about the Florida case? Anything new?"

McEnerny put down his cup, having emptied it twice, and answered.

"Yeah. I talked to those crack . . . uh, cops," he corrected after a stern glance from his boss. "Dante was murdered by gunshot wounds, two of them." He took a paper out of his pocket and read from it. " 'One penetrating shot in the abdomen with the bullet deflected by the pelvic bone and recovered from the body. Gunpowder tatooing indicates the shot was fired from about twelve to eighteen inches away.' That wound didn't kill him. 'The second shot, fired at closer range, two to four inches, was a perforating shot to the head. The entrance wound was at the left temporal bone and the exit was at the right parietal.' It was shot at an angle, understand?" McEnerny clarified for them.

"Was the bullet recovered?" queried Medeiros.

"Yeah, right nearby."

"That means he was probably killed where he was found," surmised Medeiros.

"I was coming to that." The sergeant began to read again. " 'Postmortem lividity and insect evidence indicate the body was in the same position as when death occurred or was placed in that position and location immediately after death.' A handgun found at the scene is suspected of being the murder weapon. Firearms identification is in process but both bullets were somewhat damaged by contact with bone and it may prove difficult. The gun is a Smith & Wesson Chief Special, thirty-eight special caliber, five shot, round butt, nickel finish."

"How about time of death?" asked Frank. "Did they get any closer to that?"

"Yeah, but there's a little confusion about that. It seems Dante ordered from room service and got a delivery about nine o'clock. The waiter definitely recognized him from a picture. A cheeseburger, fries, and a Coke. The medical examiner says his stomach was empty when he was done in, and it should take about six hours with that food, four hours at the least. That makes time of death no sooner than one in the morning Friday, probably more like three o'clock and probably no later than six o'clock because of the state of rigor mortis. All those times are only approximate. But the doc thinks he was dead before three o'clock because of the amount of decomposition, maybe even before one o'clock. The bug experts agree with him. But the food evidence is strong. The tray was empty when it was picked up the next morning and the waiter swears no one else was in the room with Dante.''

"Maybe he was expecting someone and ordered for her," suggested Medeiros pointedly. "Remember, Marguerite called his hotel at eight-forty-seven and we have only her word that she didn't speak to him. It would have been tight but I've been told the two hotels were close so she could have gotten there right after the waiter left, eaten, and rode with Nick to the place where he was killed, drove his car back to his hotel and left it, then walked back to her hotel and sat in the lobby so that she would be seen and have an alibi. According to the Fort Lauderdale guys, the desk clerk doesn't know what time she arrived in the lobby, just that she was there long enough to notice. That explanation would make the death earlier and make all the experts happy.''

"And maybe she ate with him at nine and came back later, about eleven, for some other reason and killed him then. Like the black widow, understand?" intimated McEnerny with a smirk. "I have one more piece of information I got off the fax early this morning. Didn't have a chance to tell you yet, Lieutenant," he explained feebly, trying to forestall a reprimand. "There was no Margaret Johnson or Marguerite Smith registered at the Hotel Tropicana on the night of January twenty-fourth, the night Nick Dante was murdered. She lied.''

Chapter Twenty-five

Though accustomed to the majestic monuments of Washington, D.C., Alex was nevertheless impressed as she ascended the wide stairway to the newly reopened Copley Square entrance of the Boston Public Library, designed by great artists of the 1890s.

The six magnificent carved bronze doors, the handiwork of Daniel Chester French, sculptor of the Lincoln Memorial in Washington, caused her to pause and examine them as she had never done in her younger days. The library seal was the inspiration of the eminent designer, Augustus Saint-Gaudens, while his brother Louis sculpted the staircase lions, mounted facing each other on the melon-tinted marble of the vaulted foyer.

Entering the library proper, she passed the central courtyard, bereft of its summer finery, the delicate plants hibernating under hardy ground cover and dead leaves. Consulting a floor map she had picked up at the entry, she noted several reference departments. Eliminating those of fine arts or music as least likely, she located the reference departments for science, social science, and humanities.

No Leah in either of the first two. Waiting patiently to speak with a harried librarian at the humanities desk, she asked her usual question but received an unexpected answer. "I'm Leah. What can I do for you?"

Alex was stunned. This must be Leah the librarian but she was most definitely not her father's girlfriend. At least sixty-five years of age, maybe more, and looking every day of it, her gray hair was tightly permed into a frizzy cap, her wrinkles undisguised by makeup. The aqua stretch knitted pantsuit and sturdy orthopedic shoes would have horrified Joseph Smith.

Blushing and stuttering, the articulate professor of English literature stumbled along. "I, er, I was looking for someone, that is, I was told there was someone, I er, mean I thought—"

Mercifully, she was interrupted by an impatient college student behind her, who thrust at Leah a paper with the name of a subject he was researching. He had at least a modicum of good manners and excused himself for jumping the line with the explanation that he thought they were just chatting. Grateful for the impetuosity of youth, she stepped to the side and rearranged her thought processes. The young man's request took some time and Alex was reoriented by the time Leah returned to her.

"A friend of mine was doing some research in this library and he was being helped by someone who I thought spoke German. Do you speak German?" Alex queried.

"No, I don't," responded Leah. "But Dolly does. She's out today. That's why I'm so busy. A death in the family."

That made no sense unless they were both helping him. She plunged on. "Do you know someone named Joseph Smith?"

"No, I don't think so. Of course, lots of people come here for help and I don't know their names. What does he look like?"

The impetuous young man was back. He needed more information. Evidently some of the colleges were back from winter break, unlike Alex's school, which was still in recess. Leah assisted the student, as well as an older woman who had been waiting patiently behind Alex.

"He has reddish-brown hair," Alex began when she regained Leah's attention, "something like mine, and brownish-yellowish eyes, something like mine, and he's tall and slim . . ."

"Something like you," Leah completed. "In other words, he looks like you. But older, maybe?"

"Yes, older," Alex confirmed.

"And why are you looking for the person who helps him?" she asked cautiously.

There were two people in line behind Alex now, shuffling papers, indicating annoyance at this waste of their time. "Do you get a break or anything? I'd really like to talk with you."

"I usually do but I won't today unless they send someone over from another desk. I'm the only one here right now. But if I do get my break it will be at ten-thirty."

"I'll wait at that table over there. Maybe I can buy you a cup of coffee."

"I can't promise anything but we'll see," replied Leah.

Alex picked up a book and leafed through it unseeingly. She was nervous and excited, her stomach in an uproar. Leah knew something. She had given it away by suggesting Joe was older than Alex. And Leah would talk. She was careful but curious. With the solution so close, Alex wished she could back away from it. She hated prying into her father's personal life. If only he had left her mother out of it.

Leah had a replacement to cover during her break. In fact, she had picked up the phone and insisted upon one. She and Alex crossed Boylston Street to a coffee shop and ordered coffee for both and a Danish for Leah. With no time to spare, Leah began immediately.

"The person I'm thinking of who fits your description is named Dan. Could this be the same person?"

"Yes, it is," answered Alex eagerly. "That was his middle name but he sometimes used it."

"Was?" inquired Leah, eyebrows raised.

Alex had been carefully using the present tense but slipped and Leah had picked up on it.

"Yes, was. He was my father but he's dead. He was translating a manuscript and I want to complete his work but I need help and I thought the person who helped him would help me." Part truth, part fabrication. "Was that you?"

"How about your mother? Is she involved with this, too?"

"Oh, no!" protested Alex. "They were divorced years ago. My mother had nothing to do with him any longer. This is something *I* want to do. You see, I'm a college professor and this would be a boost to my career." The balance was favoring fabrication.

Leah chewed her Danish thoughtfully and considered the next move. In a life constrained by her hours at the library and the exhaustion of trudging up to a fourth-floor walk-up, she rarely went anywhere or saw anyone. This was her most interesting conversation in a long time. She yielded.

"It was Dolly who was helping him."

"What does Dolly look like?"

"Hah! It always comes down to that, doesn't it? Especially when a man is involved. Let's say that you'd notice her. She has a big mop of red hair, not like yours, that bright red color, you know. And a figure she doesn't mind showing off. Dresses a little trashy for my taste."

What taste? thought Alex unkindly.

"But she's no dope. She has a master's in library science and speaks several languages, including the German you were asking about."

Bingo! thought Alex.

"You call her Dolly. Is that her real name?"

"No, it's Dahlia."

She did not pronounce it in the usual way as Dal-ya but in an elongated form as Dah-lee-a.

Alex reacted immediately. Dah-lee-a. Lee-a. Lia, not Leah. Joe probably disliked the name Dolly. Too common. She might have disliked Dahlia. So he renamed her as he had himself and she became Lia.

"Did anyone call her Lia?"

"Only your father. I used to get mixed up and think he was talking to me."

"Would you tell me her last name and her address?"

Leah was skittish. Maybe she was talking too much. "I don't think so. You'd better talk to Dolly yourself. I think she'll be back tomorrow."

"Whose funeral was it?"

"I'm not sure but I think it was an uncle. Too bad it wasn't that brother of hers," Leah added, in a tone that begged to be encouraged.

Alex complied. "Why is that?"

"He's no good. Never been anything but a problem to Dolly. She even supports him most of the time. He sometimes comes in here looking for her. Probably for money. The last time I saw him, maybe a year ago, he was a skinhead—you know, with the hair shaved off and a T-shirt with a skull. And those disgusting tattoos," she recalled, shaking her head to dislodge the memory.

"What were they like?" prodded Alex.

"On one arm he had a snake with its mouth open. On the other was a rat. When he put his arms together in a circle, the snake looked like it was eating the rat. Ugh!" She shivered at the recollection.

"What is his name?" inquired Alex.

"Desmond," answered Leah automatically. Recollecting herself, she continued, "But I'm not a gossip. I don't think I should say any more. Besides, I'm late. Lorraine will have a fit if I don't get right back. If you meet Dolly, don't say I said anything. I wouldn't want her to think I was talking about her."

"My lips are sealed," promised Alex, content with her morning's work. She was getting better at this than her mother was.

Chapter Twenty-six

Marguerite has planned their Tuesday morning's expedition with a maximum of efficiency. Preston and she drove Alex to the Braintree T station—Boston's cryptic name for its subway system—to avoid the hassle of battling downtown traffic, leaving them with only their own hassle of jousting with the heavy vehicular traffic vying for the Callahan Tunnel leading to East Boston and Logan Airport as well as Winthrop.

With Marguerite piloting, Preston wended his way through the tunnel, past the airport turnoff, and onto the exit for Winthrop. Though geographically close to Marguerite's native South Boston, she had never been there. Life's magnet had drawn her inward toward the hub, not outward toward the harbor. Winthrop was a peninsula connected to the mainland by a narrow strip of land leading to Revere. It was one of the numerous bodies of land surrounding Boston Harbor and separating it from Massachusetts Bay, making that harbor one of the great ones of the world.

Relying on a map for the local streets, Marguerite directed him to Shore Drive and Grace McGuire's house, a large, rambling Victorian, its wooden consruction unsullied by aluminum siding, its wide front porch free of louvered windows.

Grace's husband, Gerald, had used Joe's investment service for many years, and after he died ten years ago, Grace continued the association. She had met Veronica once at the office and wondered how they managed together since they appeared to lack the solidarity of common tastes and interest that provide the bedrock of a marriage after the fist flush of passion has waned. She was curious enough about his first wife to agree to meet her, though she had no good reason to do so and many reasons to refuse.

For Grace was moving. That was no small task when one was eighty-three and had lived in the same house for sixty-five years. Each morning she packed one box, spending more time reminiscing over each item and deciding whether to keep or discard than she did packing. Her appointment with Marguerite would disrupt this schedule. *Good,* she thought. For one more day she could hold onto the past. Her future held very little promise.

There was no doorbell, just an old-fashioned, elaborate, wrought-iron door knocker. Grace answered immediately and the two women inspected each other. Marguerite looked just right for Joseph Smith, but Grace would have to talk with her to be certain.

Marguerite observed a woman who was thin and brittle, aged and wrinkled, but who still cared about how she looked. Her thinning, blue-rinsed hair, something Marguerite had not seen for years, indicated trips to the beauty salon. She wore a gray flannel skirt with a forgiving A-line cut, a white blouse with only a lace-edged collar showing at the neck of a huge red sweater, thick, dark stockings, and black flat-heeled shoes. The warm stockings and wool sweater reflected winter living in a large, drafty old house. This was the one thing Grace McGuire did not expect to miss.

After the awkward preliminary greetings, Marguerite accepted a cup of tea—brewed with tea leaves, served in a china teapot—and decided to trust this woman with the truth, all of it. She began with the unexpected dinner with Joe and ended with the murder of Nick and the police suspicions of her, pausing at intervals dictated by the roar of jets, Logan Airport's contribution to life in Winthrop.

"So you see," she concluded, "this whole mystery involves two books, the one Joe and Nick were looking for, which is apparently in Eastham, and the one Joe obtained from you. Neither of them has been found. I don't think the police believe me about the first one, and they don't even know about yours. Can you help me? Do you have it?"

Marguerite had won Grace's approval. Her earnest account, the painful truthfulness about her gullibility regarding Nick, and the apparent lack of bitterness about the machinations of her ex-husband revealed a depth of character Grace admired. Her only regret was the shadow cast on Joe, whom she had always trusted and considered a friend.

Had he lost her money, too? No matter. She had little use for it. The money from the sale of the house, the monthly annuity established by her dead husband, and her Social Security checks provided as much as she needed. It was her children's inheritance that was at risk and none of them were in need. At least, she didn't think so. They rarely visited. She decided to help Marguerite if she could.

"Not any longer, but I wish I did," answered Grace regretfully. "My son, Victor, is very angry with me for giving it to Mr. Smith. He wants it back. He says it's rightfully his, it's his inheritance."

"What was in this book that's so valuable?"

"I don't know," answered Grace, shaking her head. "It was written in German. I never knew it was here until I was clearing out the house and sold the big safe in the basement. When they took it away, it revealed a hidden compartment in the floor under the safe. Very large. It could be reached by wheeling the safe away but I never even knew it was there. The men moving the safe lifted the board off the top of this hidey hole and the only things in it were an old book wrapped in oilskin and a gold coin. Mr. Smith happened to come here the next day—I have a little trouble lately getting to his office—and I showed them to him. He asked if he could borrow them. I lent him the book but not the coin. I was planning to give the coin to Victor because he collects coins. That's the last I saw of the book."

"Why do you think it was written in German?"

"That was my husband's native language. He was more fluent in German than in English."

Grace poured another cup of tea for each of them and offered Marguerite a cookie from an elaborately patterned translucent plate, its gold edging half worn away. There were four precisely placed cookies on the plate. She assumed two were for her and took one of her allotment, politely pausing for this ceremonial pouring and passing though she was bursting with questions.

"But I thought your husband's name was McGuire," she asked after an appropriate interval of sipping and tasting. "Wasn't that his real name?"

"Oh, goodness yes. That was Gerald's real name, Gerald

McGuire. I'm talking about my first husband, Vitus." Grace paused until the noise of an airplane homing for Logan subsided, then leaned forward and lowered her voice to a whisper as if afraid to be overheard. "His real name was Viktor. Just like my son, except spelled with a k, Viktor Krebs. But he changed it to Vitus Krogh because he was pretending to be Danish. It was easy for him because he spoke Danish, too. That's because he came from a part of Germany that had a lot of Danish people. Schleswig. Right on the Jutland peninsula."

Totally unprepared for this revelation which was spoken like a confession, Marguerite stalled by taking another cookie.

"Are you familiar with that part of Germany?" Grace inquired.

"No, I'm afraid not."

"Neither was I until I met Vitus. It's amazing how ignorant I was," she confided with a little laugh, her mouth covered with her brown-speckled hand as young ladies of her day were taught to do when their mouths were open.

"Why did he pretend to be Danish?" asked Marguerite, fearful that she already knew the answer.

Grace sipped her tea slowly, put down her cup and saucer, and looked around the room before she answered. Years of secrecy dictated her actions.

"Because he was an illegal. He jumped ship. He thought he would be less conspicuous as a Dane. You know, this was after World War I." She paused with a frightened look in her eyes. Maybe she had said too much.

Afraid that Grace would stop talking, Marguerite said in her most disarming manner, "Lots of men did that in those years. The waterfront was full of people from ships. It was just a matter of survival." She had not yet been born in that era but she sounded as if she was personally familiar with the situation and Grace welcomed the absolution.

"That's just what it was. Survival. Vitus told me how terrible it was in Germany after the war. Inflation was rising every day. Paper money was worthless. People lost everything. His parents lost all their savings. He had no future in Germany. But the northern part of Schleswig was given to Denmark in the Treaty of Versailles. He lived right near the new border and already spoke Danish so he slipped into North Schleswig and pretended to be Danish. He managed to get fake papers. You could buy anything if you had the money. His parents gave him the last of their silverware to trade for the papers. But he couldn't risk living there because everyone knew everyone in those towns and he had been in the German army. So he kept going further north into the old Denmark where no one knew him and got work on the docks. Eventually, he was hired as a deckhand on a ship going to America and he jumped ship in Boston. He started out working on the docks here, too. Wherever he could get work—Charlestown, Boston, all over.''

Another jet interrupted her. Grace sipped her tea slowly, reflecting. She was being reckless, speaking of things hitherto forbidden. It was a release. Somehow it was easier to talk to this stranger than to her own children. She no longer had friends her own age, or any age, and was lonely.

Marguerite found Grace's recital fascinating but useless. She had to get back to that book. Gently but insistently she prodded. ''Is that what he recorded in the book in German? And then hid it because he was afraid to be deported?''

''Oh, no. That book seemed to be about his business. It was a ledger. He never talked about his origins. I didn't even know the truth until two years after we were married. I was pregnant and he thought I had the right to know his history. Because of the baby. He swore me to secrecy.'' A smile lit her face, transcending the wrinkles and the age spots, hinting at the beautiful girl encapsulated in time, and her eyes gazed into the past. ''Meeting him was the most exciting thing that ever happened to me.''

There was no way to avoid it. Grace was not going to be rushed to the end of the story. Marguerite would have to hear every chapter if she wanted to be present for the denouement. Nervously, she picked up another cookie and asked on cue, ''How did you meet him?''

''I met him at the house of a friend from the Necco candy factory. I had to work, you see. That embarrassed my father. The Sloan women had never worked. But he lost all his money in the stock market crash and wasn't able to get a job. He had no experience at anything. He had never worked. So we all had to get jobs, my two brothers and me. I was only seventeen when they hired me at Necco in Cambridge,'' she proclaimed with pride.

Marguerite permitted no pauses. ''Why was he at your friend's house?''

''He was improving his English. My friend, Alice her name

was, had the same situation as I did. So her mother was earning money tutoring English. There were lots of foreigners in Boston and the ones who could afford it preferred private lessons. Vitus was so handsome. And he was dressed in the finest clothes. He even wore a diamond ring. I never saw a ring like that on a man."

"How could Vitus afford expensive clothes? And a diamond ring? You told me he worked on the docks."

Grace put her hand over her mouth as if she had said too much. But she had let the genie of repressed memories out of the bottle and it refused to return. She continued, although a little warily at first.

"He didn't work on the docks anymore. He was in business. The boat business."

"Building boats?"

"No. Operating them. He was a bootlegger," she said flatly, looking boldly into Marguerite's eyes.

Marguerite reached for the cookie dish and bit the end off a chocolate wafer before she realized this was the last one. Too late now. She had eaten all four cookies. Grace didn't seem to care. She was gorging on sweet thoughts.

"You mean he ran a speakeasy?" asked Marguerite.

"No, no. He never had anything to do with the retail end. He just brought it in for the people who ran those places." She pronounced "those places" disdainfully, as if it was a lower calling than her husband's.

"How did he bring it in?"

"By boat. You see, he arrived in this country in 1920, shortly after Prohibition began. He worked on the docks whenever he could but it was hard because he was an illegal and had to be careful. Sometimes he couldn't get any work at all. Then he met a man who said he needed someone who knew his way around a boat for a private run. Vitus had been around boats all his life. He took the job and it turned out to be a boat bringing liquor in from Canada. He was just a hired hand but he paid attention and learned the business. After a couple of years he got his own boat and started his own runs. He was very successful."

Marguerite was incredulous. This sedate and proper old woman was talking about her husband's success in business as if he owned a clothing store. Grace must have sensed a modicum of disapproval and hurriedly explained, "Of course, I didn't know about this when I met him. Although I suspect that my father had some idea of it. He didn't want me to marry Vitus. It wasn't his choice of a husband for the daughter of Endicott Sloan. A flashy foreigner with no background, he called him. But he couldn't stop me. My job gave me independence.''

''What did he tell you he did?''

Ignoring the direct question, Grace resumed her narration. ''By the time I met him he wasn't going on Canadian runs anymore. The business had changed. They now had mother ships outside the U.S. limits and smaller boats came out to buy the cargo. At first it was three miles, then it became twelve miles out. Most of the mother ships were registered in other countries because the Coast Guard had more power over where they could intercept American ships.''

Marguerite was fascinated. She had heard tales of speakeasies but had never thought of the business end of bootlegging, particularly the transportation of whiskey into the country. This woman was reciting the inside story of an illegal operation aimed at undercutting the most blatantly abused amendment since the enactment of the Constitution.

Grace took another little sip and continued without any urging.

''He had speedboats, several of them. They brought the cargo into shore at all different places, frequently right here in Winthrop because it was out of the way. Never into our dock, though,'' she said defensively. ''He was careful not to involve us. Even the boats weren't registered in his name. And he didn't go out much himself anymore. He hired people to do that. He just went out once in a while to keep his men honest. They never knew when he would show up.''

Ironic, thought Marguerite. Vitus was keeping his men honest.

''Anyway, to get back to your question, he told me he was the sales manager for a boat company. That's why we had access to so many boats. We used to go out on them for picnics, usually on the *Blue Bell*. All around the islands in Boston Harbor and the north and south shore. It was great fun. I didn't know the truth until I was pregnant, and there was nothing I could do about it then. Besides, he didn't live long after that.'' Her eyes were downcast, grieving for a lost husband, criminal though he was. Marguerite understood the emotion.

''How did he die?''

''He drowned. It was one time when he was going on a run himself. Our baby was very young. He told me to go to my mother's house to stay that night. I didn't want to but he insisted. It was raining. I think they went in and out the house a couple of times because there was mud tracked in the basement. There was fog, too. They ran into a storm and sank. There were usually four men on a boat but that night there was only Vitus and Paulie. A fishing boat came along and saved Paulie.'' Her recitation was funereal.

''Was the boat recovered?''

''No. Vitus's body floated to shore. No one was interested enough in cases of whiskey to dive for it. Diving was very dangerous in those days. The boat and the cargo would have been seized by the Coast Guard anyway.''

''Who was Paulie, the man saved?''

''He was a young man who worked for Vitus. One of the few he trusted. I think the *Blue Bell* was even registered in his name.''

''What was his last name?''

''Oh, let me think. Paulie, Paulie . . . I can't remember. I know it was Portuguese. He was a Cape Verdean. I'll probably remember after you're gone. That's how my memory is these days,'' she said apologetically.

''Mine, too,'' Marguerite assured her. ''If you remember, would you call me? It might be important. I'll leave my number on your mantel,'' she concluded, already extracting a small notebook from her purse and writing her name and number. She took the opportunity to make some notes she was afraid she would forget. She wrote, *Paulie, Blue Bell, Vitus,* and then looked up at Grace inquiringly. ''What did you say Vitus's last name was?''

''Krogh. K-r-o-g-h,'' she spelled.

''And when did he, er, have this accident?''

''October 12, 1933. It was in the last days of Prohibition. Vitus had been winding down his business. He was going legitimate. I don't know why he made that last trip.'' The pale eyes misted.

Marguerite tried to offer comfort. ''At least he left you and your son provided for.''

''That's the funny part. He didn't. Of course, I had this house, it was paid for. But he had very little money in the bank. That didn't surprise me because he didn't trust banks. But he didn't have any other money that I could find either. Luckily, he had an insurance policy that kept me going for a while. It was really the Necco candy factory that saved me,'' she said with a sly little smile.

"Did you go back to work there?"

"Oh, no, it was too hard to travel there from Winthrop in those days. And I had a baby to care for. But I got a toothache. Too much candy, I guess. That's how I met Gerry. He was the dentist I went to. He was just out of school. We hit it off right away. Neither of us had much money but I had a house and he had a profession. Eventually he did very well when business picked up. He's the one who provided for me. And our children. We had two daughters and, of course, I had Victor."

Grace's posture was collapsing. She sat slumped tiredly in the chair, her catharsis at an end. Marguerite had many more questions she wanted to ask but compassion overcame her curiosity and she took her leave, asking if she could call again. Grace reluctantly agreed. Her excursion into the past had exhausted her. She was not anxious to repeat it. And then there was Victor. He had warned her not to speak to anyone about his father or the book she found. She would need to hide this visit from him. She wished she had thrown that old book in the garbage.

Marguerite wished so, too.

Chapter Twenty-seven

The police investigation continued through the day on Tuesday, the steady, plodding, routine, attention-to-detail kind of work that solved cases. One item after another was ticked off their list of things to do, people to see.

Their hottest must-do item, questioning Marguerite once more about her alleged night at the Tropicana, was frustrated by the ringing of her telephone in an empty house. They left a message three times and sent an officer to the house to verify that no one was at home except the dog.

Progress was made verifying Joe's list of appointments on Cape Cod for January fifteenth. He had five meetings listed in his appointment book and through his secretary they obtained the addresses. Three of those people were interviewed and confirmed as legitimate long-term business accounts, retirees who had moved from the Boston area where they had begun their association with Joseph Smith. He had convinced two of them to increase their investments with him.

The two other investors on his list of appointments had gone south for the remainder of the winter. Both were located through neighbors who had telephone numbers for emergencies, and by late morning the police had finally spoken with the last one, a widow named Dorothy Kelly, who also happened to have been the last scheduled appointment on the day in question.

Joe had arrived at her house about four o'clock, declined the martini they usually had, and opted for hot tea, explaining he had a cold. They reviewed her portfolio as they routinely did twice a year, he unsuccessfully tried to persuade her to put additional money in her account, and he left at five or a little after.

There was still no clue as to where Joe had been between five o'clock and seven-twenty-five when Marguerite claimed he arrived at her house late, explaining that he had an unexpected meeting.

Was Marguerite lying about when he arrived?

Or was Portia lying when she said she had waited for him at his motel until seven-thirty but he never arrived? There was no confirmation that she had been in her car all that time.

Were they both lying? Or were neither of them lying and there was still an unknown quantity in this mixture? A wife and a brother who happened to be a business partner could conceivably have motives for murder, and neither had an alibi for the night of January fifteenth—if that was the night of the murder. Nor could they disregard angry clients whose money Joe had lost. A sophisticated investor would have been able to pierce Joe's veil of secrecy.

And what about the Florida murder? Were these two crimes unconnected or were they inextricably linked? There was no proof yet, only Marguerite and her stormy relationships with both men.

Finding the Mercedes the day before had clarified two points. The murder could have been a one-person job because the food stand where the car had been hidden was only a short distance from the motel. If the murderer had driven Joe's car to the lighthouse—a smart move because no traces of the murdered man would be left in the murderer's car—and then drove back and hid the car behind the food stand, the person had only a short walk back to the motel and his or her own car. It was more important than ever to try to get some identification on any other cars in the motel lot that night.

The car yielded one more intriguing piece of evidence. Joe had been alive but sick when he entered it. Traces of vomit were found on the floor, dashboard, and door of the passenger's side. Someone had wiped it up, but evidently did not have the time or facilities to scrub it clean. Why had the murderer bothered? It was Joe's car, destined to be abandoned and presumably discovered.

There were as many theories as there were theorists. The

murderer was a meticulous housekeeper who routinely cleaned up any mess. The murderer had a weak stomach and was unable to drive the car without removing the offensive odor. The murderer wanted to remove any evidence as to Joe's last meal which would be present in the vomitus.

That Joe had probably been able to walk to his car bolstered the possibility of one murderer, even a woman. He would not have had to be carried into a car, possibly in full view of anyone in the motel. Dragging him out of it at the lighthouse was a less arduous task and one that could have been accomplished safely in the darkness surrounding the Three Sisters.

Joe's cellular phone, found in his luggage, had a redial option that flashed on the screen the last number dialed. They had obtained the name and address of the person to whom that number was assigned but the recipient of Joe's call had not been at home yesterday, and was not one of his clients. They were hoping for better luck today.

Phone records had been subpoenaed and the calls on Joe's cellular phone for January fifteenth scrutinized carefully. Except for that last call indicated on the redial that the records showed was made at ten o'clock at night, there was only one other call he made that did not match any of the clients' numbers. It was to a Victor Krogh at an insurance office in Braintree and had been made at five minutes before three in the afternoon of January fifteenth.

"There's something here doesn't make sense," claimed McEnerny. "If he left off this Marguerite at a little before ten, as she claims," he added snidely, "then went back to his motel, why didn't he use the phone there at ten o'clock instead of his cellular phone? It means he didn't go back to his motel room. So either she's lying about when he left her or he called someone on his cellular and went to meet that person instead of going to the motel. Maybe the murderer."

"Maybe," agreed Frank, pleased that the sergeant was at least willing to consider an explanation that exonerated Marguerite. "There's another possibility, too. Did you ever try to use the phone at a hotel and find out it wasn't turned on?"

"No, I don't think that ever happened to me," answered an embarrassed McEnerny, who never traveled except on the rare occasions when the State Police sent him on an out-of-state investigation.

"The phones aren't automatically on," explained Frank. "They're supposed to be turned on when a person registers, but sometimes the clerk forgets. You can always call the desk but can't make outside calls. It's possible his phone wasn't turned on for outside calls and nobody at the desk answered. Remember, it was a slow night. The desk clerk might have fallen asleep watching television. It was easier for Joe to pick up his cellular phone than to walk over to the office. One thing that call does tell us, though. Marguerite was telling the truth about his leaving her before ten. If he was at her house, he would have used her phone."

"Maybe, maybe not. But was he healthy when he left?"

Chapter Twenty-eight

Trooper Stephen Fleming took a late lunch break in Braintree before interviewing Victor Krogh. He had done a lot of traveling that day. His feet felt as if they had walked the distance so he slipped his shoes off at the backs as he ate today's meatloaf special. That was the kind of meal he loved. Lots of food with gravy, no decorations, and no coriander.

His first mission had been to transport a white towel in a paper bag from the Sunset Motel to the crime lab in Boston. From there he tackled the congestion of downtown Boston streets and arrived at the State Street office of Wilson Smith shortly after noon. It was difficult to find even an illegal parking spot. Mildred Jones, the secretary, greeted him.

"You've missed Mr. Wilson. He's gone to lunch and probably won't be back until one-thirty. He likes his lunch. He always says it's the only decent meal he gets," she explained, echoing the frequently heard complaint.

Working for Joseph Smith, Sr., had been her first job. She had continued with his sons after he retired and never had a reason to seek other employment. Now sixty, she planned to work five more years and hoped Wilson had the fortitude to remain in business that long. With Joe gone, the office was like a morgue, with Wilson listlessly ambling between his own desk and his brother's, moving papers around aimlessly, never making a decision. He had never had to. Joe was the idea man; Wilson tended mostly to his law practice, not an onerous task as he turned away many clients.

"I'll wait," said Fleming.

"I hope you don't mind if I eat my lunch while you wait," she said as she ran her hair through her short, heavily sprayed hair, as if to smooth what was already rigidly in place. "I usually eat at my desk because I don't like to leave the office unattended and I could never be sure if one of them was going to be here," she explained in a whine indicating unappreciated self-sacrifice.

"Don't pay any attention to me," said Fleming, as he began to study the pictures on the wall, particularly the family pictures. He recognized a young Marguerite in one of them, dressed in shorts and a halter top, her long, dark hair blowing away from her face except for one strand over her forehead, a happy smile focused on the photographer, her head leaning slightly on her husband's upper arm, her hand in his. He paused a long time in front of this photograph, long enough to draw Mildred's attention.

"That's Joe, Wilson's older brother. He's the one who's been murdered. But I guess you already know that or you wouldn't be here. That's his wife, his first wife," she amended, "Marguerite Fallon. Everyone was surprised when he married her. She wasn't the type the Smiths usually married. And Joe had his pick. All the girls loved him, all those society girls. Lots of others, too," she added with ill-disguised lamentation.

An astute Fleming quickly estimated her age. Close to Joseph Smith's, he concluded. He decided Mildred Jones had more than a professional interest in her former boss. She was worth cultivating.

"Do you know Marguerite?" he inquired.

"Of course. The Smiths were just like family. I started here when I was nineteen. We were all very close."

Not close enough for you, suspected Fleming.

"He left her, you know. It took a long time, but he left her." After a meditative pause, she went on. "But at least I'll admit that she was better than that second wife of his, Veronica. What a mismatch! But you know how men are. They fall all over the young blonds."

"Didn't they get along?" prodded Fleming.

"Not enough to keep Joe from roaming. It was only a matter of time. He would have left her, too. He already had her replacement lined up. He used to call this new one every day. It would have served that snip right.''

"What was her name?"

Nothing could stop Mildred now. Forty years of perceived neglect by Joe Smith regurgitated itself as sour detritus, maybe even revenge. "Leah. I don't know her last name but her number is in the memory on his telephone. It's number two. At least he had the courtesy to put his home as number one."

Without even asking, Fleming went to the office Mildred indicated and pushed number two of the memory. "Boston Public Library," he heard. Without speaking, he hung up and wrote down the information.

Mildred had finished her lunch and stood up to wipe some crumbs from her navy-blue knit dress with a white collar insert that could be removed for laundering. It was one of her more expensive dresses but had the unfortunate characteristic of accentuating the lumps of flesh between bra and belt.

Sensing his time was running out as well as her lunch, Fleming casually remarked, "I guess the brothers were very close."

"I suppose you could say that. They weren't the kissing and hugging type of family. But they stuck together in public. Put up a front, you know."

"Wilson will have to handle the business himself now, won't he?"

"I hope he'll continue. I don't want to retire yet. But you never know. He was never the one with the head for business. And now with that policy he'll collect on, he might just close up or sell out."

"What policy?"

"Didn't you know? They had partnership insurance for a million dollars. But you can ask him yourself. I hear him coming in. Don't say I told you," she whispered conspiratorially.

He didn't tell, but thanks to Mildred, he knew what questions to ask. Fleming decided to concentrate on the insurance. He already had a lead on the girlfriend and suspected that Wilson would plead ignorance of his brother's peccadillo. The Smiths stuck together in public, he had been told.

The easy questions came first. Had he remembered anything additional about Joe's activities of January fifteenth since they had last spoken with him? No. Had he recalled anyone in particular who might have a grudge against his brother? No one in particular, but it might have been any of his clients who discovered he lost their money.

With Wilson feeling comfortable going over this old ground, Fleming asked, "What about this business? What happens to it now?"

"It belongs to me. That is, if I can ever straighten it out."

"What about your brother's wife? Doesn't she inherit his share? Or his children?"

"No, that's not how our agreement is drawn. We always kept the women out of it, same as our father. That keeps the business intact. The trust fund will go to his children."

"Some men have insurance on their partners. Did you?"

Wilson's face, already florid from lunch and a glass of wine, turned a red that was almost purple.

"Listen here, young man, my business affairs are my business. Personal and private. You are exceeding the boundaries of civility and making unwarranted assumptions."

"Did you?" repeated Fleming.

"Of course, we had insurance. That's how businesses are run. I realize you don't have to worry about that with a paycheck coming in every week but we have to scramble for our living."

Fleming had a flashing image of Wilson, overweight and red-faced, scrambling around the room to grab dollar bills as they fell from above. *No, make that fifty-dollar bills,* he corrected himself.

"How much was the insurance?"

"One million dollars."

"Isn't that high?"

"Not in today's money it isn't. It'll probably take that much or more to straighten out Joe's mess."

"Thank you for your time. Would you direct your secretary to give me the name and address of the insurance company?" He arose and left the office, trying to walk without favoring the left foot where the latest blister had broken exposing tender skin.

Fleming was still elated from this visit as he finished the meat loaf and passed up dessert. It was getting late and he had to see Victor Krogh.

Victor looked at his watch as the trooper entered the office, his face indicating displeasure. Fleming was fifteen minutes late. The man he saw before him was what his mother would have described as unprepossessing. Short and bulky, with a face that lacked definition, he looked at Fleming sideways with his head tilted, a look at once wary and suspicious. Thin, gray hair with a trace of its original blond was combed over the top and to one side. He gestured with pudgy fingers toward the chair next to his desk.

Fleming decided to get right to the point and waive the preliminaries.

"What was your relationship with Joseph Smith?"

"I had no relationship with him."

"He called you from his cellular phone on the afternoon of January fifteenth."

"That's correct."

"Why did he call you?"

"He was returning my call."

"Why did you call him?" Fleming persisted.

"He handled my mother's business affairs. She's selling her house and moving. There are a lot of changes in her life. She's also very old. I wanted to arrange a meeting with him and my mother to discuss her financial situation."

"Why didn't you call his office?"

"I did. The secretary told me he was on the Cape. She gave me the name of his motel but he wasn't in so I called her again and asked for his cellular number. I thought I might be able to set up an appointment for that week."

"And did you?"

"Yes. It was tentative, though, until I confirmed it with my mother. She has her own ideas."

"Did she agree to the meeting?"

"I never asked her. When I called, she seemed very upset about moving so I decided to wait before giving her any more decisions to make."

"Did you try to contact Joseph Smith to cancel?"

"No. We had left it that if I didn't call him back to confirm, the meeting was off."

Further conversation was unproductive. Fleming obtained the name and address of Victor's mother, Grace McGuire, with the promise not to disturb her unless absolutely necessary, as she was very frail. Since she did not live on the Cape and was not on Joe's list of appointments, Fleming doubted if they would need to talk with her.

As he drove back to Cape Cod, one thing puzzled Fleming.

Why would a man who was so precise in his conversation and so anxious to contact Joe Smith that he called him on his cellular phone, make an appointment that was so ambiguous?

Chapter Twenty-nine

The blinking light on the answering machine glowed scarlet as Marguerite entered the house carrying groceries she had insisted they purchase on the way home from Boston. Her ebullience at the day's revelations was squelched by the somber tone of Chief Nadeau's three calls requesting that she phone him immediately.

No need to look up the number. It was etched in that part of her memory where bad dreams are stored.

"Marguerite, where have you been?"

"Occupé, Frank. *Qu'est-ce qu'il y a?"* (Busy, Frank. What is the matter?)

His tenuous French failed him. "Uh, we'd like to come over to see you. Sgt. McEnerny has, uh, a few questions for you."

She bit her lip before the sigh escaped.

"Je n'ai pas le temps. Peut-être demain?" (I have no time. Tomorrow, perhaps?)

"Maintenant, Marguerite! *Maintenant!"* (Now, Marguerite! Now!)

"Très bien," she conceded, replacing the phone slowly.

Alex and Preston were not at home. They had driven off scouting for a liquor store that could furnish just the right wine to accompany the Chinese dinner Marguerite planned. They might also take a walk, Alex had advised her as they changed into their sneakers.

Nervously, Marguerite thrust the perishables into the refrigerator and left the remaining items scattered on the kitchen counter. Then she checked the mirror.

The basic black dress that had seemed so chic this morning now seemed basic blah. It reflected her mood. "Never let them see you down" had been her mother's advice to which she strictly adhered, so she ran upstairs, replaced the pearls around her neck with a colorful scarf and the ones on her ears with large gold hoops, ran a lipstick over lips dry from anxiety, combed and fluffed her springy hair. Ready!

She waited for the second knock on the door before she answered. *Act cool!*

Wearing the same navy-blue parka, brown suit, and green tie as he had the day she first met him in Fort Lauderdale, McEnerny stepped awkwardly back, almost off the landing, as she opened the door and a barking Rusty jumped at his legs.

"Down girl, down!" commanded a surprised Marguerite. The dog always barked at a knock on the door but never jumped at anyone. Secretly pleased at the dog's good taste, Marguerite grabbed Rusty's collar and led her away, the dog still barking furiously as she was gently pushed through the door to the basement.

Frank Nadeau sheepishly slipped through the door behind McEnerny. That was not his style. Frank never slipped around— he strode and commanded attention. She was really in trouble.

"That's a dangerous dog you have there," groused McEnerny. He hated dogs. In his adolescence he had been bitten on the leg by a German shepherd and had the scars to reinforce his bias. No matter that he had been taunting the dog mercilessly with a stick and poked it in the eye before it bit him. The dog had been condemned to death; the boy to a life of fearing dogs.

Before she could muster a defense of Rusty, the sergeant shot from the lips, without preamble, without even removing his parka. "Okay, Mrs. Smith, let's have it again. Where did you go last Thursday night, January twenty-fourth, when you left the Sea Club about eleven o'clock?"

"I've already told you that I went to the Hotel Tropicana."

"Wrong, Mrs. S. That's what you told us but it's not the answer. There was no Marguerite Smith or Margaret Johnson registered there that night. Try the truth this time. Understand?"

She was aghast. This was like a B movie. The next scene would be of her in prison garb as the cell door clanked shut.

"B-but that is the truth. Maybe there's more than one Tropicana."

"Nice try, but no. Only one."

"Let me give you my picture to show the clerk. He'd probably
remember me."

"What was the clerk's name?"

"I don't know."

"Didn't he wear a name tag?"

"But I've already told you I didn't have my glasses. I couldn't
even fill out the registration card myself. He did it."

"How convenient," McEnerny commented, lips barely moving.

"Marguerite," Frank interposed, "maybe you can describe
him."

"Oh, I think I can. White male, clean shaven, about five-feet-
eight or nine, medium build, brown hair, I don't remember the
eyes, looks close to fifty but is probably younger, maybe forty.
He's going to seed. I think from drink. His eyes were a little
bloodshot and he was sucking on a peppermint candy but it
wasn't quite strong enough to cover the whiskey smell."

Frank smiled encouragingly at her and turned to McEnerny.
"That should help."

"It does. The night clerk at the Tropicana is a thirty-year-old,
dark-skinned Hispanic with a mustache."

Silence.

"Now tell us about your gun."

"What gun?" exploded from Marguerite and Frank simultaneously.

"I didn't have time to update you on this, Chief," claimed
McEnerny. "The report just came in a little while ago. It seems
the gun used on Dante was registered to a Marguerite Smith.
Boston address but it's the same Marguerite Smith. The address
is her former one."

"Oh, *that* gun," she cried. "But it wasn't really mine. Joe
bought it. There was a burglary in our neighborhood and he insisted I needed a gun in the house for when he wasn't home. He
even made me go down to the gun shop with him and apply for
it in my name. I couldn't stand looking at it and never touched
it."

"But you took it to Florida with you, didn't you?"

"No! I haven't seen it in years. Not since my divorce. Joe

must have taken it with him when he left. I never even thought about it till now. Beatrice would know. She could tell you I didn't have a gun with me. She saw me unpack.''

"And how can I get in touch with this Beatrice?"

"I don't know," admitted Marguerite. "She's traveling and I don't know where she is."

"Let's go over this again, back to Thursday, January twenty-fourth. You claim—"

"No, Sergeant! We're not going over anything again," Marguerite interrupted defiantly, lips compressed, face white—the color of fury. "I have tried to cooperate with you in every way possible by telling everything I know. But you've never believed me. Right from the beginning you doubted me. If you had taken me seriously when I told you Nick threatened me and if you had held him he might be alive today. Instead you prefer to harass me and accuse me of lying. No more! I have nothing more to say until I consult a lawyer. You'll have to figure these murders out yourself!''

She managed to make it sound like a threat. He was dumb with surprise and said nothing as she regally rose from her seat, carefully slid the chair under the dining room table, faintly nodded to Frank, and marched out of the room, the music of the grand procession in *Aida* playing in her head.

It was a great exit for a B movie, but her high faded the moment she closed the door behind them, refusing to meet their eyes. Shaky legs carried her to the living room. Trembling fingers rubbed her forehead, as if to clear the web entangling her.

Alex was appalled at the transformation. They had left an optimistic Marguerite and returned to find a dejected one. She slouched in a chair and recited her story in a listless monotone.

Mother never slouched! Not ever! She had relentlessly corrected the shoulder slump of a prepubescent Alex, tall for her age and trying to hide it. And Mother was never depressed! Alex mobilized for action—just like her mother would have done.

"Mother, you're absolutely right about those policemen. They're too incompetent to find the real murderer and are concentrating on you. Of course, they have no evidence except some stupid gun of Dad's but we can fix that. Veronica must know that Dad had that gun. I'll ask her. We also have to locate your friend Beatrice," she continued, ticking off items on her fingers, "talk to Lia or Dolly or whatever her name is, try to locate that book in German that seems to have caused all the trouble, and let's see, what else?''

"How about a lawyer? Isn't it time for that?" suggested Preston.

"Of course. You're right," agreed Alex.

"I'll call Portia," said Marguerite in a somnambulent tone.

"Perhaps she can suggest someone with more experience than she has," Alex tactfully proposed.

No answer. Alex resolved to return to this topic later. For now, a shift in tactics was necessary.

"Well, how about dinner? Let's get started. How can I help?"

That shook Marguerite from her lethargy. "You can cut the chicken breast into bite-sized pieces. And wash it first," she added, unsure if Alex knew even the basics.

Taking two aprons from a drawer, Marguerite handed one to Alex in deference to her expensive suit and called to Preston. "You can set the table." Things were humming again.

While Alex coated the chicken with cornstarch and five-spice powder, Marguerite blended the remaining spices, chopped vegetables, and brought a pot of water to the boil for the lo mein noodles.

Table set, Preston asked Marguerite for an inspection which she promptly performed and would have whistled if she could. He had used white brocade linens, her wedding china, and sterling silver tableware with a profusion of forks and spoons. Lacking a centerpiece, he had taken from the living room a vase with an assortment of dried flowers featuring silver dollars, astilbe, and sedum. Preston clearly knew his way around a dining room. She hoped he knew as much about the kitchen as she led him back there and produced a large knife and a head of Chinese cabbage. He performed very proficiently after first removing his jacket and tucking a clean kitchen towel neatly into his belt.

Most of the work of the dinner was in the cutting; cooking was rapid. In no time, the coated chicken had been sautéed with chili peppers, garlic, ginger, and green onions; the noodles added to the stir-fried cabbage, bean sprouts, bamboo shoots, and seasonings; and the wine popped.

As Marguerite transferred the food to serving dishes, she took a generous sample of each and added it to Rusty's dog food.

"That's for your greeting to the sergeant," she giggled.

Chapter Thirty

The route to Boston was so familiar by now that on Wednesday morning Preston needed no directions until he reached the downtown maze. With a little help from Marguerite, he wheeled agressively into Devonshire Street and deposited her in front of Portia's law firm, then, under Alex's guidance, maneuvered to the new garage under Boston Common where they parked the car.

Preston was getting into the swing of detecting and had abandoned his diplomatic attire today in favor of twill trousers, a light-blue buttoned-down shirt, and a crewneck navy-blue sweater topped by a fleece-lined suede jacket. Alex appreciated the warmth of the dark green wool pants suit she wore today. A dove-gray silk shirt was mostly covered by a sweater one shade darker. The belt of her camel's-hair coat was pulled tightly around her.

They walked through the wake of their condensed breaths, the cold air hurrying them along. The streets were clear of snow and the sky was blue, not a spectacular blue but a washed-out blue; nonetheless, a treat in wintry-gray Boston.

Alex immediately spotted Dahlia in the reference room. Her father would have noticed this woman. Anyone would. Her hair was as red as Leah had described but Alex was not prepared for the extravagance of it. Curly, long, and unrestrained, it sprang up and out on all sides, creating a critical mass. She was spectacular without being classically beautiful. Her lips were full and pouty, contrasting oddly with narrow brown eyes, dark-rimmed as if

149

from sleeplessness, and a thin slash of brown-penciled eyebrows. Alabaster skin, clear and smooth—no freckling, no high color— was unusual for a redhead. The nose made her real. It had a bump at the bridge.

She had been expecting them. On reflection, Leah had regretted talking so much and decided to give Dahlia an abridged and censored version of Alex's visit. Dahlia looked up as they approached and a flicker of recognition passed through her shrouded eyes to be quickly extinguished as she turned to Preston and asked, "May I help you?"

"Yes, I'm Preston Trowbridge and this is my wife, Alexandra Smith Trowbridge." Dahlia concentrated on Preston, not even acknowledging Alex. "We believe you were working with Alex's father, Joseph Smith, and helping him translate an old book from the German."

"You must mean Dan, Dan Smith. Yes, I was helping him." She volunteered nothing.

Preston gamely continued, aware that Alex was being snubbed. "As you probably know, Mr. Smith has been murdered and the book seems to be of some significance. Do you have the book or the translated pages?"

Leah, hovering nearby eavesdropping, looked up sharply. Alex had deceived her, saying she merely wanted to continue the work on the book. *You can't trust anyone, can you? Now if Dolly gets in trouble she'll probably blame me,* Leah thought.

The conversation was tortuous and fragmented, interrupted frequently by library patrons in person or by telephone. Dahlia answered tersely, prolonging each forced pause in the conversation.

No, she did not have the book or any pages of the translation. Dan kept everything. She could not imagine why anyone would commit murder over that old book. It was the record of a bootlegger, cases of whiskey received from certain ships, cases of whiskey sold. No names were mentioned so it wasn't even useful for backmail. She couldn't understand why Dan was so interested in it unless he was planning to write a book himself.

The telephone rang again. It appeared to be a personal call and Dahlia looked somber. Replacing the receiver, she addressed Preston. "I can't talk to you any longer. I have to leave."

Alex and Preston looked glumly after her. With Dahlia gone, Leah moved in, her fear of recrimination weakening.

"It must have been about the funeral arrangements," she offered. ''Remember that death in the family I told you about? She was waiting to find out when the funeral was. It was a waste for her to even travel in today. She's leaving so early and I'll be stuck with all the work.''

''Does she travel far''? asked Alex.

''From Brockton.''

Brockton, Brockton, where have I heard that recently? pondered Alex.

She was still trying to resolve that as they walked down the library steps, past the copper statues. Preston noted a man walking up the steps with striking white hair and an azure tie.

''Alex, that was Sgt. McEnerny. What is he doing here?''

Chapter Thirty-one

The law firm of Hopkins, Potter and McNamara reflected a world before plastic, with their mahogany desks, worn Persian rugs, comfortable leather chairs. Having recently decided to enter the twentieth century as it receded, they had provided their secretaries with word processors, the glaring new monitors proclaiming this a place of business rather than the gentleman's club that it resembled.

This was Marguerite's first visit to the sanctuary where Isaiah Hopkins, senior partner and attorney for the Newcomb family, presided with grace and acumen. He had personally brought Portia Fallon Newcomb into the firm and rescued her from the high-pressure, eighty- to ninety-hour work week of her former association.

Portia greeted her aunt with a warm hug and a keen look. Marguerite had changed. The guileless blue eyes were clouded, the smile weak. Worry wrinkles had surfaced where none had been visible. As soon as she had Marguerite settled into one of the tufted leather armchairs, she tried to restore her spirits.

"Aunt Meg, I've spoken to Raymond Carlyle about Uncle Joe. I thought it would be all right to mention it now because I knew about it from you. He said he had told Uncle Joe he had no case. The house was yours. But Raymond had the impression Uncle Joe was still planning to use this threat against you in some way. Uncle Joe was bluffing. That should calm any fears you have about Veronica following up on it."

"Yes, it does. Thanks, Portia. However, it doesn't help me with this cloud of murder I'm under because I obviously didn't know that Joe had been told this. Of course, my own lawyer told me the same thing but he's out ot touch. Just like Beatrice."

"What does Beatrice have to do with this?"

"The gun that killed Nick Dante was registered to me. Joe bought it for me years ago and still had it but the police think I did. Beatrice could tell them she never saw it in my luggage but she's traveling and I don't know where."

"This could be called the case of the missing witnesses. You'd better update me."

Portia listened intently, never interrupting until Marguerite mentioned her visit to Grace McGuire and how she learned the story of the boat, *Blue Bell,* registered to a Paulie, last name and whereabouts unknown.

"Aunt Meg, do you think that boat is important?"

"I don't know. I can't even guess what's important. But that book in German keeps popping up as well as the other one that's supposedly on the Cape. And where is it? If it wasn't valuable, why would Joe hide it?

"Since the book was Grace's husband's, and since he was drowned on the *Blue Bell,* I'd also like to know more about him. Especially about that last trip. Prohibition was just about dead. Grace said Viktor had phased out the bootlegging and was planning a legitimate business. Why did he go out that night? Why did he insist Grace leave the house on a rainy night with a baby? And why the muddy footprints in the basement? That's where the safe and the secret compartment were.

"And why didn't he leave Grace much money? He was making lots of it according to her and they lived modestly except for the fact that he bought that house for cash. Paulie was the only witness. Maybe he's not even alive, but I'd like to know."

"I think I can help you there. Jeb could probably find out the owner of the *Blue Bell.* All boats are registered. I'll call him as soon as we're finished here."

Jebediah Newcomb was president of Newcomb & Stowe, ship chandlers. He was a reluctant president, hating the nitty-gritty details, loathing the confines of an office, preferring the free-wheeling life of a real estate speculator, at which he had failed miserably. Rescued by his aged and wealthy aunt, Rachel Stowe, he had sheepishly resumed his responsibilities at Newcomb &

Stowe but was still grateful for diversions. Portia knew he would gladly accept this challenge.

"Tell him to work fast. I don't have much time and I need to investigate this myself. Sgt. McEnerny doesn't believe anything I say and he'll probably arrest me soon. What a hard, bitter man!"

"He may not be as hard as you think. Maybe that's just his public shell in a tough job. I learned something about him. But you must promise not to tell him you know, no matter how angry you get."

"Me? Get angry? How absurd!"

"I had lunch with a friend yesterday. She had been to a wedding last Saturday—a relative of her husband. When I heard the name McEnerny I paid careful attention. My friend said she was delighted the bride had met such a nice man because her life had a difficult start. The bride's mother—Kathleen McEnerny, your sergeant's sister—had the girl out-of-wedlock twenty-five years ago when it wasn't as acceptable as it is now, particularly in her very religious Irish Catholic family. They insisted she go away and have the baby secretly, then give it up for adoption.

"She stubbornly refused to do that or to marry the father who she wouldn't name. The family disowned her—all except Charlie. His life had been floundering till then, always on the fringe of trouble, but this gave him an incentive. He studied for the State Police test, made a high mark, and was appointed. From that day he helped Kathleen become independent, devoted himself to her and her daughter. Last week he gave his niece away in marriage. His sister must feel very indebted to him."

"Humph! It sounds to me like his sister rescued him. Probably would have been in jail by now without her giving his life some direction."

Charles McEnerny was unredeemed.

Chapter Thirty-two

Sgt. McEnerny almost missed Dahlia. Informed by Leah that Dahlia had just left her desk to go home, he asked where she kept her coat and quickly intercepted her. She was rushing from the staff room and nearly collided with Trooper Fleming, who accompanied the sergeant.

McEnerny was as stunned by her appearance as was everyone who met her and was not surprised that Joseph Smith had been attracted to her. He was following the progression of Joe's women: Marguerite, the brunette, a good looker in her day but now over the hill; Veronica, the blonde, an early-fading cheerleader type; then Dahlia, a stunning redhead to round out the catch.

That this was Joe's girlfriend they had no doubt. Fleming had been informed of her existence, even her name, by a most reliable source—Joe's secretary. The last phone call Joe had made from Cape Cod on his cellular phone was to a Dahlia DeJonghe at a Brockton address. Medeiros spotted the connection between the name Dahlia and Lia. Reaching only the answering machine at her home, they had contacted the library, affirmed her employment, and gone to find her there.

The staff room was devoid of any other employees. She was firmly wrapped in a long winter coat and seemed ready to spring out the door in flight. McEnerny recognized the symptoms of fear. He got right to the point.

"It is our understanding that you were a, er, good friend of

Joseph Smith.'' The words ''good friend'' had a verbal question mark.

''Not a good friend but I knew him,'' she answered defiantly. ''As Dan Smith.''

''What was your relationship with him?''

''I don't know that that's any of your business.'' Her enveloping winter coat had opened at the bottom, displaying long black-stockinged legs minimally covered by a short black skirt.

''Murder is my business, understand? The last telephone call Joe Smith ever made was to you at ten o'clock on the night of January fifteenth from Cape Cod. I guess you know he was murdered?''

''Yes, I know. It was in the papers.''

''Then I repeat again. What was your relationship with him?''

''I was assisting him to translate a book he had. It was in German. About bootlegging. I assumed he was going to write a book about it. Our relationship was professional.''

''Were you paid for this work?''

''No,'' she answered reluctantly.

''Then maybe your relationship was more than professional.''

''How dare you make that assertion! I was interested in helping him only because I'm bored with this job and relished the opportunity to use my skills. It was intellectually challenging because the book was written in an old-fashioned script and was faded.'' Her reply was delivered condescendingly.

''I'm impressed,'' he said sarcastically, having caught her tone. ''Joe Smith must have also been very impressed with your, er, skills to call you at ten o'clock at night from the Cape about some translation.''

''He was concerned because we had reached a point that was giving me trouble. He called to see if I thought I would be able to continue with it.''

''That means you have the book.''

''No, I never had it. He always took it with him. The translations as well.''

''Where did you, er, work?'' His eyebrows lifted. The implication was clear.

''Mostly at my house.'' She rewrapped the coat around her legs, ending Fleming's preoccupation.

''Do you live alone?''

''No, my brother lives with me, my brother Desmond.''

"How well did you know Nick Dante?" This was a shot in the dark. The Brockton connection had been nagging him.

"Nick Dante?" she repeated, narrow eyes closing to a slit.

"Yes, the policeman from Brockton who was murdered in Florida. A smart girl like you must have noticed it in the paper."

"Oh, *that* Nick Dante," she recalled, as if the world was replete with Nick Dantes. "I knew him slightly. Just to say hello to."

McEnerny persisted. She knew nothing about Dan Smith's private life. Couldn't help them there. Nick Dante was a casual acquaintance. She couldn't help them there. Why was she leaving for home? Personal business. What personal business? That's why they call it personal. It's private.

He let her go, his mind spinning with possibilities. Did black widows work in pairs? Two women were involved with both of the male victims. Was there a connection between the women? Or was the connection between the men?

Or was it just a coincidence? Like the one in Florida that had been nagging at him. The sergeant didn't believe in coincidences in a murder case. Everything that happened had a reason. That's why he made a call to that Florida cop, Lyle Fairchild, and asked him to check out a couple of things on the qt. No use giving it to homicide yet. Fairchild could do that if it panned out. He hoped the sunglassed kid was smarter than he sounded.

Before leaving the library they returned to the reference desk and Leah, the font of information. She recognized the picture of Nick Dante.

"Oh, yes, he sometimes comes by to see Dolly. I don't know what she sees in him. He looks kind of, you know, kind of unsavory," she whispered confidentially. "I must admit he speaks well, though. Always quoting someone or other. He certainly impresses Dolly. And with her looks she could have anyone."

On their return trip to Cape Cod, Fleming mentioned Victor Krogh. That interview was gnawing at him and he was convinced Victor was hiding something. Timidly, he voiced his suspicion to McEnerny and was promptly chewed out for not following up immediately. He dared not compound his misstep by mentioning lunch, although he would love that meat loaf again. Or maybe pot roast. No, better forget it. The tight muscles in the sergeant's neck were a warning signal.

They detoured to Braintree and sought out the office manager of the insurance company for which Victor Krogh worked. It was an easy mission. All the agents kept a log that was turned into the office manager weekly to support their expense accounts. On the afternoon of January fifteenth, Victor had been in the office from one o'clock to three-fifteen, after which he left to meet a prospective client named Robert Meyers.

Could the office manager check the records to see if any policy had been issued to Robert Meyers? Yes, he could, and no, no policy had been issued. It must have been a bad lead.

McEnerny felt magnanimous toward an embarrassed Fleming. "How about lunch?" he asked.

"I know just the place," replied the chastened trooper.

Chapter Thirty-three

Thursday dawned warm and rainy, not a torrential rain, but a soft one that dampened little more than spirits, a temperate one that guaranteed fog would slink in as the mild, humid air cooled and condensed.

Marguerite arose reluctantly. It had been one week ago today that her life had come tumbling down. The opulent sunshine and blue skies of Fort Lauderdale, the heady anticipation of an evening of dining and dancing with an intelligent, debonair gentleman, had exploded in a nightmare, the shrapnel targeting her.

Breakfast was a desultory affair. They had no agenda for today but were awaiting the harvest of the seeds they had sown. Waiting for Grace McGuire to remember Paulie's last name. Or for Jeb Newcomb to discover it as the registered owner of the *Blue Bell*. Waiting for Veronica to find Grace's book. For Laura to find anything. Would Marguerite be arrested today?

The phone rang while she was walking Rusty. Luckily so, for Veronica would have hung up if Marguerite answered.

"Alex, I found something. I finally got the safe opened. The book you were looking for was in there."

"Wonderful, Veronica. Can I drive to your house this morning to get it?"

"I'm not sure what to do with it. After all, it was given to Dan, so it's mine now and if it's valuable I'm entitled to the money."

159

Marguerite's predicament was clearly not a priority with Veronica. Alex had to handle this carefully.

"You're absolutely right, Veronica. And I don't want to deprive you of it. If I could only borrow the book perhaps I could find something to help solve Dad's murder. You want that, don't you? I'd return it to you."

"I don't want to let it out of my hands. And what good would it do you to see it? Do you read German? And what good would it do me? It won't bring Dan back."

"I can read a little German. I studied it for a couple of years at college. Perhaps I can translate it with the help of a dictionary. Then I'd be able to tell you if and why it's valuable. But I'd have to go to the library and would need the book."

"No way! The book stays with me."

Her adamant tone caused Alex to retreat slightly. "How about letting me copy it? If you have the original you're protected."

Alex crossed her fingers as she said this. From her mother's conversation with Grace McGuire, it seemed likely that Grace could claim ownership of the book. She had merely lent it to Joe.

"That sounds okay. Maybe instead of you coming here I'll meet you somewhere on the Cape. I have nothing to do today and I'm going nuts here. Not at your house, though."

"How about the Hyannis Yacht Club? Do you know where it is?" Alex knew Marguerite was a dining member and she would borrow her card.

"I think so. I've been there with Dan. What time?"

"Twelve-thirty. Do you mind if my husband comes with me? I think he can be helpful."

"No, I don't mind. But no one else! Twelve-thirty."

Veronica's idea of dressing for lunch at a yacht club was to don navy-blue leggings, a navy and white striped long-sleeved shirt with a red scarf around her neck, red high-heeled shoes and pocketbook, and a mink coat. She carried a slim leather briefcase.

They were seated at the corner table on the glassed-in porch. The bobbing sailboats that enhanced the warm-weather view were missing and the disconsolate sky weeped at their absence. Flotsam and jetsam of winter storms littered the beach; the water rippled calm and gray; an occasional boat horn released a diaphanous sound at once mournful and romantic.

Alex had the forbearance to delay until the waitress served

their glasses of wine and took the lunch orders before asking excitedly, "May I see the book?"

Leisurely, Veronica took a sip of Chardonnay, leaving a crimson imprint on the glass, and reached for the briefcase tucked protectively between her stiletto heels. She unzipped it and, at a maddeningly slow pace, gingerly extracted an old ledger book. It was fragile, the pages yellowed, but intact.

Alex eagerly reached for it but Veronica cautioned her first, "Remember, it's mine."

The waitress brought oysters Moscow for an unperturbed Preston, no appetizers for the women. Alex carefully turned the pages and surveyed the writing. It would give her trouble. The script was an old-fashioned one, written not for a stranger's eyes but for the author's own. However, even a cursory look alerted her to the fact that this was not merely the bootlegger's record it was purported to be.

The dates gave it away. About one-quarter of the way through the book, the entries changed in form, with each one of them preceded by a year but no month or day, some of the years well before Prohibition, before World War I, before Vitus Krogh jumped ship and condemned himself to operating in the shadows. This was a record of something besides whiskey. As Alex concentrated on faded German handwriting, Veronica attempted conversation with Preston, enchanted by his good looks and courtly manners. She ordered another Chardonnay and lighted a cigarette.

"I hope you don't mind," she cooed, blowing the smoke away from him and toward Alex.

"Not at all, Veronica. I had a fling with smoking myself and still relish the aroma." He was determined not to offend her.

"Since you're so understanding of my only naughty habit, I have something you might like to see," she teased.

There was no right answer to this double entendre so he smiled and ate another oyster. Too late he realized that might not have been such a clever reaction considering the mythical powers of oysters.

She reached again for the briefcase and removed a single piece of paper, coyly extending it toward him. On it were the rubbings of both sides of a coin, the kind of pencil rubbings with which children amuse themselves reproducing pennies. Only this was not a penny. It was an elaborate and beautifully designed coin, evidently minted in high relief since the crude tracing revealed every element of design. A full-length Liberty was pictured on one side and the profile of an eagle, wings upraised in flight, against the background of a fourteen-rayed sun on the other. The date in Roman numerals, MCMVII, identified it as minted in 1907.

Preston was a numismatist, had been one since his childhood when his grandfather gave him a starter coin folder. But Preston never had one of these magnificent coins, which he thought he recognized as a double eagle, specifically one of the twenty-dollar gold pieces designed by Augustus Saint-Gaudens and considered to be the most beautiful United States coin. Grace McGuire evidently did not know much about coins, nor did Joseph Smith. A coin of this value should never have been rubbed or even handled.

"Veronica, where did you get this?"

"It was in the safe, right underneath that book. There were two of them. They looked the same."

She blew a smoke ring which wafted away to collide mutely with the window. The waitress hurried over to remind Veronica that they were in the no-smoking section. With a final smoke ring and a look of bravado, she stubbed out the cigarette in her bread dish.

Preston avoided the disapproving eyes of the waitress and addressed Veronica. "Since you have two of these, may I borrow this one? It appears to be the rubbing of a gold coin. I'd like to look it up in a coin book but I need this picture. Did Joe, uh, Dan, collect coins?"

"Not that I know of, but there seems to be a lot I didn't know about him."

The word "coin" had penetrated Alex's concentration. Her heartbeat accelerated until she imagined everyone could see the pounding pulse pushing against her skin.

"Preston, are you sure about that being a gold coin?"

"Yes, but I'm not a hundred percent certain of the type or present value."

Facts were gelling in Alex's mind. Grace McGuire had found a gold coin along with the book but had refused to give it to Joe. He must have suspected its significance and value so made a rubbing—twice to be sure.

Wary of revealing too much to Veronica who might withdraw the offer to let them copy the book, she casually closed the ledger and announced, "This book will take a lot of work. I really need a German dictionary. Oh good, here comes lunch. I'm starving."

Chapter Thirty-four

The homicide detectives in Fort Lauderdale were ambivalent about Marguerite and content to keep her on ice in New England under the watchful eye of Sgt. McEnerny. Though the gun used in Nick Dante's murder was registered to her, it had been purchased seventeen years ago. Guns had a way of changing hands. There were no fingerprints on it and no one could place her in Nick's company after he left her room when the police arrived.

According to Lyle Fairchild, she had seemed genuinely disturbed by Nick. If true, and if their relationship was adversarial, how would she have managed to get the drop on him and shoot him twice—an armed, experienced police officer? Even if they had settled their quarrel, the scenario was implausible.

Fingerprints from several people were found in Nick's car, but only Nick's on the driver's side. The car had not been wiped clean except for the front door handles on both sides. There was no proof that his car had even been used that night, but they needed Marguerite's fingerprints and those of her friend, Beatrice, to sort out the other prints in Nick's car.

The desk clerk at the Sea Club could not be more specific about the period of time Marguerite had sat in the lobby or if she had been there continuously. He had been on a break part of the time, such as when the phone message came for her. His only clear recollection of time was that she hurried from the hotel and into a taxi shortly after eleven o'clock. That presented another conundrum. Nick's hotel was half a block away. Why a cab if she was going there?

The detectives had one more piece of information that they had not yet shared up North. The Hispanic night manager of the Tropicana had been in that position only since Saturday, January twenty-sixth, two nights after Marguerite claimed to have spent the night there. His predecessor had been an Anglo, clean-shaven, forty-two years old, who had resigned suddenly on January twenty-sixth and left no forwarding address.

Marguerite's phone rang incessantly that dreary morning, each call clearing the gloom overshadowing her spirits, one cloud at a time. First was Veronica's call about locating the book. Then the secretary for Marguerite's lawyer phoned to say that Andrew had contacted her from Provence and left a number where Marguerite could reach him.

Beatrice surfaced shortly before noon. She was bored with traveling alone, the Florida weather had turned cold, and she was on her way home, was, in fact, calling from Virginia. Were Marguerite's problems resolved?

She scoffed at the notion that Marguerite could be implicated in Nick's murder, of which she had read in the Florida papers, and promised to call those foolish policemen immediately to confirm that Marguerite could not have been concealing a gun in her luggage.

Marguerite was almost giddy as the phone rang again with Portia on the line.

"Aunt Meg, Jeb's found the name, the owner of the *Blue Bell.* I told you he would," she proclaimed proudly.

"Who is it?"

"His name is Paulino Santos from New Bedford. Of course, that was in 1925."

"He's probably not even alive."

"Maybe not, but he could be. Or he might have a surviving wife or children who know something. That's a job for the police. They have access to all kinds of records."

Yes, and I know someone else who does, Marguerite thought but did not say.

"That's a big help, Portia. Thank Jeb for me."

She ended the conversation abruptly, rather ungraciously for a doting aunt. There was so much to think about, so much to do.

But it would be hours before Alex and Preston returned with the pages from that blasted book. No sense in calling that lawyer friend of Portia's now that everything was falling in place. She'd bake a cake. That should clear her head. What kind?

Heady from all the morning's news, she succumbed to a sick bit of humor. Why not a rum cake? This whole problem seemed to have started with a rumrunner.

The cake was just in the oven when the phone jangled again. George Atkinson suggested bridge tomorrow night if she knew of anyone to make a fourth. It would do her good to get her mind off her troubles. Would be good for Laura also to stop rummaging through those old books. She was coughing from the dust when he called her.

Marguerite said she would get back to him and threw on a coat to run over to Ed Rogers's house. Dressed as usual in a T-shirt, he seemed oblivious to the chill in that inadequately heated cottage. His artistic fervor must keep him warm, she thought as she glanced at several paintings propped on the living room chairs. He'd be available tomorrow night for bridge but he warned her not to expect too much.

"Don't worry. As long as you're my partner, no one will complain. It'll even up the odds a little," she bragged.

That matter settled, she called George and then turned her attention to the cake. It was ready to be drenched with a rum mixture.

The telephone was deceitful. It jingled merrily when it should have warned her. Chief Nadeau was on the line. Could she come down to have her fingerprints taken?

"Why?"

"We need your prints to sort out the ones that were found in Joe's car. There are some that are not his."

"Mine won't be there. I was wearing gloves. It was freezing out. So you don't need them."

"We still need them, Marguerite. Just for the purpose of elimination. Besides, they want them in Florida, too, for the same reason. To sort out the prints in Dante's car."

"Well, I was in his car. I've told them that."

"Yes, but they don't know which ones are yours and which ones are someone else's. Could you just come down and cut out the twenty questions?"

Frank was grumpy. It was supposed to be his day off but he

had come to his office planning to spend a couple of hours assaulting a mountain of dreaded paperwork. He could not blame this backlog on the rush of tourists. It was January. It was all Marguerite's fault, the time he was spending on this murder case.

"I'll be down as soon as I finish the cake I'm in the middle of making."

"What kind?" He brightened a little.

"Rum."

"How about cutting off a little piece for me?"

"Why, Frank Nadeau! I'm ashamed of you. Drinking on the job!"

Nevertheless, she did cut him a piece and wrapped it carefully. Marguerite believed in the power of food. It made the nice hormones circulate and calmed the aggressive ones. She hoped that nasty sergeant wasn't there. There wasn't enough sugar in the world to help him.

He wasn't. Sgt. McEnerny was busy off-Cape tracing the sinuous threads of this case. Marguerite would have been surprised to know that his focus today was other than she. There were multiple motives woven into this mystery and each had to be discarded or affirmed. Victor Krogh, Wilson, Veronica, Dahlia, anyone connected with Joe had to be considered.

Marguerite presented her peace offering. After the nasty job of fingerprinting was completed she claimed a chair in Frank's office and began her recital of good news.

"Frank, Beatrice called me. She says she knows absolutely that I did not have a gun."

"I know. She called." He tasted the cake.

"My lawyer has been in touch with his office. I plan to request him to call you to confirm that I spoke with him about Joe's threat just as I told you I did."

"Good, but that was probably after the murder. I don't think it'll help much."

"Laura Eldredge thinks Joe was after one of her books. Something to do with land claims. You should ask her."

"We did." Another bite of cake went down.

"There's someone else you should look into. Joe had a girlfriend."

"Yup, name of Dahlia." It was half gone.

"Well, do you know where Dahlia is from?"

"Yup. Brockton. Same as Nick Dante."

"Doesn't that mean anything to you?"

"Not as much as this cake right now. Why don't you give me some peace so I can enjoy it?"

"I have just one more piece of information to assist you. Then you're on your own. It's about Joe's brother Wilson."

"Are you going to tell me about that insurance?"

"I guess not."

Frank was mashing his fork into the crumbs, trying to capture them. Should she tell him about Grace McGuire and the book Joe had in his safe? No, not yet. She had told him enough. Better wait until Alex and Preston copied the pages and interpreted them. She was tired of doing all his work for him.

Chapter Thirty-five

Charles McEnerny felt as if he was swatting at gnats, pesky little insects that one could barely see but, if you didn't get rid of them, they kept nipping you. His gnats were people, the individuals in Joseph Smith's life who were hovering in the background of this investigation. Each motive, each alibi, had to be investigated before he could concentrate fully on his chief suspect, Marguerite Smith.

Stephen Fleming had been dispatched to show Nick Dante's picture to Dahlia's neighbors and to talk with Veronica to elicit more specific details about her whereabouts on January fifteenth and sixteenth.

Two neighbors and the superintendent of Dahlia's building identified Nick as a frequent visitor to Dahlia—Dolly, they called her. They confirmed that she lived with her brother, Desmond, a noticeable disdain curling their lips as they spoke the name. Although admitting they rarely saw him, a picture emerged of someone dressed like a Hell's Angel, a wastrel with bad manners who worked sporadically and sponged on his sister. Dahlia apologized for him, claiming his service in Vietnam had damaged him.

At Veronica's house, Fleming received no answer to his rings and noted there was no car in the double garage. As he turned to leave, a pickup truck pulled into the driveway and a young man of about nineteen took an armful of clothes covered in dry cleaner's plastic and walked into the open garage to hang them on a rack. He pushed the electronic door closer and slipped out under the slowly descending door.

Intercepted by Fleming, he introduced himself as Kevin and explained he ran errands and did miscellaneous jobs for a growing list of customers. It helped with his college expenses. What had he done for Mrs. Smith this month? Taking his appointment book from a hip pocket, he enumerated various chores including removing snow once and taking her car to be washed, vacuumed, and polished. When was that? January seventeenth. He had been surprised because it was shortly after a snowstorm and the car was sure to be splashed by spray and salt.

McEnerny concentrated on finances. ''Follow the money'' was a good rule in murder investigations. Joe's financial problems initiated the chain of events. They knew Veronica was in financial difficulty but were not certain how much she knew before Joe had been murdered.

Wilson Smith's situation was interesting. His law practice was mostly facade. Though he loved being a lawyer and participating in the camaraderie of fellow attorneys, he disliked working at the law. Or at anything, it seemed. Joe had been the worker, handling the investment business very successfully until escalating expenses impelled him to recklessness. To his credit, Wilson did garner some of the business. He was a jovial man, indulged in daily lunches and frequent dinners at restaurants, and was not loath to drumming up clients as he ate and drank.

He had been temporarily spared financial ruin because he had some investments separate from those of the partnership and his wife had money of her own. But her income was a fixed annuity, cheapened by inflation, and Wilson had been selling stock. One million dollars would relieve his economic pinch.

Nick Dante was profligate. He drove a Lincoln town car, wore custom-made suits, and drank fine wines on a policeman's salary. His credit was not only stretched, it was screaming. The car was leased and two payments behind. He kept transferring credit card balances to new cards to avoid the current month's payments. Nick needed money.

So did Joe. And Wilson. So did Veronica (if she had known). And Marguerite wanted to keep her home. Did she also sense there was money to be made? It all hinged on books—the one

Joe was looking for in Eastham and now this one Dahlia had
been translating from German about bootlegging. Bootlegging?

This case needed a librarian, not a policeman, he complained
to himself.

Chapter Thirty-six

By nine o'clock Friday morning the Trowbridges were busily at work, Preston nimbly operating his laptop computer, Alex alternately poring over books on coins and a German dictionary that she had borrowed Thursday afternoon from the Eastham library. Marguerite restlessly peered over their shoulders, asking questions, hindering progress. They were relieved when Rusty started pawing at the front door and Marguerite took her for a walk.

Preston was tracing Paulino Santos through the bureaucracy in which all are enrolled knowingly or not, willingly or otherwise. There were a number of recorded Paulino Santoses in New Bedford in the 1920s. Immigration from the Cape Verde archipelago had been steady from the mid 1800s through 1917 when it slowed due to new immigration laws.

Eliminating for age, he focused on three likely candidates. Army records revealed that one became a career soldier and was killed in action in World War II. Among the death certificates in New Bedford he found one for the second Paulino Santos. One Paulie remained—the last possibility.

If still alive, Paulie would probably be enrolled in Social Security and Medicare, but those records were sacrosanct—at least by legal means—and Preston did not wish to compromise himself. He followed other trails that were familiar to him through his State Department experience—the armed forces, police and FBI, the Coast Guard, motor vehicle registry, credit bureaus,

passports, real estate—finally zeroing in at noon on pension records. And there he was! Paulino Santos, born 1907 on the island
of Brava, Cape Verde Islands. Emigrated to the United States in
1916. Became a citizen in 1935. Employed by the railroad in
1942; retired 1972. Present address was in Falmouth, Cape Cod.

Was it the right Paulie? It had better be. It was the only one
they had.

Marguerite had the telephone book out before Preston could
copy the information on the screen. No P. Santos in Falmouth.
Now what? He was old, eighty-nine if that birthdate was correct,
and probably lived with someone or in a nursing home.

Preston knew what they needed—access to a reverse telephone
listing, the kind that is arranged by address. It should be easy
enough to find on his computer. If not, he would e-mail his office,
where he knew the information was accessible. But later. His legs
were stiff and his back sore from hunching over that miniaturized
computer keyboard and screen. "What's for lunch, Marguerite?"
he asked aloud.

Alex gratefully heard the clatter of dishes as a table was set
for lunch. She rarely concerned herself with what or when she
ate but her eyes were bleary from straining to decipher the faded
German script of the copied ledger pages. She missed as many
words as she translated, but grasped enough to make sense of the
record.

It was an extravagant lunch. Marguerite felt celebratory with
the recent progress of her private investigatory team despite their
failure to question Veronica about Joe's gun. Taking the hint that
she was disturbing Preston and Alex, she had driven to the fish
market and purchased cooked lobster tails and claws. With a little
mayonnaise and some dill from her freezer, she prepared a lobster
salad and stuffed it into hot dog buns, producing lobster rolls.
Preston was ecstatic. Alex nibbled one end of the overstuffed bun
and decided it was time to satisfy her mother's mounting curiosity.

"That ledger I'm translating is really two records. It started as
a listing of cases of whiskey received and delivered, bootlegged
whiskey since this was in the 1920s, but that record ended
abruptly and it became a record of gold coins."

Marguerite's attention shifted from the succulent lobster to the
juicy news.

"Gold coins? Like the one Grace McGuire found, the one you have the tracing of?"

"Yes, and a lot of others besides. There are eagles, double eagles, and Indian head eagles, some of the coins dating from the 1800s. Then there's another group under a heading called commemorative and that includes a couple that I think are called Panama-Pacific. I couldn't believe my eyes but that coin, in the highest rating category based on perfect condition, would be worth as much as one hundred twenty thousand dollars. Even in the lowest rating it's worth twenty-one thousand dollars. For a fifty-dollar coin!"

Marguerite was stunned.

The numismatist in Preston was intrigued. "I've never seen one of those Panama-Pacific coins. Only pictures of it. Vitus Krogh must have been a very serious collector."

"Serious isn't the word for it. I've been totaling the value of this collection using the mid-value of each because I'm not sure what the present condition of them would be if they still exist somewhere. I haven't finished but it comes to many millions. If they're in perfect condition it would be mind-boggling."

"But why would he put all his money into coins?" asked Marguerite.

"I've been thinking about that ever since I saw the tracing Veronica gave us," replied Preston, content to talk now that the last of the lobster was gone. "Didn't Grace tell you that he came from Germany and left after the war because the economy was so bad and his family ruined?"

"Why yes, she did."

"That might explain it, at least partially. Paper money became useless in Germany. Inflation went as high as two thousand percent. The only things that retained value were silver, gold, jewels—tangible items. He probably didn't trust paper money and was protecting himself against the devaluation of currency by owning gold. He was very clever to collect coins instead of bullion. Gold bars only increase in value as the price of gold rises but coins have a collectible value that rises faster. At the time he was collecting these pieces, most of them could be bought at face value, the commemoratives a little more. The United States was on the gold standard then and gold was fixed at only twenty dollars a troy ounce. Today it's about four hundred dollars. If it was this gold that went down in the *Blue Bell*, it's been submerged over sixty years. The coins won't be in mint condition, in fact, I don't know what condition they'd be in, but just taking into consideration the value of the gold itself, it's worth twenty times what it was worth then.''

"So if Vitus had a million dollars' worth of gold by weight it would be worth twenty million now. But why would he have hidden it?" wondered Marguerite. "Even Grace didn't know he had it."

"He was a secretive man hiding many things—an illegal alien with a false name engaged in bootlegging."

"That's why he had that secret hiding place," exclaimed Marguerite. "And putting a safe over it was a red herring. Anyone who knew he was wealthy and tried to rob him would assume his money, or gold if they knew about it, was in the safe and would break that open. He probably left some money in there just in case it was broken into. To fool the thief."

"He probably did," agreed Preston. "As well as some gold pieces. If he bought in as large quantities as Alex indicates, the word would have gotten around and he would be vulnerable to theft."

"Then why didn't he keep it in a bank instead of risking it in his house?" asked Alex.

"Have you ever seen any of those TV shows about Prohibition? The ones about Elliot Ness? Most of those gangsters weren't put away for violating the Volstead Act but for income tax evasion. Putting gold in a bank would have been an invitation to the Feds to prosecute."

Marguerite distractedly poured coffee, overfilling Alex's cup until it ran down the sides. She talked as if to herself, clarifying disparate thoughts.

"Some things are beginning to make sense. Grace claims Vitus didn't have much money in the bank and she was surprised. His money must have been in gold and hidden in the basement but she didn't know it. Then he decided to move it. That last trip of his, the night he was drowned, never made any sense as a whiskey run. Grace said he rarely went out and the business was phasing out because Prohibition was ending. But the trip does make sense if he was moving his gold. He insisted she and the baby leave the house that night and she said there were muddy footprints in the cellar. But why would he move the gold? And why on a boat?''

"Didn't you say he was drowned in October 1933?" asked Alex.

"Yes, I remember October because it was the twelfth, Columbus Day."

"I read some background on gold in one of the books I was using," Alex continued. "During the Depression people started hoarding gold because they were frightened about the country's financial stability. So much was hoarded that it endangered the financial structure because we were still on the gold standard and too much of the gold was now in private hands. So when Franklin Roosevelt became president, the Hoarding Act was put in place and all gold had to be turned in to the government. There were severe penalties including jail sentences. The act became law in late October 1933. Vitus must have moved his gold right before it took effect."

"But even so," queried Marguerite, "why move it? No one knew he had it."

"I guess he was afraid he would never be able to use it in this country unless he turned it in immediately and converted it to cash. But if he didn't trust paper money he wouldn't want to do that, so he was sending it to another country where he could cash it only as he needed it. Not to mention the tax and legal problems he would have if he showed up at a bank with all that money. His gesture was in vain, too," explained Preston. "Within a short time that act was amended to exclude coin collections. It was mostly the bullion they wanted back. His coins would have been exempt from the law."

Alex was still puzzled by Vitus's action. "But Grace said he drowned in the *Blue Bell,* a speedboat. Where could he have gone in that? Canada, maybe. But in the rain?"

"Oh, he wouldn't have had to go far," answered Marguerite. "Grace told me how they operated. There were large ships called mother ships that remained outside the territorial limits and supplied the smaller rumrunners. Vitus must have had connections with several of them and since the business was slacking off the ship owners would have been looking for other income. He must have made a deal with one of them to transport his gold. The *Blue Bell* only had to travel about twelve miles out."

"And never made it," commiserated Alex. She was imagining the dark rainy night and the small boat tossing about in the massive waves, the terror of its occupants.

"No, but Paulie did. I have to talk with him because that's what this is all about. Gold! Joe wasn't interested in this little house. He was after the gold and just wanted to use me to help him find it. But how? What kind of book was he after?''

Alex had been thinking hard about the shipwreck. "He had to locate the gold first, Mother, and learn where the boat sank. As I see it, there are two ways to find that information—look for the survivor, Paulie, or look for the log of the fishing boat that rescued him. Dad probably discovered the name of the fishing boat and learned that it belonged to the family of one of your bridge group. He was after the ship's log or whatever kind of record a fisherman keeps.''

"Maybe he did find the name of the fishing boat, but we've found Paulie. I've got to speak with him.''

Brusquely clearing the plates from Preston's setting, Marguerite advised him, "Lunch is over. Back to work!''

Chapter Thirty-seven

Victor Krogh was sweating, not from the temperature but from the heat supplied by Charles McEnerny. The question was simple: "Where did you go on the afternoon of January fifteen when you left your office at three-fifteen?"

"Let me check my record."

Victor opened the right-hand desk drawer and extracted a daily calendar book. "I was at a meeting with a prospective client, Robert Meyers." He smiled, his round face swelling, further obliterating any hint of cheekbones.

"And his address?" The heat was delivered coolly.

Chubby fingers leafed through the book, searching.

"I don't seem to have it," he apologized.

"Where did you meet him?"

"At a restaurant. The Olympia."

"Who gave you his name? How did you contact him?" The relentless blue eyes rarely blinked.

"He called me. Someone gave him my name as a reliable insurance agent."

Victor withdrew a handkerchief from his pants' pocket and wiped his brow. Piggy eyes were retreating under folds of padded eyelids.

"And this so-called reliable insurance agent never took the address, phone number, or any information about a hot prospect. Cut the bull, Krogh! You're only making it harder on yourself, lying to the police. Now, where were you?"

177

McEnerny leaned forward, invading the personal space of Victor, causing him to jerk backward, nearly tipping over his swivel chair, and making him look ridiculous as he clutched the edge of the desk to save his rotund self from a physical crash. The mental crash had already occurred. His florid face was shiny from perspiration that reflected the light in such a way that one beet-red side appeared eggplant purple. McEnerny knew the value of personal humiliation.

"I was on personal business," Victor admitted, eyes downcast. "That's why it wasn't in my log. It was during working hours. I wasn't really cheating, though. I work a lot of extra hours nights and weekends cultivating people and never take credit for that."

"And when did you cultivate Joseph Smith?"

Victor voiced no denial. He knew it was futile. But, like the good salesman he was, he tried to put a favorable spin on it. He had never met Joseph Smith before he called him but knew that Joe handled his mother's finances. She was selling her house and, as a concerned son, he wanted to make sure the money was safely invested. She was elderly and had to be protected.

Upon calling Joe's office on January fifteenth, Victor learned Joe was on the Cape, obtained his cellular number, contacted Joe, and said he wanted to meet him. Joe demurred at first but finally agreed to meet Victor if his schedule permitted. He called Victor a little after three and accepted Victor's suggestion that they meet at five-thirty in the bar of the Yarmouthport Inn. Joe arrived at about five-forty-five and they talked amicably for about an hour, maybe more. Then they parted. That was all.

Victor relaxed as he talked. Selling was his trade. McEnerny asked for and received specifics of their conversation. He asked what they drank, where they sat. Answers were forthcoming at an accelerated pace. The sergeant sensed that at least part of the story was true; they probably had met at the time and place Victor was claiming. Of course, he would try to verify it but it would be difficult to get an identification after all this time.

Of the reason for their meeting, McEnerny was less convinced. Joe Smith seemed to have had a definite agenda for his Cape visit. Would he have interrupted it to meet with a stranger and discuss an old woman's investments, one whose money he had probably lost? Doubtful. In fairness to Victor, he had good reason to be suspicious of Joe. But if Joe had mishandled Victor's mother's account as he had the others, he would have stalled and avoided meeting Victor as long as possible, since he would not have been as easy to fool as his elderly mother. So why did he agree to meet Victor that very day?

Did Victor have the opportunity or motive to slip the poison into Joe's drink? A motive had not yet surfaced. Even if Victor knew Joe was swindling his mother, murdering him would not have recovered the money. He did have the opportunity, in fact had created it, by insisting on meeting Joe that day at a bar. Alcohol was an excellent solvent. But Victor would have had to use a powdered form of the poison. He could hardly float seeds, crushed or otherwise, in Joe's scotch.

Better check out if abrin was available in that form and, if so, could Victor have obtained it? The timing was possible. Joe could have been poisoned at six or so and still met Marguerite for dinner due to the delayed symptoms.

Portia was half off the hook. She was evidently telling the truth when she said her uncle did not return to his motel between five o'clock and seven-thirty while she was waiting outside in her car. But she could have seen him later, at ten, if she had lied about leaving the motel at seven-thirty.

The faster I run, the behinder I get, thought McEnerny as he drove to Brockton for his interview with Desmond DeJonghe whom he had reached by phone at Dahlia's the previous evening. *Let's see what little brother has to say.*

McEnerny was armed with information about Desmond. Fleming had noted the neighbor's comment about Desmond's service in Vietnam. Army records showed he received a medical discharge as a schizoid personality, more dangerous to fellow soldiers and Vietnamese allies than to Vietcong. After a series of accidents and deaths attributed anonymously to friendly fire, he was decreed too unstable even for that dirty war. Especially since he was aiming in the wrong direction.

Charles McEnerny was not the type to live and let live. He despised Desmond the instant he saw him. Dressed in black leather boots and pants, a black long-sleeved shirt with a skull leering on the front and a snake lunging on the back, and a red bandanna tied as a cap on his head with a ponytail of coarse brown hair showing at the back, Desmond sullenly greeted the sergeant and rubbed his unshaven face tiredly.

"This is a little early for me, man."

"Early for what?"

"Hey, don't get an attitude. I said I'd talk to you."

And talk he did. About the ills he suffered at the hands of a Communist government, a Fascist army, a greedy society. When asked what he did for a living, he hedged.

"I'm in construction."

McEnerny knew construction workers. Desmond would not have lasted long among them.

"What company are you with?"

"Wherever they need me. My friends let me know."

"Where was the last place you worked?"

Slowly and painfully the facts emerged. He and a couple of friends worked sporadically for a couple of non-union contractors when they needed extra hands for unskilled work—loading, unloading, fetching, and carrying.

"It must be off the books since you're collecting disability."

A tirade was unleashed. Desmond was preparing to sue the Army for ruining his livelihood. They had illegally discharged and labelled him. He was one of the best soldiers they had and was blamed for mistakes of incompetent officers. They always blamed the little guy.

"Where were you on January fifteenth?" McEnerny demanded suddenly.

"Where were *you,* man? That was weeks ago. How do I know? One day at a time, I always say."

McEnerny recognized the motto of Alcoholics Anonymous and was not surprised. Desmond's record indicated a propensity for addiction—both drugs and alcohol.

Shown the pictures of Joseph Smith and Nick Dante, he admitted to having seen both of them once or twice. His sister had a lot of friends. Had the sergeant seen her? His eyes brightened as he spoke of Dahlia.

Unsatisfactory meeting ended, the sergeant headed for the nearest diner. He needed some black coffee to clear Desmond from his craw.

Lt. Medeiros called the Fort Lauderdale police, impatient with their lack of contact with him.

Marguerite's fingerprints had been found in Nick's car in two places—on the rear door of the passenger's side and a thumbprint on each side of the visor mirror above the front passenger's seat. Nothing on the driver's side. Medeiros chuckled at the prints on the door to the backseat. She had evidently been promoted forward at some point. Or was it vice versa? No prints of hers were found in Nick's room.

One more piece of news cheered Medeiros. The night clerk at the Tropicana had abruptly quit two days after Marguerite claimed to have registered there. The peripatetic owner, Tomás Fernandez, had finally been pinned down long enough to be questioned about the clerk, William Morrison, and had admitted that he forced him to resign rather than be fired. Fernandez did not want Morrison to be able to file for unemployment benefits. It might increase the premiums.

Fernandez suspected him of stealing cash receipts. On the night of January twenty-fourth, Fernandez passed the Tropicana at midnight and noticed the NO VACANCY sign lighted. But when he checked the receipts for that night, one room was listed as vacant. He had suspected the clerk for some time, since he rarely received cash for rooms rented when Morrison was on duty but frequently received cash for rooms rented by other clerks. Faced with this accusation, Morrison had summoned the tatters of his dignity and announced that he quit.

Morrison's description fit the one Marguerite had given. Perhaps she did register there after all, thought a pleased Medeiros. Of course, this didn't clear her yet. She could have shot Nick before or after she registered, although the likelihood of her having killed him before she registered was diminished by the confirmation from the phone company that calls had been made from a pay phone at the Sea Club at ten o'clock on January twenty-fourth, one to Washington, D.C., and one to Seattle, just as Marguerite claimed. That meant she would have had to kill him between eight forty-seven when she called Nick's hotel and ten o'clock when she made those calls, or between ten o'clock and when she picked up the message from Beatrice at eleven o'clock. Not impossible, but difficult.

No one could verify whether she had left the hotel at any time after registering. According to the Lauderdale detectives, there was a stairway leading directly to a back door that could have been opened from the inside and left propped open with a wad of paper.

As to why she would have registered there if she had already killed Nick and was in no danger from him, Medeiros could not guess. Unless it was to convince the police that she believed Nick to be alive and a threat to her. She made sure the clerk would remember her by asking him to fill out the registration card. It was still iffy for Marguerite, but he decided to tell Frank the news.

Frank shook his head on hearing Al Medeiros's report. If Marguerite had been able to read the clerk's name tag, her story would have been more credible and the police less suspicious. *That will teach you to stop being so vain and to wear your glasses,* he lectured an imaginary presence who scoffed at his admonition.

Chapter Thirty-eight

The bridge game was less than scintillating. Ed had told the truth when he said he was a beginner. Marguerite could not succeed in turning him to the same mental page as she.

At first Laura was delighted, as she and George easily won the first rubber. They did not change partners as was customary in social games and even her victory staled as the second rubber wended its way toward an uninspired conclusion with Ed still trumping Marguerite's tricks.

The conversation began to digress more to Laura's search through land records than to bidding. Marguerite was circumspect. Although she was convinced that land claims had nothing to do with Joe's murder and suspected that either George or Laura would soon be intimately involved in its solution, she did not want to initiate premature rumors of sunken treasure. Not until she had spoken with Paulie. If she had located the right Paulie. Though Preston had obtained the telephone number for the address on the pension records, it was listed in the name of A. Barros and no one had answered Marguerite's several attempts at calling.

It was not difficult to withhold information. Laura was content to detail book by book by paper every step of her research through Eldredge history. She was certain it wouldn't take much longer to solve Marguerite's problem.

With the game on hold, the recitation endless, George became sleepy and his eyes drooped, his hands folded over his stomach, slipping occasionally as his slender physique did not provide a comfortable prop.

"Laura, you'd better get the coffee going," suggested Marguerite. "We're losing George."

As Laura clanked around her old-fashioned kitchen, Ed followed the noise and offered to help her.

"You'd be more in the way than helping. I know just where everything is."

"Do you mind if I sit here out of the way? I love old houses, especially the unrestored ones."

Laura had heard her house called many things, usually uncomplimentary. Unrestored had a positive ring to it. He was an astute young man.

Noting a pad and pencil on a splintery wooden counter, he began to sketch Laura as she worked: setting cups on a tray with cream and sugar; cutting into four pieces sandwiches taken from the refrigerator; uncovering a cake sparsely sprinkled with coconut atop thick white frosting.

By the time refreshments were served, Ed had a rough pencil sketch of Laura, excellent to Laura's eyes, flattering in the opinions of Marguerite and George who refrained from saying so. But prettified or not, it was a very recognizable Laura and gave Marguerite an idea.

"Ed, did you ever draw a picture from a description, you know, like they show on television when they're looking for a criminal?"

"No, I never have."

"Do you think you could?"

"I don't know. I guess it would depend on how good the description was."

"Would you try? If I described someone, would you draw him?"

"Not now, Marguerite, The coffee will get cold," protested Laura.

Colder, thought Marguerite.

Ed assumed a weary George's usual role of peacemaker. "Why don't I come by in the morning? That will give us more time."

"Good, Ed. Is nine too early?"

"Not at all. I'll be there with my sketch pad. Don't expect too much, though."

Everyone mollified, attention turned to the food, dismissed in

Marguerite's mind as cold coffee, stale sandwiches, and tasteless cake with gooey icing.

Laura's brothers were the restaurateurs. She had always resented her housekeeping role, and it showed.

Chapter Thirty-nine

E d Rogers knocked on the door at nine-thirty Saturday morning, sketch pad in hand along with a case of pencils.

"Do I smell coffee?" he asked.

"Yes, I just made a fresh pot. How about a cup? There are some fresh bagels, too. Preston went out this morning to get them."

"That would be great. Who's Preston?"

"My son-in-law. He's leaving tomorrow, so Alex and he are getting ready to go out. Preston's never seen the winter dunes. They've been tied down with me all week. There's nothing further we can do today, except this, of course," she concluded, indicating the sketch pad.

"Let's get down to it then," said Ed, downing a piece of bagel with coffee. "I guess we should start with the shape of the face."

"Nothing unusual about the shape of his face. Sort of oval, but a thin oval, not a fat one."

Ed drew his interpretation of a thin oval. Before he could ask the next question, Alex and Preston came down the stairs, were introduced to Ed, said good-bye to Marguerite, and opened the door to find Frank Nadeau, arm raised and thrust forward as he knocked at the space from which the door had just been pulled.

Convinced their excursion had been thwarted, Preston asked if he had come to question Marguerite further.

"No, just a social call. In fact, I bring good news."

As they listened, he told Marguerite the tale of the fired/resigned hotel clerk who fit her description of him and who was suspected of destroying the registrations of guests who paid cash. A jubilant Marguerite waved off Alex and Preston, telling them to enjoy their day, and brought Frank into the dining room, insisting he have coffee and a bagel as a reward. She magnanimously refrained from saying "I told you so."

Setting a place for Frank, she explained what they were doing.

"I know Sgt. McEnerny has Nick's picture but he'd never give it to me. I doubt if he's even shown it around, he's so convinced I'm the guilty one. But I'm just as sure that Nick either murdered Joe himself or was in on it with a partner who later murdered him. If enough people see a picture of him, someone will recognize it and confirm he was here when Joe was killed. His picture didn't appear in the local papers."

"Marguerite, two people have been murdered. Stay out of it!"

"I wish I could but all of you have dragged me into it. Now hush, Frank, and let Ed work."

He complied, mostly out of curiosity.

"How about the hair, Marguerite? Let's do that next," suggested Ed.

"Okay." She closed her eyes, summoning Nick's face. "Dark hair, receding in the front. Pretty long though, long enough to cover the top of his ears. Not combed over to hide the missing hair in the front. Parted and combed down straight."

Ed complied, sketching in the hair with a part and combed over to the left. Marguerite suggested he put a little more hair in the front. It didn't recede that much. She stood back, studied it, and approved.

"He had a mustache, too. Mostly dark like his hair but showing a little gray. Just a touch." She waited, then proclaimed, "Good!"

"How about his lips and chin?" asked Ed.

"I don't remember anything special about his chin. It must have been an average chin. His lips were a little thin, though."

Ed worked on the lips and chin, with a few directions from Marguerite.

"Now the eyebrows. Thick, thin?"

"They were thick but not extremely wide. Long, though. They extended far on each side and into the center. Very noticeable. And dark."

Ed penciled in a ridge of eyebrows, then, at Marguerite's

direction, a nose that was a trifle large but straight with fairly prominent nostrils, and Nick's dark eyes.

With a few more touches, a somber Nick stared at Marguerite.

"That's him, all right, when he was serious or mean. He had a wonderful smile, though." She sighed.

Her moment of reminiscence over, she began clearing the table in a hint that the tête-à-tête was ended. It was time for both of them to leave, as she had plans.

Thanking Ed for the drawing and Frank for the good news, she ushered them out, with Rusty following at Ed's side ready to leave with him. The dog was less friendly to Frank, whose gruff voice offended her.

Marguerite was out of the house almost on their heels, her red convertible headed toward the nearest copy shop to obtain a sheaf of duplicates of Ed's sketch. She had added her phone number at the bottom to be contacted if anyone recognized the man in the drawing.

Starting from the Orleans Rotary, she stopped at every Eastham motel that was open in the winter. If Nick had been on the Cape on January fifteenth, the day Joe arrived, until January seventeenth, the day she left for Florida, he had to sleep somewhere. She assumed he would have been close by and not in Orleans or Wellfleet. Winter staffs were small. It was easy to question the day help and leave the picture to be shown to the night help. Nick's looks were distinctive enough to remember.

He would have had to eat, too, so she included all Eastham restaurants and coffee shops in her dragnet. Luckily, the winter selections were limited but it still took hours, as she had to repeat her query anew in each business and to each employee.

It was two-thirty when she returned home footworn, dry-throated, and hungry. Having neglected the larder, her only lunch choice was tuna fish. Tiredly opening the can, she added a dollop of mayonnaise and mixed it halfheartedly.

Then she remembered Paulie. She had been so absorbed in the production and distribution of Nick's picture that everything else had slipped her mind. Tuna fish abandoned, she hastened to the phone and dialed the now-familiar number—but this time with a difference. A woman answered.

Nervously identifying herself as a friend of Grace Krogh's (she omitted the McGuire), Marguerite inquired if this was the residence of Paulino Santos from New Bedford who had been shipwrecked on the *Blue Bell*. The woman stiffly affirmed that it was and identified herself as his daughter, Amelia Barros.

Marguerite asked if she might interview him.

Amelia bristled. ''No way! He's an old man and that part of his life was over a long time ago.''

Marguerite realized her error in using the word interview. Amelia probably thought she was a reporter. She tried to recoup.

''I'm not a reporter, Mrs. Barros. Or a policewoman. I'm trying to help Grace Krogh, Vitus's wife. Why don't you tell this to your father and see if he would agree to see me before you say no again? You would be performing a great kindness.''

''Hold on.''

The wait seemed eternal; it was three minutes.

''My father doesn't think he knows anything to help you but he'll talk to you because he felt sorry for Mrs. Krogh when she was widowed with a baby. But not today. He gets tired in the afternoon. Come tomorrow morning at ten. He's good then.''

With a few brief directions to her house, Amelia hung up.

The tuna fish looked insipid to a revived Marguerite. She snipped a few strands of chive into it, spread the mixture on two halves of an English muffin, topped each with pimento and cheese, and thrust them into the toater oven for a tuna melt.

She would skimp on dinner.

Chapter Forty

At eighty-nine years of age, Paulino Santos still had a twinkle in the eye that was not clouded by a cataract. Curly gray hair framed a face whose deeply entrenched wrinkles and crow's feet were etched cooperatively by age and sun, his earliest years having been spent in the cranberry bogs and strawberry fields and his young adult years on the water. Caramel colored, with a broad nose and slender lips, he was that unique blend of African and European ethnology—mainly Portuguese—that was a Cape Verdean.

The windswept, drought-plagued Cape Verde archipelago off the west coast of Africa became a colony of Portugal in the mid-1400s and a crossroads in the slave trade, furnishing vessels with various supplies including salt. The sparse Portuguese population intermingled with the slaves, some of whom fled landowners who scampered to the mountains during pirate raids, and others who were granted manumission.

The population pressure on the barren islands caused many young men to sign onto New Bedford whalers in the mid–1800s. Emigration began as a trickle and swelled from the early 1900s to 1917 when the United States passed a literacy law for immigration. The packet trade bearing immigrants ended in the early 1930s as the Depression in the United States presented an additional obstacle to immigrants. Cape Verdeans proudly proclaimed that they were the only Africans who migrated here voluntarily.

Paulie was in a small television room seated in a faux leather recliner before a sunny bay window, with a shawl around his frail shoulders. Marguerite was led into the room by Amelia, who had the same gray hair as her father but lighter skin, high cheekbones, and almond-shaped hazel eyes. She had just returned from Sunday Mass and was tying an apron over her peach woolen dress when Marguerite arrived. Speaking first to her father in Crioulo—a blend of Portuguese and West African—she then advised Marguerite to speak loudly, as Paulie's hearing was bad.

Marguerite introduced herself and spoke clearly, looking at him directly. She knew that people with declining hearing compensate by watching lips.

He smiled and told her he was pleased to have a young lady for a visitor. Marguerite smiled in return and protested the compliment—weakly. Young was a relative term. Paulie had few contemporaries.

She told him about her visit to Winthrop and the revelation by Grace Krogh that Vitus had been a bootlegger. Paulie's face darkened. This was something he never discussed. Marguerite tried to recover her lost favor with him.

"I know you were not in charge. Vitus was. And I am not here to talk about bootlegging," she explained, enunciating distinctly, avoiding confusing contractions. "I am only interested in that last trip when the *Blue Bell* sank. You were not carrying whiskey, were you?"

She hoped he did not ask why she was interested in that trip as she did not have a ready answer. The truth was complicated.

"What do you know about that trip?" he asked.

"Grace told me some things. Do you remember Grace Krogh?"

"Yes, nice lady, that Grace. She was very young, too young for Vitus. And too, er, er . . ." He struggled for the word.

"Innocent," Marguerite suggested.

"Yes, that's it. Innocent. He should marry a showgirl, fancy like him."

"He seemed to love Grace."

"I think so, too. But it was not a good life for her. Look what happened."

"I would like to help Grace." She blushed at this half-truth. "It is important to learn about that last trip. What were you carrying?"

His arms moved upward and he flipped his hands palms

uppermost, in a gesture that meant either he didn't know or wouldn't say.

"Was it whiskey?"

Paulie shook his head, economical with speech.

"Was it in boxes?"

He nodded.

"How many boxes?"

"Maybe ten. Maybe twelve. Very heavy. Took two of us to carry."

"Did you take the boxes from Vitus's house?" She was clearly leading him but saw no other way. He was not prone to volunteer information.

"Yes, from basement. Under floor."

"Was there anyone else on the boat except Vitus and you?"

Another shake of the head.

"Did Vitus or you carry guns?"

The head shake was accompanied by a spate of words.

"No, no. Me and Vitus never carry guns. He hire men for that. This trip he left them out. Not much danger from gangsters anymore. And never shoot at Coast Guard. We had rainy night for cover."

"Where were you going?"

"To meet the big ship. Vitus made a plan."

"What happened?"

Paulie looked inward to a night that cataracts did not obscure. It was clearly not a pleasant memory. He began to talk slowly, then faster and excitedly, alternating between English and Crioulo, creating gaps in the narrative lost to Marguerite. But she understood enough.

The light rain falling when Paulie and Vitus left Winthrop was not a problem, even without the experienced seaman who usually navigated the *Blue Bell* on whiskey runs. They had gone out on worse nights to evade the Coast Guard cutters and Paulie had learned the route and its hazards. But the rain became heavier and the visibility poorer, confusing the fledgling navigator. En route to Race Point a squall developed.

The waves became mountains, the boat tossed around like a splinter and finally swamped. He grabbed a life preserver as he went over and held onto that and the sinking boat for a while. But the boat went under and he would have drowned when, as suddenly as it started, the squall passed and the night cleared.

The water was cold, very cold, and he became numb, almost unable to hold onto the life ring. Just in time, a boat getting an early start to the fishing grounds came along. It was a miracle that they passed so close to him and that there was a full moon. He used all his ebbing stength and yelled. A man checking the lines on deck heard him. There was no sign of Vitus, although they searched for him.

There were tears in Paulie's tired eyes. The memory exhausted him.

"Just two more questions. Do you know where you went down?"

The familiar negative head shake responded. Then a clarification. "I got lost in storm."

"Do you know the name of the fishing boat that rescued you?"

"I will remember it till I die. It was *Laura Ann,* God bless them." He made the sign of the cross as he reverently said the name of the boat.

Marguerite thanked him profusely and said good-bye, which he probably did not hear since his head was bowed on his chest as he communed with the spirits of those revered fishermen.

Making her way to the kitchen, Marguerite found Amelia busily cooking. The aroma was tantalizing and Marguerite could not resist peeking over Amelia's shoulder and into the enormous pot. Amelia responded to her implied curiosity.

"I'm making manchupa, a stew."

"What's in there?"

"Oh, some potatoes, some squash, linguica—Pop loves that—and the thick stuff is corn meal. Would you like to try it?"

Of course Marguerite would and did. "Delicious!"

"Thank you. It's simple food but it's what Pop likes." In a more serious tone she added, "I hope you didn't upset him. He never likes to talk about those years. He still thinks he can be arrested."

Marguerite knew she had, so she skirted the issue. "He's been very helpful and I promise I won't reveal that I spoke to him. Thank you so much."

Amelia was not finished. "Please don't call again. I'll have to refuse you."

"Promise."

With a final waft from the pot, she left, trying to remember the name of that delightful restaurant near the harbor in Woods Hole.

Chapter Forty-one

There was no car in the driveway when Marguerite returned from Falmouth, but the door to the house was unlocked. She felt a frisson as she cautiously pushed open the door a crack and peered in. The murders had changed her perception of safety and she had become assiduous about locking doors and windows.

While debating whether to enter or run, a familiar bark sounded behind her as a red-cheeked Alex and a panting Rusty strode into the driveway. *How silly of me! I forgot Preston was leaving and driving to the airport in the rented car.*

The dog was exhausted! Alex's long-strided pace was too much for the aging dog. As Marguerite patted and consoled the tired dog, the phone rang and she ran to answer it.

It was a hangup, discourteous at all times, disconcerting now in her altered state of wariness.

"The phone just rang and someone hung up," she told Alex.

"That's strange. Preston and I went out for lunch and when we returned there were two calls on the answering machine but no messages." Realizing she was frightening her mother, she added, "I guess someone keeps dialing the wrong number."

"Perhaps. But let's not worry about it now," said Marguerite, brightening. "I have wonderful news. Paulie remembered the name of the fishing boat. It was the *Laura Ann*. He doesn't know exactly where the *Blue Bell* went down in the storm but it must have been near where he was rescued. The log of the rescue boat might have recorded the location, if fishing boats keep a log. Joe must have known or assumed they do and that's what he was after. If he found the log he might have been able to locate the gold and solve his financial problems. He evidently wanted to obtain the log secretly, using me to steal it so the owner wouldn't realize its value.

"Paulie doesn't seem to know what was in those boxes although he knows it wasn't whiskey. Even if he suspected it was something valuable, he would have been too afraid to do anything. He had been working with a bootlegger and wasn't even a citizen at that time. He might have been jailed and later deported. In fact, he's still hesitant to talk about those days."

"There's also the possibility the government would confiscate the gold. Don't they seize money from illegal activities?"

"They do now. Maybe Joe was worried about that, too," agreed Marguerite.

"But someone murdered Dad. He evidently didn't keep his secret very well."

"He couldn't because the book he obtained from Grace was written in German. He used Dahlia to translate it and she must have realized its value and gotten very cozy with him. I'm sure she's connected to Nick. That's the link. Nick killed Joe."

"Then who killed Nick?"

"There are so many possibilities it makes my head spin. It could have been anyone in whom Nick confided—perhaps a cop friend. They're good with guns. Remember, Nick was armed and someone was still able to shoot him.

"Or it could have been someone else who murdered Joe, maybe someone like a professional diver. Joe wouldn't have been able to find and bring up that gold himself even if he did learn the approximate location. And let's not forget Veronica. According to you, she knew Joe had a girlfriend. She might have suspected he was about to leave her and wanted that treasure for herself. We have only her word that she didn't know what he had found and that she didn't know the combination of the safe."

"Then why would she give me the book to copy?"

"Because she had the same problem as Joe. She needed the fishing boat log to locate the gold. She needed an ally and decided to trust you. Maybe she's going to offer you a cut."

"I'll take it, too," teased Alex.

Marguerite was not in a jocular mood, and ignored her daughter's comment. "And let's not forget Victor Krogh, Grace's son by Vitus. Grace was surprised that Vitus hadn't left more money. She might have mentioned this to Victor over the years. Then when she found the coin and the book in that hiding place, he started piecing it together.''

''Then why would she give the book to Dad?''

''She's old and probably wasn't thinking fast enough. Grace had relied on Joe for years and he might have taken the book and left with it before she had a chance to consider what she was doing. But when she gave the coin to Victor, that alerted him to the possibility of more coins. She said he was angry and wanted the book.

''Do you see what I mean? It's so complicated. But first things first. Paulie told me that the fishing boat was named *Laura Ann*. Does the name Laura ring a bell?''

''Laura Eldredge! And her father was a fisherman.''

''So was her grandfather. I'll call her right now. Once the log is located and turned over to the police we'll all be safe. They can sort out who owns the treasure, if there *is* any treasure.''

''You'll be safe from the murderer but not exonerated.''

''One thing at a time, Alex. I just have to outthink Sgt. McEnerny. That ought to be easy.''

Chapter Forty-two

The first two telephone calls on Monday morning were hangups. Alex answered the third call and it was for her. A college friend whom she had called yesterday but who had not been at home was returning the call and inviting her to lunch. Alex hesitated. She would need her mother's car, leaving Marguerite without transportation if Laura called. Marguerite encouraged her to go, saying it was no problem—Laura had a car.

The wait seemed interminable. What was taking Laura so long? Afraid even to walk Rusty, Marguerite opened the door and nudged her out. "Go exercise yourself," she commanded, knowing full well the dog would leisurely sniff the perimeter then rest. She was not an athlete.

It was one o'clock when Laura called. "I have it! The log of the boat. Come right over."

Marguerite was ecstatic. Then she remembered that she did not have a car. "Laura, can you come over here with the book? Alex has my car."

"Impossible! These books are very fragile. A change in temperature might be disastrous. And it's cold out."

Not much colder than your house, thought Marguerite, but said, "Laura, can't you wrap it up? Or carry it under your coat?"

"Marguerite, I've gone to a lot of trouble, devoted a week of my time to your self-inflicted problems. I'm out of patience with you. Do you want to see this book or not?" Marguerite could hear the sniff.

"Of course I do. I'll be over there as soon as I can."

Glancing out the window in the vain hope that Alex would be returning, she saw Ed Rogers pulling into his driveway. Not bothering to put on a coat, she ran out the door waving and calling to him.

"I have an emergency. Can you drive me to Laura's house? She found a book I need."

"Okay, but you'd better put a coat on first. I'll take my packages into the house. Meet you in five."

Marguerite grabbed a coat, penciled a brief note to Alex, and ran to Ed's car.

Laura greeted her with a pursed mouth. "I knew you'd find someone to take care of you. You always do."

Marguerite bit her tongue, then opened her mouth enough to ask, "Where's the book?"

"Follow me. I would have found it sooner but that Owens woman is back and dropped in yesterday afternoon to ask about the church bake sale. Took up my time chattering. Glad she didn't show up today."

Marguerite and Ed trailed Laura through three rooms connected one to the other without benefit of a hallway and each crammed with books and boxes in no apparent order.

"In here, in the library," she announced.

The library's only distinction from the other rooms was the presence of a leather armchair, aged and cracked beyond redemption, an unmatched footstool similar in age and decrepitude, and a wobbly side table with a lamp shedding more heat than light. On the table was a book, its cover showing incipient mildew. Marguerite lunged for it.

"Be careful!" shouted Laura. "It's very delicate."

"It certainly is," agreed Marguerite as she tenderly opened the book. "But it's dark in here. Do you have a brighter lamp?"

"Nothing wrong with this one for them that have good eyes. But since you don't, I'll carry it into the living room."

The procession reformed and retraced its steps, Laura majestically leading and carrying the book as if for an offering. Able to see better in the natural light of the living room, Marguerite noted the title page and was disappointed.

"Laura, this is the record of the *Lorann*. I said *Laura Ann*."

"Nonsense! You didn't hear it right. Your ears are as bad as your eyes. The Lorann was the only Cape Cod fishing boat with a name like that working these waters in the 1930s. I ought to know. It belonged originally to my grandfather who named it after his mother Ann and his daughter Lorraine. When my father replaced it he called his boat *Lorann II.*''

Marguerite said the name aloud several times. It did sound like Laura Ann. And Paulie's pronunciation was a little indistinct. She started to read the first page and immediately encountered difficulty. The writing was hard to decipher, some words were smudged—she could picture the salt spray dotting it—and small patches of mildew marred the record further. What she did read appeared to be about fish—mostly cod and haddock.

''It will takes me ages to interpret this book. Can I take it home with me?''

''Absolutely not! You can see the condition it's in. It'd go to pieces in that overheated house of yours.''

''Very well, I'll do my best. You don't have to wait for me, Ed. Alex will be home in time to pick me up.''

''Okay, I'll go home. I haven't had lunch yet,'' he said, looking at Laura, his green eyes in full color, blond curls falling over his forehead.

''Well, come right into the kitchen. I'll fix something for you.''

Marguerite had an hour of peace. She made some progress with the old record but had not gotten beyond fish.

''Well, have you solved the mystery yet? Whatever it is you're looking for?'' asked Ed.

''No, not yet. It will probably take me a week.''

''Maybe I could do it faster,'' he volunteered.

''That sounds like a good idea,'' agreed Laura, who was not anxious to have Marguerite underfoot for a week. ''Why don't you let Ed do this? He could work here and you could attend to your other affairs.'' Marguerite detected a faint emphasis on the word *affairs.*

''No,'' she answered firmly. ''This is too important to me. I have to do it myself no matter how long it takes. Besides, I know what I'm looking for and Ed doesn't.''

''And maybe I do,'' he replied, smiling. ''Maybe I'd like to know where the *Lorann* rescued that man from the *Blue Bell.*'' The smile annealed to hostility.

Both women were mute. Their gestures spoke—Laura with hand to forehead in confusion, Marguerite with hand over mouth in disbelief. Ed Rogers knew about the gold! How?

"I'll take that book," he said, walking slowly toward Marguerite, hand outstretched, countenance rearranged from cherubic to menacing.

"It won't do you any good. We know you and can prove you stole it from Laura. Maybe you even had something to do with the murders."

"Shut up, Marguerite!" hissed Laura, afraid Marguerite would taunt him too far. She always went too far.

"You only think you know me. Ed Rogers will disappear like my shadow when I walk out of here. Now give it to me!"

"No!" answered Marguerite, defiantly hugging the book to herself. She had more to lose than Laura—an old book versus a murder charge, maybe two murder charges.

"Then I'll take it," he snarled, stepping smoothly behind her, wrapping his left arm around her throat and holding her right arm with his. In desperation, she flung back her left arm, still holding the book, hoping to hit him in the eye. She missed all but the corner of his left eye, but it was enough to inflict pain and his left arm sprang involuntarily to his eye, releasing her neck but not her right arm.

As she struggled to free herself, he quickly recovered from his shock and attempted to control her. She lost her balance and fell to the floor, taking him with her. It was an uneven match. Ed was in command and had one arm pinned to the ground while he bent her other arm back until she released the treasured book.

No one paid attention to Laura, who reached stealthily into the magazine rack next to her favorite chair and extracted a gun—a large, old, mean-looking gun. As she cocked it, Ed heard the click and whirled his head to face an enraged Laura pointing a gun at him. Unable to shoot without hitting Marguerite, she decided to prove she was serious and fired across the room. A huge recoil and an ear-splitting sound disconcerted Laura most of all. She fainted. The telephone rang.

The bullet sped across the room only inches from Charles McEnerny as he burst through the door yelling, "Freeze! Police!"

Ed frantically turned to check the door behind him and discovered another, much larger presence—Stephen Fleming—rushing in from the kitchen.

"Don't shoot," Ed whined, still kneeling over Marguerite.

"Look! I'm unarmed. I have witnesses. You wouldn't dare shoot me."

"Oh, I'd dare all right. Just breathe too heavy and see what happens," said McEnerny, those normally cool blue eyes emitting sparks like the sun rays bouncing off a glacier.

Fleming ordered a trembling Ed to crawl away from Marguerite, then moved forward to handcuff him as tears began to flow from eyes wide with terror.

McEnerny stepped forward and proclaimed in a monotone, "Desmond DeJonghe, you're under arrest for assault and battery, attempted theft, and driving a car with stolen license plates."

"Stolen license plates?" exclaimed Marguerite, instantly comprehending the significance of his being Desmond, Dahlia's brother. "What about murder? Two murders."

The telephone was still ringing.

"Someone pick up that blasted phone!" shouted McEnerny.

A recovered Laura started to rise but Marguerite stopped her. "Laura, you'd better sit down after that fainting spell."

"I've never fainted in my life, Marguerite Smith! I was knocked out trying to save your life. Little thanks I get for it. At least you could stop that confounded phone."

Marguerite sheepishly complied. It was Alex.

"Mother, what took you so long to answer? I found your note and have important information."

"It's a long story, Alex. What's so important?"

"Veronica called a little while ago. She's been trying to contact me for two days but either the answering machine picked up or you did and she hung up. She's been clearing out Dad's desk and found a book shoved way in the back of the bottom drawer. It was a collection of sea stories about life on a fishing boat and had a bookmark placed at one of the stories. Many lines were highlighted in yellow so she became curious and read the story."

"I know what you're going to tell me. The boat was the *Lorann*, not the *Laura Ann*."

"What gave you that idea? It was the *Laura Ann* just like you said. Sailing out of New Bedford."

Marguerite's interest was piqued. New Bedford, not Cape Cod. That was why Laura didn't locate the right boat. Alex went on.

"The story was about the day they rescued a man whose boat had sunk—the *Blue Bell*. They searched for a second man and couldn't find him."

"We already know that." Marguerite was growing irritable at missing the drama enfolding around her in Laura's house.

"But did you know that according to the introduction to the book, the author kept a journal giving all details of location, knots traveled, depth of water, weather, wind speed, catch, and so on? He didn't include all those details in his stories but he probably recorded in that journal the location where they rescued Paulie and that would be a good indication of where the *Blue Bell* sank. The book Dad wanted was that journal, not the log of a fishing boat."

"I guess Laura found the wrong book."

"She could never have found the right one. She doesn't have it. The man who kept the diary later became a journalist, not a fisherman. He's probably dead now but his family might have his diary."

"Don't tease, Alex. Who wrote that book?"

"George Atkinson. Your friend's father."

Chapter Forty-three

Desmond begged Fleming not to hurt him as the large trooper ushered the slim, manacled prisoner to the police cruiser. McEnerny showed uncharacteristic concern, asking if the ladies were all right, did they need medical attention.

"No, just answers," replied Marguerite. "That must be Dahlia's brother. What was he doing here?"

"Spying on you just like he spies on his sister. He was hoping Joe or you would lead him to the book everyone wanted."

"Then he must have murdered Joe. Maybe even Nick. Why didn't you charge him with that?"

"Because those cases are solved. We arrested the murderer this morning." His expression was smug, even for McEnerny.

"Who? Who did you arrest?"

"Beatrice."

"Beatrice Owens?"

"That's one of her names. She has a string of them. Her husbands drop like flies. A regular black widow."

"But what did she have to do with Joe? She never even met him. What could she know about him?"

"Only what you told her. Remember the night he took you to dinner? She called you when you were out and you returned the call. You must have been very upset because you blurted out what happened and told her about the book he wanted. A lot more than you told us when we questioned you in Florida."

"But how did she get involved so fast? Why murder Joe? And what about Nick?"

The sergeant would say no more but hinted that Beatrice was cooperating with the DA in an attempt to have Massachusetts try her, evidently hoping that Florida would drop its murder charge, which she was vehemently denying. Florida had capital punishment.

Without even a good-bye, McEnerny strode to the door, stopping to point to the bullet-shattered woodwork and commenting, "You ought to be more careful who you point a gun at. Understand?"

Marguerite sank back on the itchy sofa.

"Laura, I think we could both use a drink. Do you have anything?"

"You know I'm a teetotaler. But my father kept some brandy in the cabinet. For medicinal purposes, you know."

"Well, bring it out. It should be well aged by now."

Chapter Forty-four

Beatrice Owens, née Havarian, hated the small-town life in Ohio; hated the small bedroom she shared with her two sisters, adjacent to the small bedroom shared by her three brothers; hated the mean house on the wrong side of the tracks when small towns still had railroad tracks. From the age of ten she worked at every job she could find from farm work to baby-sitting and hoarded her money, never telling her parents the truth about what she earned. It was enough for nurse's training, after which she moved to Chicago and obtained a position in a hospital's private pavilion, where the wealthy people stayed.

William Mansfield, aged sixty-five, widower, financially secure, had terminal cancer. Good-looking, young, smart, and skillful, Beatrice coddled and convinced him he would live longer and better at home under her expert care. He succumbed to her charms and checked out of the hospital with her in attendance as a private nurse and, in a short time, wife. He lived six months.

She moved to Philadelphia, lived a luxurious life for ten years, then obtained a nursing job in a private hospital. Carl Kozinski recovered from his illness but not from the carbon monoxide that overcame him when he fell asleep in his car, drunk, with the motor running and the garage doors closed. Moderate in his habits, Carl had never been known to drink more than one wine spritzer.

Beatrice was charged with murder but never brought to trial. However, she was fingerprinted and those prints turned up in the

FBI files to be compared with hers taken in Eastham when she returned from Florida and also matched prints on the toilet seat cover in Nick Dante's hotel room in Florida.

Carl's money lasted ten years. Then Beatrice turned up in Michigan and found employment as a nurse at an auto plant, not as the executive assistant she later claimed to be. Although forty-five years old, she was still strikingly attractive and wooed by several executives. She eschewed the married ones and the younger, healthy ones, settling on Cecil Owens, an overweight smoker. He lasted longer than most—six years—before he succumbed to a heart attack. There had been no autopsy. The family doctor was also a friend. Grosse Pointe police were now considering exhumation of Cecil Owens.

Afraid her extravagant life-style would outlive her money, Beatrice had grasped the opportunity Marguerite unwittingly offered in her tell-all phone call. Her nose twitching from the scent of money, she went immediately to Joe's motel, revealed she knew about the book, and proposed a partnership. She was in the bridge group and had the same access as Marguerite.

Too ill to make a serious decision, he promised to think about it and see her in the morning. Unable to sleep well, Joe checked out early and went to Beatrice's house, taking a motel towel with him, either absentmindedly or because he felt nauseated. He agreed to her proposition, telling her he wanted the record of the *Laura Ann.* Whether from illness or latent mistrust, he did not clarify that it was George Atkinson's journal about the *Laura Ann* that he was seeking. Assuming she knew all and that the book was a fishing boat log in Laura's possession, Beatrice prepared a lethal breakfast. She never shared money.

On a Caribbean trip with her last husband, Cecil Owens, she had been given a pair of earrings by him, the dangling type she favored, decorated with exotic black and red seeds. Beatrice rarely wore them because they were clip-ons, not the type for pierced ears, and the tight clips were uncomfortable.

About six months ago, while sorting through her jewelry, she noted them. Attracted anew by their bright color, she decided to take them to a jeweler to have the clips changed to posts and left them on her dresser. The next morning her cat was violently ill. About to take her to the vet, Beatrice noticed one chewed-up earring on the floor. Ever alert to future contingencies, she fed the cat some hoarded opiate, buried her, and pretended Ling had been killed by a hit-and-run driver. The intact earring was pre-served and the poisonous seeds identified in a botanical book. The police were digging in Beatrice's yard, searching for the remains of the cat.

On the morning of Joe's fateful visit, she had removed the seeds from the earring and pulverized them in the food processor. She added the large dose of ground seeds to granola along with cinnamon to disguise the taste and coconut flakes to encourage thorough chewing. Beatrice ate the same breakfast, minus the poison.

Racked with a headache and fever from the flu, Joe agreed to lie down after breakfast. Later in the day, as the poison began to take effect, he became violently ill. She pretended to be taking him to the hospital. Noting the towel, she put it over the driver's seat, forgetting that the towel fibers would cling to her coat, where they were later discovered. As she drove him around in circles, he vomited, convulsed, and became comatose.

Convinced he would never regain consciousness, she boldly parked the car in her garage, waiting until the early-morning hours to drag him, still faintly breathing, into the lighthouse where she had noted a broken lock recently on one of her daily walks. Safely hidden, he would die soon and she would be out of town when the body was discovered. It was difficult to drag him out of the car and into the lighthouse, but nurses were trained to move incapacitated patients and she managed.

Before she abandoned the car behind the food stand, she used the motel towel to remove the vomit. She knew the police would examine it and preferred that they not learn Joe had eaten break-fast. It was more convenient for her that they think he died after dinner with Marguerite. She discarded the towel in a wooded area on her walk home, a long way from where she hid the car.

Beatrice adamantly denied murdering Nick Dante, although her fingerprints were found in his bathroom and she could offer no proof that she had been in Boca Raton that night as she claimed. A suspicious McEnerny, wondering about the coincidence of her having called Marguerite that night in Florida on some flimsy excuse about a telephone number, checked Fleming's notes and discovered that he had automatically written the name, K. Cough-lin, and the phone number.

The sergeant had asked Lyle Fairchild in Lauderdale to check Coughlin out. Kenneth had not seen or heard from Beatrice since

he retired four years ago although he had been home the night
she said she intended to call him. He supplied them with the name
of their other coworker with a home in Boca and she had not
seen Beatrice either.

The supposition on the part of the police was that Beatrice
made no attempt to secure the book during the one day before
she left for Florida because of the difficulty in locating it and
because she considered her secret safe. Joe had told no one else
the exact nature of the book. She apparently became wary of
Nick's fortuitous meeting with them, his initial interest in her,
and his shift to Marguerite. She watched him carefully, pretending to go to Boca Raton but following him and calling Marguerite
when she saw police enter the hotel and Nick leave without Marguerite. Faced with Marguerite's anger at Nick during their brief
phone conversation, Beatrice became convinced he had made his
move. She went to his hotel and proposed a partnership but he
refused, a fatal refusal.

She evidently had stolen Joe's gun from his car or luggage.
That was her most serious mistake. It tied Joe's murder to Nick's.
The bathroom fingerprints could have been explained away on
the basis of a tryst with Nick. She disclaimed all knowledge of
the gun and claimed Marguerite must have had it all along. But
it was Beatrice who left fingerprints in Nick's room, who lied
about her whereabouts that fateful night, and who admitted to
one murder in her quest for treasure.

The police had one more lucky break. Noting a newspaper
delivery box in front of Beatrice's house, they questioned the
delivery woman. On the morning after the snowstorm of January
fifteenth, she had noted a Mercedes in Beatrice's driveway at
seven in the morning. She was sure of the date because the snow
plows had created a snowbank and she couldn't reach the delivery
box without getting out of her car. She was surprised to see the
Mercedes because Beatrice never had house guests.

When they came to arrest her early Monday morning, she was
packing her car. She had known since they fingerprinted her on
Saturday that she had to leave but thought she had the weekend's
grace before they unearthed her past and the dead men who littered it. Unknown to her, the Boca alibi had already been broken
and the fingerprint check tagged as an emergency.

Beatrice needed Monday morning to gather her assets, which
were very fluid. Her money was in cash deposits at several banks

and a safe-deposit held valuable jewelry. The house had a large mortgage and would be abandoned. She made one attempt on Sunday afternoon to find the book at Laura's but the enormity of the task overwhelmed her and she left rather than kindle Laura's suspicions until she had her money and was on her way to a new identity.

The police had a search warrant. In the space between the wall and the bed in the guest room, they discovered a crumpled but expensive man's linen handkerchief with the monogram *S*. A brownish-gold hair was nestled in a fold of the handkerchief.

Dahlia was distraught over Desmond. Beautiful but tortured, he had been her albatross since childhood when their mother died and their father washed his hands of an errant son. Even the Army could not discipline him.

Desmond had been taking a new medication and seemed dramatically improved. He had given up his skinhead friends, let his hair grow, dressed normally, and claimed to be looking for a job. He had even undergone laser surgery to remove those hideous tattoos. Dahlia had borrowed the money for the treatment from Nick. But the changes were mostly cosmetic.

Obsessively possessive of his sister, he spied on her constantly; knew every detail of the gold coin saga; knew that her boyfriend, Nick, encouraged her to play along with Joe until they had enough information to recover the treasure themselves; learned about Joe's plan to enlist Marguerite to aid him and even learned where she lived; listened in on the telephone conversation when Dahlia told Nick that Joe had failed with Marguerite and that Victor Krogh was pressuring Joe to return the German book; heard Nick tell Dahlia he would follow Marguerite himself. While secretly renting the Eastham cottage, Desmond returned nearly every night to Dahlia's to keep abreast of developments. He planned to recover the treasure himself and cut out both Joe and Nick. He hated all her suitors.

His only recent reversion to his old persona had been when he donned his old clothes and a fake ponytail to greet Sgt. Mc-Enerny. With appropriate changes in facial expressions, intonation and language, he became the skinhead at which he had played being. He had never discovered who he really was.

* * *

Wilson and Veronica were immensely relieved at learning the truth of Joe's murder. They had both known or suspected his affair with Dahlia and, upon consultation on January sixteenth, had agreed to delay reporting him missing, assuming he had deserted his wife for another woman, déjà vu. Veronica wished to avoid embarassment. To Wilson, it was a matter of family, first and always.

Marguerite had been summoned to police headquarters to read and sign her statement about the events at Laura's house. If not invited, she would have come anyway. She wanted more information; she was entitled to it.

She received very little and was irate at the unfair exchange. Patiently, Medeiros explained that the murder cases were still under investigation and Joe's was in the hands of the DA.

"Well, you can at least tell me why Sgt. McEnerny and that nice young trooper were at Laura's ready to play gang busters."

"Good old-fashioned police work," crowed Frank. "I became suspicious of Ed Rogers the day I saw him draw Nick's picture. I attended a seminar once on composite sketches and, at best, they're not perfect. Ed drew that picture too well. When you said Nick's hair was parted, he immediately drew it parted on the right without you saying so. Most men part their hair on the left. Nick was an exception. Ed also drew in ears without asking you about them and drew them very close to the head, just like Nick's. I checked his ID picture later. The drawing was too good, especially for someone who never did this before."

"That was all you had?"

"Of course not. I sent David Morgan to the house on the pretense that a call had come in about a prowler. Ed said he hadn't seen anyone but invited Morgan in. He noticed there were no paints in the house, no easels, no canvasses, only some completed stuff in the living room. The paint was completely dry and they looked like they were done by different people, something about the brush strokes. Morgan made some comments about painters and painting styles and Ed agreed with everything he said, even the things he made up. Ed Rogers was not a painter."

"But he did have artistic ability. How about that drawing of Nick? And he made a sketch of Laura?"

"He always could draw well, according to his sister. She tried to interest him in painting, even paid for a course, but he only went once or twice. It was too disciplined for him.''

''That information didn't lead you to Laura's. What else did you learn?''

''Morgan took down his plate number and we ran it. The plates were stolen from a car in Stoughton. We got the VIN from the car. It belonged to Dahlia. She rarely used it in the city and was letting her brother borrow it while he looked for a job.''

''Evidently the job was watching me. He almost had me fooled,'' she commented, at which Frank and Al looked at each other with raised eyebrows, ''and he certainly fooled Rusty. So much for dog sense! But you still haven't told me why the troopers were at Laura's house.''

''Beatrice Owens had been arrested early in the morning but we didn't have all the facts yet. Ed's connection with Dahlia and Nick was troubling us,'' said Medeiros, ''and the fact that he was at that cottage under false pretenses. McEnerny was supposed to question him and find out if he was Desmond or somebody else connected to Dahlia and Nick or even Joe. When he and Fleming approached the cottage in their car, you ran out of your house without a coat, waving your arms and calling Ed. They watched you return for a coat and get in his car. McEnerny wasn't sure at first if it was Desmond but he had a hunch something important had happened, so he followed. Lucky for you.''

''Lucky for you, too, Lieutenant. Imagine how embarrassed you'd be if Laura and I had been hurt due to police negligence.''

''But you weren't, were you? You ought to think a little more kindly about Sgt. McEnerny. He rescued you.''

''I guess so,'' she admitted. ''If only he wasn't so hard to take.''

As if on cue, the sergeant entered the room and cursorily greeted her. He had to speak with Medeiros—privately.

''I was just leaving,'' she said. On an impulse she added, ''Sergeant, I'm preparing a special dinner tonight. My daughter is leaving for home tomorrow and I want it to be a treat. I'd be pleased if you would have dinner with us, sort of as a thank-you for helping me. I was thinking of making French onion soup, and oxtail ragout—in the Quebec style my mother always made— and maybe a mousse or a tarte tatin.''

McEnerny was taken aback, in fact, stunned. The only dinner that awaited him was a frozen one.

"That's nice of you, Mrs. Smith. I'd like to come. But couldn't you make steak or pork chops or some other regular food? I don't go much for that frog stuff. Understand?"

Epilogue

The gold coins, if there were gold coins on the *Blue Bell*, remain hidden in the sea somewhere off Race Point, Cape Cod. George Atkinson never had his father's journal of a year aboard the *Laura Ann*. Along with the manuscripts of his books, the senior George Atkinson had bequeathed it to his alma mater.

Upon request, the university head librarian located the card for the journal among those of a special collection but could not locate the book itself. Was it lost in the bowels of this archaic building, or stored in a basement trunk along with other college memorabilia of a former student?

Or perhaps the librarian was planning an early retirement.

For the reader who wishes to explore in detail the customs or events mentioned in this book, I recommend the following resources:

Lighthouses

Clemensen, A. Berle, et al., *Historic Structure Report*. U.S. Department of Interior, 1986.

Snow, Edward Rowe, *The Lighthouses of New England*. New York: Dodd, Mead & Company, 1973.

Rum-running

Willoughby, Malcolm F., *Rum War at Sea*. Washington, D. C.: United States Government Printing Office, 1964.

Post–World War I Germany

Davies, J. S., *From Charlemagne to Hitler*. New York: Barnes & Noble Books, 1994.

Gold Coins

French, Charles F., *1993 American Guide to U.S. Coins*. New York: Simon & Schuster, 1992.

Cape Verdean Americans

Halter, Marilyn, *Between Race and Ethnicity*. Urbana and Chicago: University of Illinois Press, 1993.

—Marie Lee